# VALLEY
# OF
# THE
# KINGS

## Books by Cecelia Holland

*An Ordinary Woman*
*Railroad Schemes*
*Jerusalem*
*Valley of the Kings*
*Pacific Street*
*The Bear Flag*
*The Lords of Vaumartin*
*Pillar of the Sky*
*The Belt of Gold*
*The Sea Beggars*
*Home Ground*
*City of God*
*Two Ravens*
*Floating Worlds*
*Great Maria*
*The Death of Attila*
*The Earl*
*Antichrist*
*Until the Sun Falls*
*The Kings in Winter*
*Rakossy*
*The Firedrake*

For Children
*The King's Road*
*Ghost on the Steppe*

# VALLEY  OF THE KINGS

## A NOVEL OF
## TUTANKHAMUN

### CECELIA HOLLAND

 A Tom Doherty Associates Book

VALLEY OF THE KINGS

A Forge Book
Published by Tom Doherty Associates, LLC
175 Fifth Avenue
New York, NY 10010

Forge® is a registered trademark of Tom Doherty Associates, LLC

Library of Congress Cataloging-in-Publication Data

Holland, Cecelia.
   Valley of the Kings / Cecelia Holland.
      p.  cm.
   "A Tom Doherty Associates book."
   ISBN 0-312-86334-9 (hc)
   ISBN 0-312-86862-6 (pbk)
   I. Title
PS3558.O348V3    1997
813'.54—dc21

                                                                              97-5499
                                                                              CIP

First Forge Hardcover Edition: June 1997
First Forge Trade Paperback Edition: August 1999

Printed in the United States of America

0  9  8  7  6  5  4  3  2  1

This book is dedicated to Marion Hardy
for reasons that she alone knows

# PREFATORY NOTE

A few years ago I had the good fortune to spend a few hours in the company of the present Earl of Carnarvon, son of the Carnarvon who with Howard Carter discovered the tomb of Tutankhamun in 1922. The Earl told me the story of his father's search and what became of him afterward, and from that conversation this novel sprang.

My name is Howard Carter, and I am English; I am an Egyptologist. In 1902 I was working for the Egyptian Department of Antiquities, supervising the diggings in the Valley of the Kings, near the ancient site of Thebes. A long-simmering feud between me and my superior officer had flared up into hot words and threats, and when word of that got to the British Resident in Cairo, I got a summons to appear at the Residency.

The Resident at that time was Lord Cromer. Before the war, the British were officially only guests in Egypt, which was nominally ruled by the Turkish Khedive, although, of course, the place was under British domination. It was a ticklish situation, in which Cromer's diplomatic talents were given full exercise.

Exactly how polished those talents were I learned when I presented myself at the Residency. I expected a reprimand; instead I was invited to dinner.

There was a third man at the table that evening. Slightly

built, he looked frail and appeared to be in his mid-thirties, a few years older than I. His hair looked polished and his eyes looked overbright to me. I wondered if I'd have noticed that if I hadn't been told he was delicate. He was the Earl of Carnarvon, and for reasons of health he was wintering in Egypt. After we had eaten, the three of us went to Cromer's study for brandy and cigars. So far not a word had been breathed about my falling out with my chief. That was not Cromer's way.

We arranged ourselves around the snug little room that Cromer used as a private study. The servant lit the hand-painted lamps and brought out the brandy in a crystal decanter. It was a very English setting, almost enough to let one forget that only a few feet outside the window lay teeming Cairo, crawling with flies and thieves and smelling of the Nile. Carnarvon sat in a deep leather chair and plucked the crease of his impeccable trousers straight. On the bookshelf behind him, before a matched set of Dickens, was a white soapstone bust of Napoleon. Pictures of horses running and jumping hedgerows took up the wall space between the heavy bookcases.

As usual in an English study, the first words spoken were of European politics. I stood at the end of the room, reading the titles of the books behind the glass, while Cromer and Carnarvon repeated the pretenses of the ruling class.

"The Kaiser," Cromer said, pouring the brandy, "has no sense of the seriousness of seriousness. We are quite boring Carter, who has no interest in anyone not embalmed."

I took a bell-shaped glass of brandy from him. Cromer was smiling. His pale eyes bulged, intelligent and cold, from his smooth, expressionless diplomat's face.

"Sit down, Carter," he said.

"Thank you," I said, but I stayed on my feet.

"I understand you worked under Flinders Petrie in the digs at Tell el-Amarna," Carnarvon said to me.

"Yes," I said. "I worked in the crew that dug out the remains of the royal palace of Akhenaten."

"Carter knows Egypt," Cromer said. He took the chair next to Carnarvon's. "He knows everyone, he is known everywhere. You couldn't have a better man in your employ."

At that I was glad I was standing up. I looked at Carnarvon's finely kept hands cupped around the brandy snifter. He was the son of an earl; signs of labor would have been déclassé.

He said, "I understand you've fallen out with your chief, Carter."

"Flinders Petrie trained me," I said. "I have more respect for detail than some people. Are you interested in Egyptology?"

"I'm afraid I know very little about ancient history. I'm just keen on getting out of doors, you know. I spent my last season here doing word puzzles. There isn't even any decent shooting."

Cromer leaned over the arm of his chair for the brandy decanter on its tray nearby. The servant had come in behind him and was silently adjusting a lamp. Cromer said, "This isn't England, in spite of all attempts. Do any shooting, Carter?"

"I haven't the time, my lord."

"I can't say I know much myself about ancient Egypt," Cromer said. He crooked a finger, and the servant brought about a box of cigars. Cromer went on, "I don't follow the dynasties, and they had a crew of monsters for gods—the Greek gods are rather splendid, but the Egyptians—even Herodotus pokes fun at them. Monkeys and cats. Crocodiles."

Herodotus saw only the decadent Egypt, past its glory. I took one of the long, slim cigars.

"The only Egyptian I find sympathy for is Akhenaten," Cromer was saying. "The heretic." He nodded to me. "You'd know more about him than I."

"The Criminal of Tell el-Amarna," I said. "The most overrated figure in the ancient world."

3

Carnarvon was eying the cigars. The servant bent slightly to offer him the box; the golden lamplight fell on the dark Egyptian face, the lowered eyes, the mouth smiling.

"Overrated in what sense?" Carnarvon said.

"I've heard him called the first monotheist," said Cromer, combative. "He may have influenced Moses. Our whole civilization may ultimately rest on the vision of Akhenaten."

"He destroyed Egypt," I said. I had an almost personal dislike of Akhenaten. "The Egyptians understood their world in terms of their religion. When he attacked their religion, he upset their whole way of thought. They could never get back on track after him."

"What did he do, precisely?" Carnarvon asked. He took one of the cigars and sniffed it, languid.

I said, "He was a fanatic. He believed in one god, the Aten, the disk of the sun, giver of all life, that sort of thing. He abolished the hierarchy of the popular gods, whom the Egyptians had worshiped for thousands of years."

Carnarvon took a small gold clipper from the Egyptian servant. He nipped off the end of the cigar, moistened it with his lips, and fit it neatly into his mouth. The servant struck a match. Ceremoniously they waited until the sulfur had burned off. No one spoke. Carnarvon tipped his head slightly and the servant lit the cigar.

This ritual successfully completed, Carnarvon leaned back into the depths of his chair, exhaled a plume of smoke, and said, "I don't understand. Was he some sort of priest, this Akhenaten?"

I saw that I would have to begin at the beginning. Going slowly, I said, "He was Pharaoh—the King of Egypt. He embodied the connection between the world of men and the eternal world of the gods. The ancients saw things much differently from us. We live in Newton's universe. We see reality as a mechanism, like a watch: once it's started, it goes on by itself according to rational rules. The ancient Egyptians believed that the world had to be made to go on functioning, every day, every hour. Pharaoh did that. He made the sun rise and set, the Nile flood and ebb, the grain grow and ripen—all this by interceding with the gods through the proper rituals. Then Akhenaten threw all the old gods out."

Carnarvon said, "What happened?"

"What would you expect?"

I meant that rhetorically, but before I could go on, he said, "Chaos."

"It was a disaster."

"On the short term," Cromer said. "But Akhenaten's idea of One Loving God conquered the world. What's that line of Shelley's—'Look on my works, ye mighty, and despair'?"

That was certainly malapropos. I had forgotten my cigar, beside me in a little silver dish, and I reached for it.

"A heretic King," Carnarvon said. "It's a contradiction in terms."

"To our age, it is," Cromer said. "It appears that modern man will stomach rather much if the man doing it wears a crown. Akhenaten was an extraordinary man. He was ill, and died young—"

"Thirty-odd was a full age for an Egyptian," I said.

"How was he ill?" asked Carnarvon.

"That's conjecture," I said. "His images usually show him with a swollen abdomen and thighs and breasts like a woman's. There's been some attempt to prove he had an endocrine disease."

"Was he married? Did he have children? That would give a clue."

I puffed on my cold cigar. The stale residue of smoke almost made me cough. "He was married to Nefertiti."

"Nefertiti! That name I know. A legendary beauty, wasn't she?"

"The most famous piece of Egyptian art yet uncovered is a head of Nefertiti."

"And did he have children?"

"Yes."

"So much for endocrine disease," said Carnarvon. "What did he die of?"

The Egyptian servant came over to light my cigar for me. I talked around it, my eyes on Carnarvon's. "Nobody knows. Anyway, his religion failed. The King who followed him was Tutankhamun, who took the court back to Thebes and restored the old gods. The priests made sure nothing lasted of Akhenaten. They hacked his name and face off his monuments and left him out of the lists of Kings—"

"Then how do you know so much?"

"We know almost nothing," I said.

"Who was this Tut-amun?"

"Tutankhamun. Nobody knows anything at all about him. He reigned for only a few years. His tomb has never been found."

"What do you mean? Where is his pyramid?"

I cleared my throat. He seemed so clever to be so ignorant. "The pyramids were all built a thousand years before Tutankhamun."

"Oh. The Sphinx, too?"

"Yes," I said. Was he teasing me?

"Well," he said, "I'm interested, Carter. It sounds like good fun, searching around the ruins. Do you have some project in mind—something I could join in on when I'm here for the winter?"

Beside the soap-colored bust of Napoleon, Cromer was smiling at me. I realized that he had invited me here for exactly this, to give his friend an amusement, to get me off the hook at the Department of Antiquities. He had a Turkish mind for intrigues. I sucked on my cigar; it had gone out again.

"Well," I said, "if I had the money . . ."

"What?" Carnarvon said.

"I'd look for the tomb of Tutankhamun."

"Akhenaten's successor? But why not look for Akhenaten himself?"

"His tomb has been found, empty and looted, at Tell el-Amarna."

"What makes you think you can find Tutankhamun's, if it's been lost for so long?"

I wet my lips. Cromer was watching us intently. I launched myself into the arguments I had used so many times before.

"Tutankhamun was of the Eighteenth Dynasty. Except for the people buried at Tell el-Amarna, all the members of that dynasty were buried in the Valley of the Kings, at Thebes—where Luxor is now. Now, in the 1880s, some peasants discovered a cache of mummies of those kings, all packed together in a single tomb in the valley. Apparently their tombs had all been rifled in ancient times, and the priests had gathered up the mummies and put them away for safekeeping. Amenhotep II and III were there, and Thothmes III, some others, but not Tutankhamun. I believe he is still somewhere in the Valley of the Kings."

"Can you find him?"

"If I have the money, and—"

"Can you find him?"

"Yes."

"Good," Carnarvon said. "Let's give it a go."

A few days later I took Carnarvon out to the pyramids. He had been there before, of course, but he suggested going together—he wanted to hear what I had to say. That made me ill at ease, and a little didactic.

We rode out on camels, with a dragoman, more to mind the camels than anything else. Carnarvon sat very straight and stiff in his worn, rug-covered saddle. I asked him if he rode horses back in England. He gave me a wry look.

"Commenting on my seat, Carter? Actually it isn't my sport. I prefer walking. My son's dead keen on polo."

7

We were approaching Saqqara. We both turned forward. The coolness of his answer rebuffed me. He took such pains to remind me of my inferior social rank.

The pyramids loomed ahead of us.

No matter how often one sees them, they jolt the mind and senses. They are still among the largest monuments built by man. Enough of the limestone cap remains on the Pyramid of Khefren, which stands in the middle of the three, that one can visualize how they must have looked, forty-four hundred years ago, polished white and blazing in the sun.

Their shapes emulate the sun, radiating downward in a widening fan from a single point in heaven. Nothing else in Egypt so expresses the confidence and devotion of the Old Kingdom.

I explained the construction and the design of the interior tunnels and chambers, as Carnarvon and I strolled around the base of the large group. Carnarvon had little to say. He seemed uninterested. I began to worry about what the next few years would be like, trying to stir this dilettante to sufficient interest that he would pay for a lot of digging. We left the camels and the dragoman in the shade and walked away along the causeway that led from the Pyramid of Khefren to the funerary temple, a third of a mile away, in the Nile Valley. The Sphinx is there. One forgets the ruin of the temple for awe of this creation, half monster and half god.

Perhaps the original spur of rock, jutting more than sixty feet up from the sand of the desert, reminded some ancient sculptor of a crouching lion. Then he had only to touch up, here and there, and shape the huge, regal head into the head of Pharaoh.

"It represents the King as the sun god Ra," I told Carnarvon. I was sure he had heard all this before. He listened obediently, like a clever schoolboy tolerating the chatter of an ignorant tutor. We walked slowly down between the

8

colossal paws. The layered sandstone striped the breast of the lion in shades of gold.

The head towered above us into the cloudless blue sky. I said, "No King since has ruled so absolutely. He was like the sun, he was everything."

Carnarvon emitted something like a sniff. "I'm afraid I can't admire people who built such monuments to their vanity with the sweat and pain of slaves."

"Slaves," I said. "The Egyptians did not have slaves."

He turned his head; his eyebrows described arcs of surprise in his lean face. "Weren't all these monuments built by slave labor?"

"No," I said shortly. I was tired of coddling his nobility.

"How, then? It must have taken thousands and thousands of men thousands of hours."

"For four months out of every year," I said, "nine out of every ten Egyptians were idled by the flood."

"Still, it seems an odd way to spend a holiday?"

I wondered if he were having a joke on me. I glanced up at the ruined features of great Khefren. The Arabs did that, hating idols.

"I confess, Carter," he said, "that your Egyptians elude me. I can't find the key to them. Even their art, which ought to be a window of their lives—it's beautiful, some of it, sophisticated, subtle—but, damn it, the most graphic of the pictures give one no sense at all of what their inward lives were like. How they thought, how they thought of themselves. Like those friezes in the temples. There's no individuality, the people might be interchangeable. It's as if they deliberately effaced all the personality out of their pictures."

He turned his back on Khefren as he spoke. I followed him up toward the open again, away from the sun god.

"I can't see anything human in them, Carter."

"My lord, you're looking at them with modern eyes."

"That's what I'm equipped with, Carter."

"Personality—a man's individual self—those are modern ideas. These people had no inward lives, as you call it. They were not free to have inward lives—to be different from the other men around them. Nature bound them. The Nile, the Sun, the Soil, the life cycle of the millet—those were their rulers, not their own morals or judgments. How could they develop any individuality? Everything they did and felt and thought was the same as it had been for generations—shaped by the constant inflexible challenge of making life possible here."

As he walked he watched me, his hands tucked behind his back. The schoolboy pose. He seemed to be listening. His eyes were dreamy. We started up toward the pyramids again. My gaze reached for their insuperable heights.

"Pharaoh was their self. He was the Personhood of Egypt. He represented them before the gods. They built these monuments to venerate him and to make themselves great. They did it for joy, as willingly as the medieval knight hauled stone to Chartres."

We walked on in silence. I was tired of talking. Let him do some of the work. I felt old and blocked and tiresome. I pinched the bridge of my nose between my fingertips. My forehead began to ache. There was fine sand in my mustache.

We had reached the pyramids before he finally spoke.

"You see all this so differently than I, Carter." He smiled at me, enigmatic. I wondered what he meant. It was so obvious to me, what I had said: who could see it differently? He nodded to me. "It should be an interesting collaboration."

"Yes, sir," I said, guarded.

We started toward the camels, lying on their tucked legs, their heads drawn back.

# 2

For the reasons I had recounted to Carnarvon at our first meeting, when we decided to search for the tomb of Pharaoh Tutankhamun, I believed the lost tomb to be in the Valley of the Kings, in the desert near Luxor, where ancient Thebes stood. However, the Germans and the Americans had the licenses to dig there. Until they gave up, Carnarvon and I could do nothing except potter around elsewhere.

We did some digging in the Nile Delta, around Saïs, uncovering some interesting sites from the Middle Kingdom and Ptolemaic times. I confess that my attention was elsewhere. The American Theodore Davis, whose work I had supervised before I met Carnarvon, was excavating in the Valley of the Kings, and I lived in daily fear that he would find the tomb himself.

The Department of Antiquities had kept me on as Davis's nominal supervisor, but he seldom informed me of his work. I had to rely on some friends in the nearby village of Kurna to watch him for me. Then one spring, just before Carnarvon would arrive in Egypt for the season, one of my friends sent me word that Davis was into a real find.

I was in Cairo, buying digging supplies. I took the new railroad train down to Luxor. This is where ancient Thebes once stood, and in fact much of ancient Thebes is still there. Crowds of giant columns and gates cover whole acres of the east bank of the river. Some of them still retain the bright painting that decorated them when Pharaoh and his courtiers looked upon them on their way to the sacred rites and mysteries of Amun, the god of Thebes. The modern town of Luxor with its curving date palms and square white houses looks small and temporary by comparison with the gigantic structures of the ancients. The west bank is a warren of the mortuary temples of Eighteenth Dynasty pharaohs and their families. In the midst of these ruins is the village of Kurna; some of the villagers actually live in the ancient buildings, and they and their ancestors have made a local sport of tomb-robbing since the days of Rameses.

As one crosses the Nile from Luxor to the west bank, the two tremendous statues of Amenhotep III dominate the approach. They are so huge and so ruined by time that they no longer look human but, rather, like vast primeval brutes, enthroned beside the river, their heavy hands on their thighs. Behind them the alluvial plain runs back to the cliffs. Here the ruins are piled almost on top of one another. Some are no more than a square foundation, some are nearly whole. The long horizon of the desert shelf frames them.

Here one can ignore the slight modern presence and imagine oneself living at the dawn of time.

At the ferry stage there are donkeys for hire. I rode back past Deir el-Bahri, the great temple of Queen Hatshepsut, and onto the road that leads into the Valley of the Kings. As soon as I crossed into the desert I seemed to have left the modern world behind me. The barren ground, scoured by the wind, was ridged and hollowed like rock ribs. Dust hung perpetually in the air. My donkey had the frantic, steady trot of a rented hack whom everybody beats to death. The trail climbed. On my lips I tasted the acrid, poisonous dust of the desert.

The slopes of the gaunt hills had collapsed into ranks of sheer cliffs. Taking off my jacket, I folded it cleverly over my head against the bright sun. I sang a little, although I don't know many songs. I was happy to be back in the valley. I have always enjoyed this place, all honeycombed with tunnels and caves and rooms hacked into the rock.

I passed the square mouth of a minor tomb cut into the cliffside by the trail. Another appeared, halfway up the opposite slope. To the west, one lone peak reared above the flat tablelands like a natural pyramid. The ravine swerved again, and, rounding the turn, I came within sight of the tremendous scarp that stands behind the tomb of Rameses VI. It is a favorite site for people on the tour, and one can see why, although the magnificent rooms are empty and the mummy of the King is in Cairo.

In the broad yellow face of the cliff the opening of the tomb, neatly shaped and shored up to make smooth the path of the tourist, was oddly out of place: too square, too false. It always made me nervous: it looked as if it undermined that part of the cliff, as if the gigantic palisade might collapse before my eyes.

Four or five donkeys were waiting nearby as I approached. One carried panniers, doubtless full of a picnic lunch. Across the valley from them was a string of fellahin, handing up baskets of rubble from a pit in the ground.

This was Davis's dig. I took the jacket off my head.

Davis himself was sitting above the dig in the shade of a huge blue beach umbrella, one gaitered leg crossed over the other. I left my donkey and climbed a short steep path toward him. The slope was treacherous, covered with broken rock and gravel; the whole valley here is half-buried in bits of rock, the chip from the many tombs hollowed out of the cliff on either side.

"Carter," Davis said, sharply. "What are you doing here?" He stood up, his hands on his hips.

"I understand you're on to something." I said. I stopped on the path. My gaze went to the fellah in at their work, bending and swaying over the baskets of dirt.

They were working around the edge of a square pit that seemed to me to be already empty. I glanced around me for signs that they had removed anything other than rock: artifacts, for example, or pottery. The only thing on the slope was a pile of empty blue mineral-water bottles behind Davis's beach umbrella. He was glowering at me.

"Nobody asked you here, Carter," he said.

"I am your supervisor, aren't I?" I took a step toward the pit. He grabbed my elbow.

"What do you think you're doing?"

"Well, let's have a look at what you've found," I said. "Or aren't you proud of this one?"

He grunted. His hat was pushed back a little, exposing a strip of bright red sunburn above the tan of his forehead. "All right," he said. "I'll show you."

He started down the slope toward the pit. One of the men below saw him and, taking a whistle from around his neck, blew on it. The shrill sound brought the other workmen up straight. As a band they trooped off from the dig into the shade of the cliff wall and sat down. Davis and I went over to the pit.

"I have not yet made my official identification," Davis said. "But I have my strong suspicions what this find is."

I said nothing, tramping down after him across the hot flint. Davis had uncovered a number of magnificent sites, both here and elsewhere in Egypt, but he was notorious for misidentifying them. He was a careless, undisciplined digger who went by intuition more than reason, and he had no time for the grinding detail work that in the end pays off in a more total picture of Egyptian life. What Davis was after was sensation. Now he stood on the edge of the pit and gestured to me to inspect.

I looked down into a narrow hole, deep in shadows even in strong daylight. Davis said, "It was full of rubble. Took us nearly a week to empty it out. Obviously it's been looted."

"Looted," I said. "What do you think it was, anyway— a cache?" Near my feet there was a ladder extending down into the pit. I stooped to rattle it, testing its strength.

"It's a tomb," Davis said roughly. "Look at it, damn you —it's a pit tomb, and my guess is it's Eighteenth Dynasty."

"Come on," I said, and climbed down the ladder into the pit.

Midway, I passed from the sunlight into the cold grip of the shadow of the earth, and I shivered from head to foot. Davis came after me, his heavy boot soles sometimes grazing my hands. The pit was so small that he and I could barely stand side by side in it. It was a cache pit, no more, perhaps even less; the ancients very neatly buried the debris of their farewell rituals after a funeral.

I tilted my head back. The patch of blue Egyptian sky shone far overhead. The pit had been hewn roughly from the rock. It had never been painted or even smoothed out, although the work was well done. But it usually was.

"Whatever makes you think it's Eighteenth Dynasty?"

Davis shot me a fiery look. "If you'd waited until I could do a little more excavating—"

"If you'd tell me when you find these things, I might be able to help you from the beginning."

"Come on," he said.

We climbed out of the pit. He led me back across the valley, through the blazing heat, to his beach umbrella. There was a little box near his chair, and he sat down and put the box on his knees.

"See? Rather fine, don't you think? And obviously Eighteenth Dynasty."

In the box were half a dozen bits of gold. I put my fingertips to them. I was touching the past, touching them. Thousands of years in the earth. There were a few rings, a small statuette of alabaster, a couple of strips of gold foil. Lifting the foil, I held it into the sunlight.

A line of pictographs crossed the surface. Part of the writing was a name, and my nerves jumped with excitement. It was Tutankhamun's name.

"Well?" Davis said. "What do you think?"

I picked up the box with the bits of gold and walked back down the little slope and across the valley to the pit. Davis trooped after me. Midway to the pit he began to shout at me.

"You won't admit it, will you, Carter. It's the tomb of King Tutankhamun, isn't it, but you won't admit it."

I put the box down at the edge of the pit. "What kind of fill did you remove?" I squatted down and ran my hand over the top of the pit. It was dug in the sandy floor of the valley. "Was it the same as this stuff?" I looked around me again, at the heavy flint boulders and flint chip piled against the foot of the cliff nearby. That was chip from Rameses' tomb.

Davis struck at my hand. "Stop the act, Carter. There's nobody here to impress. Flinders Petrie is dead, Carter. You're old-fashioned—your methods are obsolete."

"Listen," I said. "This is important. I want you to show me exactly where and how you found these artifacts."

"Get out of here. This is my dig."

His cheeks were red under his tan. His eyes glinted with bad temper. I kept my own temper under control. It would do no good to fight with him again—not now, when he might have the key to finding Tutankhamun.

I said, "I am your supervisor, Davis. Now, just show me where you found these things."

"It's the tomb," he said. "It's the tomb of Tutankhamun."

"Damn you," I shouted into his face, "you don't know, do you! You didn't keep any records!"

He shouted back at me, standing nose to nose with me. "Nobody cares about that stuff, Carter—measuring this, sifting all the little baskets of rock—nobody cares."

"I care!"

He turned on his heel and walked away from me. I pursued him, and he shouted at me over his shoulder. "What do you think, Carter—you can't bring Egypt back, you know. It's dead, it's gone."

"People like you destroy it. You didn't even go through the chip, did you. Didn't record what was on top of the pit—"

"Get out of here! You crazy fool—"

On the opposite side of the valley, the party of tourists was coming out of Rameses' tomb. Currently, we were their attraction. Davis saw them and hushed his voice. We glared at one another. His face was flushed and his bushy gray mustache bristled with anger.

"This is an important find. You can't deny that."

"You goddamned Philistine," I said. "It might have been, if you'd do your bloody job. Now it's nothing, don't you see? Whatever significance it had you destroyed when you destroyed the context."

"What does it matter where we found everything?" Davis roared. His arms flailed in the air as with his blunt fingers he pointed around us. "We found them, didn't we? Would it be different if we'd found the rings over there, and the cup in the pit? What if—"

"What cup?"

Davis shut his mouth. His hands fell to his sides.

"What cup?" I said evenly.

"We found a faience-work cup," Davis said.

"Where?"

He kept still. Apparently he remembered the tourists; he shot a look in their direction. They were standing by their donkeys, their faces turned toward us: four white oval faces and two brown ones, the dragomen.

"Where did you find it?" I asked. I was being very civil, because I knew I had him.

"Under a rock," he said, and pointed to the foot of the slope, a few tens of yards away. "There. It was buried under the loose earth. Someone must have hidden it there. When they robbed the tomb. Just a blue faience cup. But it has Tutankhamun's name on it."

I took him by the arm and made him walk together with me down the valley; I made him show me exactly where he had found the cup. He was disgruntled. He said no more than he had to and his eyes never met mine. We both understood what he had done. Egyptian law specifies that all artifacts found in the course of a dig belong to the Egyptian people; Davis had tried to keep the cup secret from me so that he could sneak it out of the country.

I stood there looking at the slope at my feet. Turning my head, I looked back across the pit at the tomb of Rameses. The feeling welled up in me that the parts of a puzzle were there before me, if only I had wit to put them together; what I saw ought to be telling me something. But I could not grasp it. Under Davis's furious eyes, under the eyes of the native workmen and the tourists, I turned and went to my donkey and rode away down the valley.

# 3

In the Delta, Carnarvon and I spent every fall and winter season at the digs, and I began to know him a little better. He was surprisingly companionable at times. When some topic took his fancy we could talk for hours. His wife usually accompanied him to Egypt, and in the evenings she would sit by the lamp reading, while we argued and talked over the details of the day's digging, or some wider subject. As the years went on, Carnarvon's daughter, Evelyn, joined us as well, a gawky, ugly girl in the starched pinafores and long white stockings in which the English upper class saw fit to swaddle their children. She collected rocks.

In spite of all, though, Carnarvon never really became broadly knowledgeable about Egypt. He knew—often very keenly—the areas that interested him; but if a subject failed to strike a spark with him, he could not be troubled to involve himself in it.

Periodically the Countess and little Evelyn dragged me off to the bazaar in Saïs.

The bazaar covered several acres of ground; the stalls under their torn and dirty awnings were set up without any particular order, so that the crooked lanes between them were like a warren. The Countess walked along with her skirts hiked up in one hand, holding Evelyn in the other, and the governess trailing after, all the ladies circling and swerving around the garbage and dung that littered the ground. The vendors screamed at them, and sent their boys to run after them screaming, which the ladies ignored. The air was rich with changing odors, of people and beasts, leather, dust, the beans cooking in open pots on every corner; and the racket was constant and deafening. The ladies might have been taking their tour through the park at Highclere.

While they looked at woven cloth I went over to a stall I knew. On the ground, on graying canvas, was spread a mass of artifacts. In the back of the stall, in the shade, an old man sat eating figs. I picked through the masses of bits of old pottery and scraps of what purported to be papyrus. Some of the Egyptian forgers of antiquities were marvelous and could fake anything well. There were some old brass beads in a pot in the middle of the canvas. The old man in the back was watching me with gleaming eyes.

I looked over everything on the canvas. When I looked up, the old man came over to me.

"Carter," he said. "What are you looking for? What do you think I have?"

His voice was supposed to be plaintive, but he grinned at me. Evelyn was watching us from a few feet away.

"Oh," I said, "I never worry about you, sheikh. I know you never have anything really old."

The grin widened. He said, "I will show you something old."

"Don't do that. I don't like to put you to any trouble, since I know you have nothing but fakes here."

The old man dashed into the back of the stall. I glanced at Evelyn, watching raptly. She spoke rather good Arabic and understood everything she heard. The old man returned with a necklace.

"You see?"

He held out the necklace on his palms. It was made of innumerable small plates and chains linked together intricately, so that it jingled when he showed it to me. The tarnished metal seemed to be silver. Some of the plates bore an odd design. I reached for it, but the old man snatched it back.

"No, no. No touch."

"Bah," I said, disgusted, and started off. I put my hands in my pockets. If it had been genuine he would have had no qualms about letting me handle it.

"Carter! Thirty shilling!"

I kept on, strolling through the passing crowd. Suddenly the old man appeared before me, dangling his object in my face.

"Twenty-five shilling!"

"What do you take me for, sheikh? I don't spend my money on fakes."

"It is not a fake! Carter—do you think you are the only man in Egypt who knows antiquities?"

I had to stop; he was standing right in front of me. He cried, "Look! See the metal!" With his thumb he rubbed at the heavy black tarnish on one of the links, and a smutty gleam came through. "See how the links are joined! Twenty shilling!"

I grinned at him. The price was falling faster than the old lady's drawers. I said, "Clean another part of it, sheikh, ha? Or let me."

He yanked the necklace back out of range of my reaching hand again. His black eyes snapped with bad temper and bargaining zeal. For a moment we faced each other, he glaring at me, and I smiling at him.

At last, he said, "Fifteen shilling."

"Get out of my way, sheikh."

He retreated, grumbling. I glanced behind me; the

Countess and her maid, with Evelyn in among them, were watching me from the side of the lane. When they saw I was through with the old man, they started off down the lane again.

As she passed me, the Countess murmured, "Was it a fake?"

"Decidedly, my lady."

"Oh—too bad."

Evelyn smiled at me triumphantly from the shelter of her mother's grip. We went on down through the bazaar.

Near Saïs was a well called the King's Water, at the edge of a stretch of marsh called the King's House. On the strength of this puzzling name, a number of diggers had explored in the area, and each dig yielded enough material reward to keep them coming—but no one yet had cleared anything major there.

A large percentage of the artifacts uncovered at the site were from the Eighteenth Dynasty—Tutankhamun's dynasty. Therefore, as long as I could not dig in the Valley of the Kings at Thebes, I dug in the King's House.

In the evening after I had gone with the ladies to the bazaar, while I was washing out some items of clothing in my tent, the old man who had tried to sell the necklace to me put his head in through the door.

"Carter."

"Yes, sheikh." I wrung murky water out of my socks. The camp stool and the frame of my cot were draped in soggy undershorts and vests and the tent smelled dreary. "One moment," I said to the old man, and took my smoking old lantern off the table and went out of doors to talk to him.

He was not alone. Three or four other men loitered in the shadows beyond my tent, keeping well away from the light. On the other side of my tent were the tents of Carnarvon and his people and servants and the diggers. As I emerged from my own doorway, Carnarvon's voice said something sharply in the nearby tent, and there was a burst of answering laughter.

The old man and his friends drew me off into the dark a little way. We stood at the edge of the marsh. The moon was up, gleaming on the still water pooled among the rushes. I trod carefully on the uneven ground, where I had more than once put down my left foot on solid earth and my right down into the black muck.

"Carter," the old man said, "is this a fake?"

His teeth showed in a broad grin. He held out a figure no larger than my hand, and when I took it, made no effort to keep it back. Lifting the lantern, I bathed the object in the indifferent light.

It was a statue of a lion, made of soft, pale stone. I turned it over, impressed with the workmanship. On the bottom was a mark. I looked closer, and my hackles rose. It was the pharaonic cartouche of Tutankhamun.

"Where did you find this?"

The old man retrieved the lion. "We will show you. Yes? You and the Bey."

I swung the lantern back and forth, mulling this over. Something was out of joint in the whole business. "How much?" I said.

The men glanced at one another. The four Egyptians who had come with the old fellow stood close together, and whenever my light threatened to expose them, they withdrew from it. The old man turned back to me.

"One hundred shilling English."

"Let me see the lion again."

"Oh, no." The lion vanished inside the old man's loose, sashed gown. "Get the Bey and come with us."

I stared at them, warm with excitement. There was something wrong in this, but the lion looked authentic. Irresolute, I tried to make out their features, and they retreated from the swinging light of the lantern.

Out across the marsh a bird shrieked, and the wind rose, as if answering, a cool tingle along my neck and cheek. I made up my mind.

"Wait here."

They shifted together in the dark. I went back past my tent to Carnarvon's.

The Earl's tent was large enough for some stout furniture; Carnarvon was sitting in a stuffed armchair, and his wife across from him in a chair without arms. On the table between them was a litter of playing cards. Evelyn sat cross-legged on the floor; the maid was dozing in the back of the tent, beyond the light thrown by the lantern suspended over the table. As I entered, Carnarvon was saying, *"And* the ten of diamonds and the two of spades!" He tossed down cards as he spoke. His wife wailed; obviously he had won, although I had no idea what they were playing. Carnarvon looked up at me.

"Excuse me, sir," I said. "May I talk to you a moment?"

His eyes sharpened. "Yes, of course."

"It is rather late," said Lady Carnarvon. "Can't it wait until the morning?"

"Play solitare," Carnarvon said to her.

"But such a bore!"

He was already leading me out of the tent. In the dark, we walked off a few strides, out of the hearing of his wife, and I nodded to the old man and his entourage, waiting in the darkness by the head of the marsh.

"They have something they want to show us. Now. They want money. But it seems off true to me."

He gave the little group of Egyptians a searching glance and turned the same keen look on me. "How? What did they say?"

"They showed me an artifact that has Tutankhamun's reign name on it. It looks like the goods, but there's something. . . ." I shook my head. "Of course, there are many reasons why they'd insist on going at night. But it feels off, somehow."

24

"Marvelous instincts. I used to feel I'd die young." He glanced at the Egyptians again. "Are we to go alone, naturally?"

I nodded. "They want one hundred shillings."

"Wait here a moment," he said, and went back into his tent.

I raised my hand to the old man waiting at the marsh, to tell him that we were progressing. Inside his tent, Carnarvon and his wife had a brief discussion ending in a cry of dismay from the Countess. Through the tent canvas their shadows could be seen, and I watched them keenly; Carnarvon might be doing something foolish: for example, having us followed. I hoped he wasn't having us followed. He reappeared, smiling, his hands in the pockets of his jacket, and Evelyn behind him in the doorway calling, "May I come?"

"No," he said, over his shoulder. Without pausing, he walked on by me toward the Egyptians. I followed him, catching up with him as we joined the old man.

"Tell them that I have the money," Carnarvon said calmly, "but I won't pay them until we see whatever it is they have to show us."

The old man agreed to that without a murmur of protest. I could see Lady Carnarvon watching us from the doorway of the tent. We all set off together, going across the marsh.

The old man led us on a path that skirted a brackish pool rimmed in rushes sharp as daggers. The peeping of frogs sounded ahead of us but ceased at the sound of our approach. Shortly after we left the camp, one of the old man's followers slipped unobtrusively behind us. I did not glance behind me to see where he was going. He would stay on the path to warn the old man if we were followed. Carnarvon was trying to catch my eye. He was smiling.

"Carter," he said, "it's about time you brought me an adventure."

I was thinking about the lion. I had seen it for only a few moments but the figure was familiar: it closely resembled a larger stone lion that had been unearthed some years before at a quarry in the south, where it had obviously been carved. The lion was lying down, its head turned slightly, and its forepaws crossed. As I thought of the little figure I had just seen, my blood quickened, and I began to walk faster; Carnarvon had to catch my arm.

"How far is it now?" I asked the old man.

He gave me an eloquent Egyptian shrug.

We were now well into the marsh, and the insects had found us. I felt their lancet jaws at my neck and in my ears. The shriek of the marsh bird sounded again, this time to the far right. Stretches of rushes alternated with open water. The path twisted and circled around deep black pools that reflected the moon.

The lion could have been his talisman. Or a fake, of course, copied from the other stone lion. I began to fret, wondering.

Ahead, the path pinched down to a thread and wound into a tall thicket.

Carnarvon said, "Steady." He had stumbled; his hand caught my arm and he held me. Surprising. He seldom asked for any help. We went into the dark of the thicket, the lacy branches shutting out the moon.

Abruptly the old man, just ahead of me, darted off into the brush. I yelled, warned. The thicket erupted with men rushing at me and Carnarvon. Carnarvon's hand tightened hard on my arm; he was pulling me down. The Egyptians shrieked like banshees.

A piercing whistle cut through the racket. I jumped a foot at the sound. The Egyptians did not hesitate. In unison the whole crowd wheeled and took to their heels. Within seconds the thicket was deserted except for Carnarvon and me.

Carnarvon laughed. I straightened up out of my crouch, my ears cocked, and looked around. We were alone. The close quarters of the thicket made me nervous; I rushed out onto the open moonlit path. Carnarvon followed.

"Who were you calling?" I said.

My hands were shaking. I had been ambushed once before, and been badly beaten; I thanked God we had escaped that.

Carnarvon held out a silver whistle. "I wasn't calling anyone. You see the power of authority."

"Good God! Do you mean that was all? They ran from that?"

He laughed again, this time jubilant. We started down the path toward home, keeping a watchful eye out.

"Damn it," I said bitterly, after a time, "then it was a fake. Damn, damn."

Carnarvon laughed again. He tossed his silver whistle up and caught it in his hand. "A genuine adventure. Let me tell the ladies, Carter." He tossed the silver whistle up; it sparked in the moonlight.

Davis kept the licenses to dig in the Valley of the Kings until 1914, damn him, while I wasted my time in Saïs. In the course of it he found a number of tombs and some sensational finds, none more sensational than the ambiguous mummy of Tomb Number 55.

The Valley of the Kings is a narrow gully cut into the desert just to the west of ancient Thebes. At one end of this wadi, on the lower slope, Davis uncovered the doorway to a corridor that led back into the steep, flinty hillside. It ended at a chamber cut from the cold rock. That chamber was empty, stripped of all the funeral equipment that should have filled it, save for a few wrecked pieces of furniture. But in the alcove in the rear of the chamber, Davis found a mummy, laid out in the conventional pose of a woman, one fist clenched to the breast, and the other arm extended down straight along her side.

Davis, with his talent for misunderstanding what he found, proclaimed this oddly disposed body to be that of Queen Tiye, the Royal Wife of Amenhotep III, and mother of Akhenaten.

I say *oddly disposed*, because, on closer examination, the mummy turned out to be a man.

Someone had disguised him awfully well. His name and titles had been sliced off the gold bands around his torso and legs, and the single coffin in which he was buried bore no markings. The tomb had in fact been made for Queen Tiye, but there was no evidence that she had ever occupied it.

The body itself was in bad condition. Much is made today of the sacred, almost supernatural power of the Egyptian embalmers, but the truth is that the dry air of the desert, where most of the mummies have been found, would suffice to preserve most bodies. In this case, the work of the embalmers had been for nothing; water had seeped into the burial chamber and rotted the wooden bier that supported the coffin, and it had broken and pitched the coffin to the floor. The lid had fallen off, and the unprotected mummy had been reduced to little more than bones and tarry, moldering linen.

Davis, in his fashion, had broken so hastily and violently into the tomb that he destroyed any other clues to the real identity of the hidden (or disgraced) body. I saw it a few days after Davis found it; I went over the ground and through the tomb for evidence, but, finding nothing, I could make no firm guess about the mummy's identity. Yet I had a certain intuition about Davis's odd find.

The tomb was very close to the pit that Davis had uncovered some years before, almost within stone's throw of it. The fragments of evidence that had survived the harrowing years and Theodore Davis all seemed to point to the Eighteenth Dynasty. Who in that great dynasty would be apt to be so disgraced? I was sure—on no evidence but my feelings—that the misused body in Tomb Number 55 was that of Akhenaten himself.

And if it was Akhenaten, then whoever had fooled with the mummy must have done so during or near the reign of Tutankhamun, Akhenaten's successor.

I communicated none of my suspicions to Davis. In fact, he and I were hardly on speaking terms. I could do nothing except wait—while Davis like the Typhon of myth smashed and battered his way through the Valley of the Kings.

I had a house in Luxor, on the east bank of the Nile at the site of ancient Thebes. One day in 1914, after the digging season had closed, I was facing myself in the washroom mirror and trimming my mustaches. It was early morning, and I was expecting no one, so at first I overlooked the knock on the door.

At the second, louder banging, I went to the front room to answer and found Theodore Davis on my threshold.

"You have to sign this," he said. He held out a sheaf of papers, typed and folded.

He wore a black suit and waistcoat and carried an elegant soft hat in his hand. I had never before seen him in city clothes. He looked like someone's rich father.

"What are these?" I put my scissors into the pocket of my shirt and opened the papers.

"My report. I'm giving up my licenses to dig in the Valley of the Kings."

He walked into my house, and I pulled the door shut after him. My hands were trembling a little with excitement. Now I could begin the real search for Tutankhamun.

In the middle of the room, he stopped and looked around, at the window covered with a bit of cloth from the bazaar, and the desk half lost under books and papers. The rest of the room was stacked up with the crates where I kept my notes and gear.

He said, "They do pay you, Howard, don't they?"

"I spend it on women," I said.

His report was twenty pages long. I ruffled the edges with my thumb. "Do I have to read all this?"

"You should. It's the definitive archaeological description of the Valley of the Kings."

He ambled innocently around the room, pulled back the curtain to look into the room where my hammock was, and passed by my desk, his head cocked to read the letter lying on it. I sniffed. He trailed an aroma of shaving lotion behind him. He said, "Writing to Carnarvon, are you? Where will you be digging now?"

I ran my fingers over the expensive paper in my hand. "The Valley of the Kings."

"Save yourself the trouble. And your aristocratic pal a lot of money. The valley is exhausted."

"I think we'll try it."

"I went through there with a sieve, Carter!"

His report needed my signature. I patted my pockets, remembered that I had left my pen in the kitchen, and went after it. Davis stayed behind in the parlor. I heard the rustle of papers as he went through my desk. Spreading his report out on the kitchen windowsill, I held the pages down with my forearm and scribbled my name in the space marked SUPERVISING OFFICIAL.

"What's the date?"

"June 30, 1914."

I wrote that in.

Davis said, "D'you think you folks will get into this thing in Europe?"

I blinked around at him. He was standing in the doorway right behind me, rocking back and forth on his heels. I said, "What folks? What thing in Europe?"

"The fracas over the assassination."

"Oh. That Austrian prince." I folded his papers and held them out to him. "Or do you want me to file them for you? I'll have to go to Cairo for my licenses."

"The Grand-Duke Franz Ferdinand," Davis said portentously, "was the heir to the Austrian throne."

"Is he buried in the Valley of the Kings? Then I don't care."

Davis's fingers twitched at his mustaches. "You file them, if you're going to Cairo anyway."

"Very well."

I opened the drawer in the kitchen cupboard and dropped the papers in. Someday I would have to read them, but I certainly did not intend to let him know that.

"Well," he said, dogged, "if France goes in, Britain certainly will."

By now I knew perfectly well what he was talking about, but I could not resist the urge to bait him. I blinked several times at him and said, "Go in where?"

"The war, damn it!" he cried. "The war. But don't count on the U. S. of A. coming to rescue you!" He put on his soft hat and tugged the brim down. His gaze made another slow passage around my kitchen and over me. "Howard," he said, "you're a nut." He went out.

I hated Cairo. The Francophile Turks of the nineteenth century had remodeled it into a dirty version of Paris, but the succeeding hundred years had filled up the open spaces and streets with dumpy little hovels and dumpy little shops. Giza was close enough that from certain rooftops one could see the pyramids, but otherwise Cairo was like a foreign island in Egypt. Even the bank of the Nile was paved. Down the Corniche, stained with donkey dung beneath its shedding palms, an occasional motorcar swerved in and out of the carts and plodding beasts of burden, its klaxon horn braying every few feet. A dead cat floated in the water at the quay where my boat tied up. I went along the wharf and up toward the street. At the kiosk under the palm trees a man in a tweed waistcoat and a fez was stacking newspapers with headlines in French and English. Two Egyptian students waited, coins in hand. The assassination of the Archduke was still the most important news. I took my valise to my boardinghouse and went over to the Government Building.

Outside, this rambling structure of shaded courts and colonnaded porches was all Turk; inside, all English. There were umbrella stands inside every door, pictures of the

King overlooked the work of typists and clerks, and everybody wore shoes. The Department of Antiquities was on the third floor.

Behind the counter two young men sat at desks typing. The fan was broken. The blades hung motionless in the air and the string was black with flies comotose in the heat. While I was standing at the counter making out the filing ticket for Davis's report, a young Englishman rushed in through the door behind me.

"That's it," he called. "No fancy free trips to Luxor and Aswan. The whole junket's been canceled."

The two men at their desks stopped typing; their heads bobbed up, their faces wrinkled with dismay. "What?"

"Lord Kitchener. He isn't coming. Cancel the whole schedule. He's been called up to be War Minister."

They wailed. My pen jagged a dark line across the white form I was filling out. Something slipped into place in my mind. There was going to be a war. If there was a war, Carnarvon would not come to Egypt. I signed the form. My hands were trembling. Without Carnarvon to pay for the digging, I would have little chance to use my licenses.

I dashed around Cairo, from office to office, making out the applications. Everything had to be done in double. There was one set of forms for the government of the Khedive who reigned and one for the British Commissioner who ruled Egypt. I went up the steps to the Department of Antiquities five times that afternoon, never one at a walk. I was passionate to finish. If I could only begin the dig, I might drag Carnarvon into a commitment to it, even with a war on. The last train to Luxor left Cairo at sundown; and I felt that I had to be on it, or my heart would break.

The bureaucrats sensed it. They did everything with slow deliberation. I could understand it of the Egyptian clerks, who never did anything any other way, but the British drove me almost to a screaming fit. By five my clothes were sodden with sweat, my feet burned inside my shoes, and my hands were crippled with writer's cramp. With my licenses in my pocket I reached the railway station two minutes before the train left for Luxor. I collapsed into a seat. The train was passing through the maze of switches at Helwan on the outskirts of Cairo before I realized that I had left my valise back at the hotel.

The flood came in less than a week later. I had hired as many of the Copts who had dug for me at Saïs as I could find and filled out my crew with other men of that city, the best diggers in Egypt, the only ones who really appreciate what they are doing. I took them into the valley and we laid out the dig. I felt like a man trying to walk against a strong wind. The war was sweeping up the whole world. By mid-August, England was in, and there was a strong chance that Turkey would be forced in on the side of the Germans. Two German ships had escaped a British fleet in the Mediterranean and steamed into the Black Sea, where they promptly raised the flag of the Ottoman Empire and fired on Russian forts along the coast. The Turks denied any connection with it, but it was clear that they would have to join the Germans.

I wanted to dig in the area of the Valley of the Kings where Davis had uncovered the pit tomb and the mysterious mummy of Tomb Number 55. The department forebade it, since that would block the access of tourists to the tomb of Rameses VI, which, as I have said, was a most popular attraction. I went to Cairo to argue with them that in times of war no tourist was very likely to find his way down the Nile, but nobody would listen to me. They were all too nervous about what might happen if Turkey entered the war against England; surely the British Army would have to take over Egypt. I simply could not bend their minds to the mere matter of an archaeological dig.

I went back to Luxor. Two days later, Britain declared war on the Turks. The Crown took over direct administration of Egypt, and I received an "urgent invitation" to report to Cairo.

# 4

I was attached to the staff of Lord Allenby, the commander in chief, as a civilian liaison man. Thereafter I spent my days at the impossible job of interpreting English orders to Egyptians, and Egyptian reactions to the English.

Whenever I could get leave, I went up to Luxor. Most of the men from the town and the nearby village of Kurna had gone to feed the war. The Copts, also, had gone. I could not begin any new digs, but in my free time I could finish half-done things. I cleared out the tomb of Amenhotep III, discovering that Queen Tiye had actually lain there with her husband, nowhere near the mysterious tomb up the valley where Davis claimed to have found her.

I spent some time turning that over in my mind. I would sit on the veranda of my house wondering how it all fit together: the tomb that had apparently been built for a queen, which had housed the body of (perhaps) her son, disguised as a woman; the pit with its bits of gold, incised with the name of Tutankhamun; the blue cup, also bearing that name. They all fit. If I have any faith at all, it's that history makes sense. Sometimes, as when you stare up at the stars, and around the corners of your vision see other, invisible stars, I could contemplate my clues and glimpse the order that linked them.

But it was impossible to do anything sustained or innovative. The war was a kind of foul generator. The more the war consumed, the louder it chugged along.

One night, two years after Franz Ferdinand was assassinated, while I was sitting on the veranda of my house with a book, a man from Kurna came to me. He was an old man, important in the village, and had often spied for me on Theodore Davis. We trusted each other.

"Carter," he said, "we need your help. Someone in the village has found something in the valley—"

I put down my book and got to my feet.

"And some of the other men have gone out to try to steal it. There will be a quarrel. Carter, someone will be hurt."

"What have they found?"

The old fellow shrugged, his palms raised, eloquent. "You know the people of Kurna. But you are not one of us, you can be impartial, and they will accept your word. Go, make them give up whatever they have found, and come back to Kurna before they hurt each other."

I went back into the house for a coil of rope, a lantern, and my sturdy boots. When I returned to the veranda, the old man was walking away down the path. I ran after him.

"Come and show me where this is taking place."

"Hurry."

We crossed the Nile and went up the sloping valley toward the desert escarpment. The moon was rising. The flat surfaces of the ruins that litter the east bank of the Nile were painted in the blue light. Over where the village of Kurna was huddled in and among the relics of the past, a few yellow fires shone. My heart quickened as I walked. They were old hands at finding the secrets of the valley;

more than one of the great discoveries there was found first by a man of Kurna.

We took the narrow foot path that leads along the upper edge of the valley, along the verge of the desert plateau. With the moon at our backs we could hurry. It was much colder on the cliff than below. I carried the rope first on one shoulder, then on the other. My old friend seemed tireless. He had not been sitting around in an office in Cairo signing papers. The path was worn a foot deep into the stone of the cliff; doubtless it had been here for centuries—millennia. Near the top it was steep, and I paused to rest a moment.

Behind us, far below, was the broad flood plain. The river that had brought it into being cast its loops through the darkness into the north. Once this cliff had joined the one on the far side, and the whole of Egypt had been one flat tableland, until the river cut this valley from it. It moved me to think of it. Don't ask why: the enormity of time involved, perhaps, the great passage of time.

I looked in the other direction, over the desert. Far down on the top of the cliff something moved in the dark.

"Come on," I said. I put my feet under me.

On the desert shelf a bitter wind met me. The rope weighed me lopsided and I had to step short to keep from stumbling. The moonlight confused my eyes. I began to wonder if I did not see something glowing, up ahead. A moment later, a shot cracked out, and I exclaimed and broke into a run.

There was a light ahead on the edge of the cliff. I tripped over a rock and fell to my hands and knees. The elder from the village huffed and gasped in my tracks.

Ahead of us someone shouted.

My knees hurt. I staggered on a few steps and stopped. Before me in the middle distance was a group of men, standing near the edge of the gorge that opened to my left. One of them was carrying the light. They were arguing, but one of them saw me and pointed, and they hushed.

"It's Howard Carter," I called. "I'm coming up; don't shoot." I strode toward them. I couldn't give them a chance to think; I had to take charge of them. I walked straight in among them, standing as straight and tall as I could.

There were four or five of them, mostly boys. One had a large revolver that he was aiming around him, first at one boy, then at another. His face was wild. I put out my hand for the gun.

"Now, what's this?" I said, in the loudest, firmest voice I could muster. "Give me that gun. Yes, give me the gun. The rest of you, stand up straight, hands at your sides, there."

The frightened boy with the gun put it in my hands as if he were glad to see it go. The others stepped self-consciously together, although none of them straightened up or put his hands to his sides.

With the gun in my hand, I really was in charge, and I lowered my voice considerably.

"What are you doing? The valley belongs to the government, you know—and everything in it. Tell me exactly what you are doing here."

The old man reached us. His glance raked the boys, whose faces were lit by the lantern the middle of them still carried. My old friend turned to me.

"Ahmed is not here. It is Ahmed who does everything evil in Kurna, now that the men have gone to the army." He turned back to the boys. "Where is Ahmed?"

The young man who had held the gun pointed down over the edge of the gorge. "There. He is in the cave."

"What cave?" I went to the lip of the Valley of the Kings. Black shadow filled it. Near my foot a rope was hanging over the edge. I followed it back with my eyes and saw it was secured around a great rock. "How many feet down is it?" I said, and knelt, and tested the rope.

"I was standing guard," said the boy behind me. "These —dogs—swine—"

The other boys growled at him. Wildly he went on,

"They tried to scare me away! So they could rob him, when he comes up!"

"Who is Ahmed?" I asked of the old man. I made my own rope fast to the boulder.

"Young," the old man said. "Bad. A very restless bad young man. What are you doing, Carter?"

"I am pulling up Ahmed's rope," I said. I did so. The other boys were watching me, standing close together, Ahmed's sentry with the others. "Go home," I said, "and put your heads under your pillows, and don't come out until your mothers call you for breakfast."

"My gun," the sentry said.

The other boys were already moving off, relieved, I suppose, that I wasn't arresting them. I had no authority to do that, naturally, nor any inclination. With Ahmed's rope raised, I dropped my own rope, which I trusted, down over the cliff.

"What are you doing, Carter?" the old man said. "You cannot go down there tonight. Are you mad? You have trapped him—he cannot get away now. Wait until morning."

"When I signal," I said, "pull the rope up, and don't let it down again until I call you."

"Carter!"

By morning Ahmed could have broken into anything he found in the tunnel. I shook my head. The old man wagged his from side to side, bemused. He pointed to the boy who remained with us.

"You stay here and help me."

The boy nodded. I swung myself down over the cliff and climbed down the rope.

I had lowered my rope in exactly the same place as Ahmed's, but still I did not see the hole in the cliff until I had almost passed it. It opened out a yard and a half to my left, a narrow keyhole shape in the face of the rock. I took my electric torch from my belt.

For a moment I swung there on the end of the rope, one

38

leg coiled around the rope to brake my weight. The cave was far enough down from the top of the cliff that Ahmed might not have heard the shot or the arguing or the scuffling above his head. There was no light inside the cave, not a sign of movement, nothing. I covered the torch's face with my hand and turned it on, opening my fingers to let out a thin beam of light.

The gleam showed me the first few feet of the cave. It was empty. I shut off the torch, stuffed it into the waistband of my trousers, and swung on the rope into the cave.

My foot hit the side. I bit my lip to keep from grunting at the pain. Ahmed was here somewhere. I still held the rope in my hand, and I gave a jerk on it and let go. A moment later the old man drew it up away from me.

I took the electric torch in one hand and the gun in the other.

"Ahmed," I called.

Abruptly I thought to look over my shoulder. I was standing in front of the cave opening, silhouetted for anyone coming from within the cave. I ducked down like a rabbit.

There was no sound from within the cave. I raised my voice.

"Ahmed!"

"Who's there?" a voice called, from the impenetrable darkness.

"It's Howard Carter," I said. "Come out, and let's talk about how you're getting home."

Silence. Although I strained my ears, I could hear nothing down there. I wondered how far away he was—if he had a gun, too.

"Ahmed," I called. "We've taken up your rope, and mine as well. Either you leave now, or you can stay here, permanently."

"You'll stay too, Carter Bey!" came from the darkness.

"I'm willing," I said. "I ate a late supper."

More silence. The wind fluttered along the cliff outside.

It was warmer in the tunnel than in the open. I wondered how far back it went, this tunnel, and what lay at the end, and my nerves quickened.

The man down the tunnel said, "Where is Fuad?"

"He surrendered to us," I said.

Ahmed began to swear. He was angry, and he made a colorful choice of words.

"Yes, yes," he said, after a series of other phrases. "I will go. You are a bad man. I will go, as you say."

I put out my head into the open and bellowed to the old man to lower the rope. Muttering at me, Ahmed crawled into the throat of the tunnel. I switched on my electric torch. My first sight of him rattled me: in spite of his youth, he was an enormous man, brawny, muscular, the true southern type. His eyes rolled at me. His breath hissed between his clenched teeth. The rope slapped down against the cliff wall nearby us.

"Go on," I said.

"English pig."

"What did you call me?"

He reached out for the rope and swung agilely across the face of the cliff, paddling in the air with his feet, and hoisted himself out of sight up toward the clifftop.

The tunnel was mine. I sat still a moment, shaking off the tension gathered in the routing of Ahmed. The place seemed much larger now, inviting. On hands and knees I started into the tunnel, pushing the torch on ahead of me.

"Carter," the villager called. His voice was faint.

I slid backwards to the mouth of the tunnel again and put my head out. "Just a minute. I will come up presently."

"Carter!"

With the torch lighting the way, I crept on hands and knees into the tunnel. Ten feet from the opening in the cliff the walls pinched in so narrow I had to slide through sideways. I held the torch ahead of me but all it showed me was the rough wall of the fissure. That was all it was, a fissure in the cliff.

My breathing sounded very loud. The stone ground at my back and scraped across my chest. My neck was twisted awkwardly and began to hurt. The tunnel curved, and I squeezed into the bend and then was caught as if in a vise.

The cliff had me clamped in its grip. I could hardly even expand my chest enough to breathe. How Ahmed had gotten through here I could only wonder at. Perhaps he had stopped here. I strained to free myself. A spur of rock dug into my side from the back. Panicking, I wrenched myself backwards.

My hand with the torch struck the rock and I dropped the torch. It went out. Utter darkness closed around me.

At first I could not breathe for fear. Slowly I came back to myself. After all, other people knew I was here. The open air was less than fifteen feet behind me. I collected my wits. Perhaps I could go forward. I pressed my back to the stone and inched ahead.

The rock scraped across my chest; I heard a button pop off my shirt. The pressure eased. I was through. I took a step forward, surprised to find that the close-pressing cliff walls fell away from me, and I seemed to be standing in the open, as if in a great room.

Matches. I fumbled in my pockets until I found a box and struck a light.

The faint light steadied. I held it up so that I could see around me. I was in a large chamber. The walls had been smoothed and squared; so once it had been used, for a cache, perhaps.

It was all but empty now. The match light flickered on the smooth, female curves of a jar lying on its side against the far wall, half-inundated in centuries of dust. There was nothing else there but me. Whatever this room had held once, it had long since been looted. The match went out.

"Carter?" a voice called, at the other end of the tunnel.

"Yes," I said. "It's all right. I'm coming." I wiped my hand wearily over my eyes.

The following morning, when I came back from the market, my house had been broken into, and my desk maliciously handled: nothing taken, just papers strewn around and books thrown on the floor. My teapot was full of mud and there was a dead bird in my bed. I sent for Ahmed, the tomb robber of Kurna.

When he came I was on the veranda, writing in my notebook. He stood just off the path to the front steps. The railing was between him and me, like bars.

"Did you want me, Carter Bey?"

I looked him over, trying to make him squirm. I had not misjudged his great height, back in the cave; although he was standing on the ground his head and shoulders cleared the top rail. His mud-handling, bird-handling fingers were behind him. We stared at each other for several moments.

"Ahmed," I said, "I was not acting for myself, last night. I was acting in the place of the government. If you keep trying to revenge yourself on me, I will make use of the government against you."

His lips widened into a contemptuous smile. He raised his hands to the top rail and leaned on them.

"I know you," he said. "I know all about you, Carter Bey. You are a thief, like me, a tomb robber, that's all."

"Better than you," I said. "There was nothing in that cave you found, Ahmed. Nothing. And I got through the tunnel, which you did not."

He muttered an oath at me and walked away.

In the heat of the season I often slept on a hammock on the veranda. That night the smell of smoke awakened me. I sprang up, all my hair on end; even in the dark I could see the roiling black smoke escaping from under the veranda steps.

With the broom from the kitchen I raked out a mass of smoldering rags and cotton waste that had been stuffed into the space behind the steps. My blood went hot with temper. I seemed to feel every shooting pulse. I beat the smoking heap apart with the head of the broom and sat down on the step. The wood was warm. Dry as powder, it would have exploded into flames. Fortunately the fool had wadded his tinder together so tightly that it smothered out the fire.

I looked up at the stars. In three days I had to go back to Cairo to carry silly messages about for the British Army. Everything suddenly clotted together into one festering gall: Ahmed, my job, the war, the government, the army, the looters and robbers who had got into the chamber in the cliff ahead of me. I could not begin to sleep. Until day came there was nothing else to be done, so I lay in my hammock watching the slow wheel of the stars and thinking of revenge.

In the morning I went to the army recruitment office in Luxor, where the War Office signed men into the army to be taken off and made into bait for cannons and poisonous gas. With the war going on so long, they were desperate and would take anybody. A sergeant with a hangover gave me all the proper forms. I went back across the Nile to the path that led to Kurna.

I went up the street toward the village. Ahead of me three or four Kurnite women were walking, encased in black from head to toe, with jars of water balanced on their heads. I followed them past the crumbling walls of the temples where their distant ancestors had worshiped Osiris in the form of a dead Pharaoh. The living village was made of the same mud, often the same bricks. Were they so wrong, the ancients?

I went through the twisted street to the house of my elderly friend, who had taken me out to catch Ahmed on the cliff.

His house was one square block of mud brick. In the unshuttered window, strings of mullet roe hung to dry. I smelled the beans cooking over the fire, laced with onion. The old man met me at the door and led me into his home.

We squatted down on the rugs that cushioned the floor, and he took out his tobacco and a pipe made of glass, and we exchanged the amenities and smoked. Finally I took the recruitment papers out of my pocket.

"Do you know what these are?"

To my surprise, he did. His son had gone into the army. I explained what I wanted to do, and he sat breathing smoke, his eyes half-closed. Halfway through my explanation, he began to nod.

"Very excellent, Carter Bey, but are they not to be signed? Will Ahmed sign them?"

"Can Ahmed write?"

"Ah," he said, and smiled.

"All I need is this information—his age, his full name, the names of his parents."

"Ah."

"Will you help me?"

"I am not fond of Ahmed. Of course, everyone will know it was I who helped you." He stroked his pointed gray beard. "Very well."

We filled out the forms. When we came to the space for the date of recruitment, I wrote in a date over two months gone.

"Will they accept this?" my friend said.

"You don't know the army," I said. "All I have to do is put it in the file. It may take them another two months to find it, but when they do, they'll send half the knickers in Luxor to take Ahmed."

"Carter Bey," my friend said, "you are a Turk."

I signed Ahmed's name in the proper place. Under it was a space for a witness. I signed my name there, clearly, so that Ahmed would find out. Surely someone would read him the name of the witness.

At noon the old man invited me to dine with him. We ate bread and beans and onions and rice, and argued about whether the British would let the Khedive have his government back, after the war.

"Not the Khedive," my friend said. "The Khedive is a Turk. They will give Egypt back to the Egyptians."

"The British never give anything back, once they've taken it," I said. "It would be an admission of theft."

"They have promised us. We shall have our independence."

"They won't keep their promises, they never do," I said. "Besides, foreigners have ruled Egypt for thousands of years. You ought to resign yourselves, some people are fated to be oppressed."

"Once Egypt ruled Egypt," he said. "Once. As you know."

I went back to Luxor. My leave ended at sundown the next day, and I would have to go back to Cairo that night. In Luxor, I returned to the recruitment office, asked the sergeant, still battling the agents of his debauch, to bring me a file from the back room, and, while he was swearing and ringing open the drawers, slid Ahmed's recruitment papers under a pile of other papers on the desk. I began to smile. I relaxed, drew a deep breath, and put thoughts of Ahmed out of my mind.

The war ended. The British did not allow the Khedive to return. Nor did they elevate an Egyptian government to real power. There was a little trouble over that with a labor union, which delayed the return of Lord Carnarvon to Egypt until 1920.

I went to meet them at the wharf of Luxor; Carnarvon had chosen to sail up the Nile, although now most tourists took the train. As the boat turned sedately to approach the wharf, with a start of shock I recognized the old man standing at the rail as Carnarvon. It had been seven years since our last meeting, but he looked fourteen years older.

Beside him was a young woman in a hat. I shook hands with Carnarvon, and he turned to the girl and said, "You recall my daughter, Evelyn."

"Oh. Naturally." I gave her a startled look. Vaguely I remembered pinafores, braids, black shoes, certainly nothing to prepare me for the tall, slim girl who coolly put her hand out to me and smiled.

"Hello, Mr. Carter. I'm so glad to see you again. To be here again."

A little parade of fellahin passed up and down the gangplank past us, lugging down Carnarvon's baggage. The brown leather cases were plastered with steamship stickers. I stuck my hands in my pockets.

I began, "How was your—" and simultaneously Carnarvon said, "Got through the war all right, did you?"

"Oh. Fairly. Better than I expected."

Their baggage was stacked on the wharf. I led them toward the motorcar I had hired to take them up to the hotel. Lady Evelyn walked along in front of me. She wore a linen dress; she walked with an athletic boyish grace.

Carnarvon was on my left. I shortened my stride a little, so that I would not outwalk him. "I have all the plans laid out," I said. "I judge we can cover the Valley of the Kings in six good seasons."

Lord Carnarvon cleared his throat. I knew something was wrong.

The Egyptian driver was sitting in the front seat of the motorcar. He did not get out to hold the door, and I scurried around ahead of Lady Evelyn and yanked the door open and helped her climb the single high step into the back seat. Carnarvon settled himself beside her. His gaze aimed straight ahead, he fluffed his mustaches with his forefinger. I expected him to comment on the driver's cheekiness, but he did not.

I sat in the front passenger seat. It would have been awkward to try to talk leaning back over the seat, and so I said nothing more to Carnarvon. The driver took us off with a roar and a spray of dust. He had driven lorries during the war. I had told him to take us up to the hotel by a circular route through the ruins of the Great Temple at Karnak. Now I regretted it. Something was wrong, and

I could guess what it was: Carnarvon was losing his taste for archaeology.

At top speed we raced past the tumbled blocks and columns of the Imperial Temple. The Ninth Pylon cast its shadow across the road. We passed by a heap of blocks that had come out of the core of another column. A team of Americans had begun looking them over and discovered that they had all once been part of the wall of a great Temple of Aten that Nefertiti had sponsored and that the Amunist Horemheb had torn down. Through the corner of my eye, I saw Lady Evelyn surveying the ruins, her hat clamped on with one hand. The shadows of the columns flickered over us like a moving film. I rubbed my hands on my knees. Without Carnarvon's help I could not dig.

We reached the old hotel where I had engaged them a suite, and while the servants were bringing in the crates and trunks of baggage, Lady Evelyn got her father settled in a chair in the study. She disappeared into the back of the suite. I waited nervously by the window.

Carnarvon sat there looking tired. He did not move; he seemed not to have the will to move.

"Is it too bright in here?" I asked. The sunlight poured in through the wide french windows.

"Yes," he said, and I closed the lace curtains. He said, grouchy, "Place smells awful. What d'you do, Howard, store mummies in it?"

I laughed, in case he intended that to be funny. He leaned back in the chair and crossed his legs, and for a moment I saw the old Carnarvon, perfectly turned out, supremely confident.

He said, "Sorry we couldn't get down here last year, Howard."

"I can understand that." The year before we had been face to face with the rebellious Egyptian labor union. It had required Lord Allenby's talents to lure the natives back into harness. I said, "We can go right out to the dig tomorrow morning, if you want."

"Now, there's something I must—" he began, and then Evelyn came in with a tray of tea things.

He let out a gusty sigh and sat straight up. Beaming, she put down the tray and poured his cup full and put cream and sugar in. She had not even taken her hat off yet, but when she had the cup in his hand, she stepped back, the corners of her mouth tucked back in a smile, and pulled her hat off and ran one hand over her fluffy brown hair and grinned at me.

"That's better," her father said. "You dear girl."

"Will you have tea, Howard?"

I shook my head.

Carnarvon put the saucer down on the table beside his chair. The room was stocked with old-fashioned furniture; with the draped french windows and the ticking mantel clock, we might have been back in England. An older England, before the war. The Earl sipped his tea.

"Carter," he said. "I'll be frank. I don't want to dig another six years."

"I don't honestly think we can do a fair job on the valley in less than that," I said.

"I can't afford it anymore. Money doesn't buy as much anymore—the damned war . . ." He held out his cup, and Evelyn rose to pour. "You expect too much of me," he said.

"How can we give up now?" I said. "I'm sure that Tutankhamun is somewhere in the Valley of the Kings. Now we have the licenses—the first real chance we've had to dig—"

"Our first chance," he said. "Everybody else has already given up. Egyptologists have been shoveling up the Valley of the Kings for years, Carter. Men as good as you."

"Father," Evelyn said. She held the teapot lid on with one finger while she tipped it over his cup.

"Besides, there's this problem with the local people."

I sat down in a cane-bottomed chair beside the window. Nervously I fingered the white fringe on the doily on the table beside me. "I don't think we'll have any more problem with the Egyptians."

"It was a bloody revolution," the Earl said. His head bobbed up and down over the last word. "The damned Jews and Bolsheviks—"

Lady Evelyn said, "Tea, Howard?"

"No, thank you."

She was pouring tea, anyway. "It's marvelous for steadying the nerves."

"I'm telling you, Carter," her father said, "it isn't our world anymore. The damned wogs are taking over everything."

"One lump or two, Howard?"

"I don't—one, please. Cream. The situation in Egypt is pretty much settled, my lord. Allenby won a lot of goodwill, letting the labor leaders come home out of exile." The Egyptians, new at rebellion, were naïvely appreciative of that. I let go of the white fringe to take my cup and sat there stirring and stirring the pale tea. "It wasn't anything like a revolution, actually—"

Carnarvon said, "I know what it was, Carter."

His jaw was set like the lintel on the Ninth Pylon. I stirred the tea around and around, wondering what had happened to him to make him like this. I sipped English tea.

"The damned war," Carnarvon said. He pinched his nose between his thumb and forefinger.

"Father wants to continue the digging on a year-to-year basis," Lady Evelyn said. "If everything goes well—"

"That isn't what I said," Carnarvon said.

"If the new Egypt is so bloody awful—"

"Evelyn, don't use that word."

"It behooves you to support the old Egypt. Doesn't it?"

"Bah," he said. Standing, pulling the sleeves of his coat down, he gave us both a bitter look. "I'm going up to rest before supper." He left the room. His feet were heavy on the carpeted floor.

Evelyn sighed. She went to the marble mantel to view the old clock, bracketed by cupids.

"Thank you," I said.

"Not at all. When shall we go out to the valley?"

"Tomorrow. I'll come here, eight or so, with the motor-car."

"Good," she said. "Thank you for all you've done, Howard." She smiled at me, but her eyes went beyond me, and she looked weary. Glancing at her wristwatch, she opened the face of the clock on the mantel and moved the hands carefully back to the right time.

That evening I was out on the veranda of my own house, going over a chart of the valley by the light of a lamp. Gradually I became aware that someone was standing in the darkness just beyond the steps. I peered at the huge, vague shape there in the dark.

"Yes?"

"Hello, Carter Bey."

I went cold all over. It was Ahmed, the tomb robber from Kurna. I pushed my work away across the desk. A book fell to the floor. "Oh," I said. "Hello. I thought you were in the army."

He came closer to the rail, into the lamplight. "I was." He made a mirthless smile at me. "The war is over, Carter Bey."

His face had filled out. His gaze, shifty before, was direct now, even arrogant. But he was not going to attack me. His hands hung empty at his sides. I leaned on my elbows on the desk.

"And you came back to Kurna," I said.

"Yes. I want work. I thought of my friend Carter, who was so helpful in the past. In finding me work."

"Oh, really?"

"You are digging in the Valley of the Kings? I want to work for you."

"I have my crew," I said.

He shook his dark head. His smile was gone, and he looked angry. "I will be the leader. The foreman. Not just one of the diggers."

"I'm sorry. I already have a foreman."

"Then make two foremen."

"You have no experience. Besides, as I said, I have no use for you."

"I know the valley foot by foot," he said. He leaned toward me across the railing. "I am strong—I will work harder than anyone else. I speak English—"

"No, damn you." I reached across the littered desk for the pad of paper I had been writing on. "Get out."

He made a half shrug and went away into the darkness. I sat hunched over my chart, my mind buzzing. I had forgotten all about him. Of course, he had to come back now, when I was already burdened with Carnarvon's new temperament. I forced myself back to work on the chart.

In the morning, all our donkeys had been run off. We spent most of the morning herding them up, and all the afternoon ushering Carnarvon around the valley, and got no work done at all. When I had returned him and Evelyn safely to their hotel, I dragged myself exhausted back to my own house.

The place had been ransacked. All my books had been pulled off the shelves and the pages torn.

My temper exploded. Shivering with rage, I set off at a dead run for Kurna, on the west bank of the Nile.

It was suppertime. The houses in the ruins were full of people. Talk rose from the windows with the aroma of beans and onions. The streets were empty. I dashed up toward Ahmed's house, on the edge of the village.

A brown goat was tied up to the front door. Goat droppings like pebbles covered the path. I knocked on the door. No response. I tried the latch and found the door barred. Standing back, I slammed my foot into the door, and the whole panel fell inward.

Ahmed was a big man, or I would not have caught him. He was climbing out the back window as I dashed into his house, and the window was too small for him. I got him by the back of his robe. Caught, he wheeled around to face me.

"What do you want?" I shouted. "Money? If it's money, you're wasting your time, Ahmed."

Three or four people were watching us from the doorway. Ahmed's gaze flickered at them. He put his hand to his mouth, but he said nothing. I screamed into his face.

"If you lift one finger against me again, Ahmed, I'll show you things the army never showed you!" I shook my fist in his face. I wanted to beat him to a jelly. I wished he would strike me so that I could have struck him back. He stood still, his hands between us, fending me off.

I looked around, panting. There was a shelf on the wall, lined with jugs. I yelled. Grabbing a jar, I lifted it over my head and smashed it on the floor.

The people in the doorway shrilled with excitement. Ahmed clenched his fists. I took up the next jar and threw it down on the floor, all the while watching his face. Oil splattered both of us. He did not move; he said nothing; he did not look at me. I went along the shelf casting the jars down at his feet, until he was standing in a puddle of oil and his house was littered through with the fragments of his jars. I went up to him again.

"Stay away from me!"

He blinked. I went off through the midst of a dozen people in his doorway, and went home.

After Carnarvon had been a week out on the dig, he came to me at noontime and said, "There is a fellah in Kurna I think you ought to hire."

I did not have to ask who that fellah was. We were sitting on the slope of the ravine, above the digging site. Two yellow camels were tethered just to my left, the lunch hampers slung over their backs. Ahmed must have come with them, because there he was, off at the edge of the trench, carefully not looking at me and Carnarvon.

The Earl sat spraddle-legged on the ground beside me, picking the onions out of a dish of meat. He said, "I spent most of the last hour talking to the man. He seems to know the Valley of the Kings upside down. Even better than you do, Howard."

I did not answer that. Evelyn was below us, walking along the side of the trench with a notebook in her hand. Lady Evelyn. She had her straw hat tied on with a scarf. Like everything else in the valley, her hat was dun-colored, but the scarf was bright orange.

"Howard, I want you to do as I say," Carnarvon said.

"Yes, my lord."

Carnarvon smiled at me. The brim of his hat shaded his eyes. "Good man, Howard."

I did not answer. I was surprised how I hated him for that, for using me like that. After our years together, he could have been a little more kind.

Ahmed stopped calling me "Bey." Now when he said "the Bey" he meant Carnarvon.

# 5

We began work on the floor of the valley below the tomb of Amenhotep III, where I had worked during the war, and were trenching along the foot of the slope. I set Ahmed to leading that part of the crew carrying fill from the trench up to the dumping ground to one side of the Amenhotep excavation. Periodically I went up to inspect the dirt we were removing; the third or fourth time I appeared at his work site Ahmed began to bristle.

"You think I am slighting the work," he said to me, angry.

"Not at all."

I squatted down on my heels and took a handful of the dirt and spilled it out again. Black flinty chip, the same as we had been cutting through all morning.

"Then why are you here? Playing with the dirt?"

His whole manner irritated me, and I was long in answering, so that he would know. I straightened up and faced him. "Yes: playing with the dirt. Sometimes the first sign that we're coming into something is a sudden change in the character of the fill."

His face altered; for an instant he looked ashamed of himself.

"Satisfactory?" I asked. "Or shall I put it in writing?"

That made him angry. His black eyes glittered. He began to say something, but a shout from the trench below us interrupted him.

I wheeled. All along the site, workmen were running toward the trench. On the edge, the old foreman stood waving his arm over his head. I sprinted across the floor of the valley toward him.

Lady Evelyn was kneeling in the bottom of the trench, down in the deep blue shadow. She tipped up her face to me. "Howard—it's a wall. Come show me what to do."

I jumped down beside her. The two of us crowded the space. Just behind the head of the trench, in the bottom, she had uncovered a hard worked edge of stone. My heart began to thud. Kneeling, I felt along the edge with my fingers.

"What do I do?" she said.

I was about to tell her to go up to the surface and let me clear it, but a glance at her face told me that would be a cheat. I called up for two shovels, showed her where to dig, and the two of us began clearing either end of the edge.

Babbling with excitement, the workmen packed the lip of the trench to watch. I heard Carnarvon's deeper, English voice among them. Lady Evelyn's arms thrust and pumped with her shovel. When she had exposed another two feet of the edge, I touched her shoulder, and she stepped back, breathing hard.

The air was acrid with dust. It was hard to see. I bent to grope along the stone and found a right angle.

"There's the corner," I said. "Now, let me find the corner at my end, and we can take a measure and see what we have."

Raising my head, I caught the eye of the man directly

above me on the top of the trench. It was Ahmed. I sent him for a basket for the dirt.

Before he came back, I had uncovered the other corner. I straightened. My back hurt. At my feet the neat stone edge rose out of the dirt. I shook my head.

"What?" Evelyn asked, apprehensively.

"It's too small to be a tomb," I said. The edge was only about a yard long. Ahmed landed behind us in the trench, light as a cat, and silently began to shovel up the dirt we had thrown off. I bent to examine the rock wall.

"It's a cache, maybe."

Her hand touched my shoulder. "I'm sorry," she said.

She was beginning to amaze me. She had all the exuberance and generosity a man is supposed to have and never does.

We spent the rest of the afternoon digging away from the other three walls of our find. I showed Evelyn how to record measurements and draw the diagrams to show exactly what we had found. We spent an hour over supper talking about the tools and building techniques of the ancients. In Egypt there is no wood, and that single fact, I think, explains more about Egyptian building practices than anything else.

For that same reason I discarded a pet theory of mine that the close-packed columns of the great temples had their power over the ancients because it reminded them of the primordial jungle. For a long time I had tried to imagine that the Egyptians had migrated here from somewhere to the south.

The following morning saw us removing the contents of the square pit Evelyn had discovered. It was full of rubble: chip from the tombs built nearby, probably, mostly flints, but here and there a layer of the softer white stone from the east end of the valley. I made careful records of everything and saved out samples of each type of rock. Evelyn did most of her own digging.

At noon we all stopped for lunch. I looked down the

valley, hot as a smelter in the sun. On either side the pale hillsides were veiled in the dust we had raised. The sky was the color of lapis lazuli, the blue of ancient Egyptian faience work.

"Beautiful, isn't it?" Carnarvon said, beside me. He dipped up water from the jug. "And yet nothing grows here, it produces nothing, it's utterly worthless." He dropped the dipper back into the water jug with a splash. His forehead was puckered into furrows, as if something puzzled him.

In the evening our careful digging in Evelyn's cache exposed a round of alabaster. Evelyn gave a cry. She insisted that I show her how to clear away the dirt packed around the thing, and in the course of freeing the first jar we found another, and another after that, alabaster jars lying on their sides, with handles in the shape of lotus stems. On her knees, she whisked away the dirt with a little broom and bent over her notebook, spread beside her on the rubble, to sketch the relative positions.

Around the site the gathered workmen were watching, their faces split with wide grins. They appreciated what she was doing, perhaps, even more than I did.

In all there were thirteen jars. She removed each one herself. But there was nothing else in the cache, and we found nothing else that year.

The next year was 1921. We found nothing at all.

By the end of that season Carnarvon was determined to quit. Evelyn talked to him, I argued with him, and in the end, to please her, he promised to finance my work in the valley up to January 1, 1923, but not a day or a shilling more.

I was determined to go on in my search, even if Carnarvon defected. Exactly how I would finance my work remained a problem. Then, during the flood, a photographer from the finest museum in New York City arrived in Cairo to work with the local collection.

I went immediately down to Cairo from Luxor. I intended to meet this American, but I wanted the meeting to seem unintentional. I spent two days at the Cairo Museum without encountering him, but I did find out that he was digging up old files in the Department of Antiquities, on the other side of Cairo.

The river had only begun to ebb. Cairo simmered in the heat. The streets were empty, and all the shops closed: everyone had gone indoors until the evening. Only the English offices were still open. I trotted up the steps of the Department Building and into the dusty shade of the interior.

My quarry was in the bursar's office. I loitered outside in the corridor, pretending to read notices and newspaper clippings fastened up on a board on the wall. The door to the bursar's office was ajar and I could see the young American's back as he talked across the counter to another man. The corridor was dark and stiflingly hot; my hair and shirt were soaked. Excited, I waited for the young American to come out. I would bump into him going in, apologize, and introduce myself. I began to practice the introduction in my mind.

Twenty feet down the hall a door slammed.

"Howard Carter!"

Startled, I jerked up my head at the sound of my name, while a tall, balding, red-faced man tramped down on me.

"Well, this is most opportune. There's a matter that needs your attention. I was afraid we would have to send away to Luxor for you."

"Who are you?" I asked, bewildered.

"Conway. Assistant curator in charge of catalogs."

Instead of offering his hand to shake, he lifted it slightly toward his forehead, in a half-suppressed salute. He stood four inches taller than I, and his voice boomed; I stepped away from him.

"Will you come to my office a moment?"

58

"I don't understand what you want me for," I said.

The American was coming out of the office behind me. I started to intercept him, but Conway blocked my path.

"You turned in an incomplete report of your last dig," Conway said. "You forgot to sign the last page, as required by regulations."

The American was out the door, going away from me down the hall. When I tried to pass Conway, he stepped sideways to get in my way again.

"My office is right this way."

"Sign it yourself!" I shouted. "Spit on it! Kiss it! The dig was barren, anyway."

"I say, Carter, you don't need to shout."

"To hell with you!"

"Everything they say about you is true," Conway said. He marched off the way he had come.

He left me facing the young American. The quarrel had drawn his attention, and he was eying me with blunt interest. He looked even younger than I knew he was, with his fair hair cut very close, and his pink cheeks and scalp.

He said, "Are you Howard Carter?"

I put out my hand to him, out of wind after the shouting match. We had tea together.

We drank tea and ate flat sesame-seed cakes in the courtyard of my hotel. The American's babyish looks were deceptive. He was clever enough to be guiled.

When I was sure of that, I said, "Are you interested in backing any new digs in Egypt?"

He was biting into a cake, and he chewed thoroughly and swallowed before he said, "I was under the impression you were with Lord Carnarvon."

"We did more work together before the war than since," I said.

"I don't—have you some specific—are you onto something, Mr. Carter?"

I did not answer him; I did not say no. All I did was pack my pipe.

"If you have uncovered a new site, Mr. Carter, I'm sure my boss would be interested in exploiting it with you."

"Excellent," I said, and lit my pipe.

"What exactly have you found?"

"Nothing."

He looked confused and a little angry. I smiled broadly at him. I said, "Carnarvon is still paying for it." His face cleared, and he nodded gravely at me.

"When do you begin to dig?"

"October," I said.

"We will be waiting to hear from you."

In October, after the flood had receded, I went down to Luxor again.

The first day after my arrival, I went out to look the place over, to decide where to begin work. It was a quiet day, but then days in the valley are quiet. Maybe the solitude and the silence here induced the pharaohs to dig their last houses here. I rode slowly from one end of the valley to the other. Every turning brought me within sight of another triumph of Egyptology: the splendid tomb of Hatshepsut, the woman who overthrew Thothmes II and kept Thothmes III from his throne for so many years, and the tomb of Amenhotep III, called the Magnificent, the father of Akhenaten, who built the palace now in ruins on the bank of the Nile above Luxor. Magnificent they all were, the princes of the Eighteenth Dynasty, and the power of their personalities still glimmers a little through the thousands of years. They were not brutes: in the brute world, women do not dominate men. Their wealth was only a poor outward show of the subtle richness of their culture. Yet their dynasty ended in failure and decadence (as perhaps all dynasties must) and within a few generations of their triumphs Egypt was a poor sick old man, helpless before invaders, and senile with hollow superstition.

All this we know because of the discoveries made here and elsewhere in Egypt, the scraps and treasures unearthed by archaeologists. To this evidence, for all my work, I had contributed relatively little. I had worked and worked and come up empty, or finished off other men's finds, strung together other men's evidence. The name of Howard Carter would occur only in a footnote.

If only I could have found one cup, one bracelet, one sandal that told me that Tutankhamun had been buried here! The least artifact might have helped us bridge the gap between the fall of Akhenaten and the failure of the dynasty. Brooding on this, I rode on my donkey past the ancient splendors of the valley.

Halfway to the end of it, I met Ahmed.

The big Egyptian was on foot. He stood on the path waiting for me to catch up with him. When I reached him, he said, without smiling, "Hello, Carter. One more time, ah?"

"Looking for something to steal?" I said, sourly.

"I learn from you, Carter."

After this habitual exchange of snarls I started off again. He walked beside me, and I admit that I was glad of the companionship. I was feeling pretty hopeless. I had put my head in the noose: if I did not find something worth attracting the support of the Americans, my ploy with them would discredit me with other possible backers. I was here now to find a site to begin the new dig. That was easy. Every place I looked I wanted to dig. But I had to find something fast.

We rounded the bend in the valley that brought us before the great tomb of Rameses VI, a square hole gaping below the cliff. I stopped. This place had always had a peculiar attraction for me.

On the left was the strange tomb where Theodore Davis had discovered the mummy disguised as a woman. Nearer to me and Ahmed was the pit that Davis had claimed was the tomb of Tutankhamun; even closer, almost at Ahmed's feet, was the rock where the blue faience cup had been found. I stood staring at the blank walls of the valley. I was overwhelmed by the feeling that all these finds were part of a single find; if only I could put them together, I would understand. Yet I could not understand them.

"Well," I said, out loud, "suppose the cup and the rings in the pit were loot from the tomb. Perhaps the robbers threw the things away, to get rid of the evidence before they were caught."

Now something began to form in my mind.

Ahmed was staring at me. "Carter, what are you talking about?"

"Ahmed." I clutched his arm. "If you stole—if you broke into a tomb here and were caught, which way would you run?"

"At night or in the day?"

"At night," I said. The valley would have been well guarded; only at night could anyone chance a theft.

"Down," he said. "Down into the dark."

"Into the dark," I said after him. "They would have run away from the tomb into the darkness of the valley."

My eyes followed the line from the place where the blue faience work cup had been found, back past the hole where the rings had been found, back straight across the valley floor to the low slope in front of the tomb of Rameses VI.

No one had ever dug there. Rameses' tomb was such an important tourist attraction that the authorities refused to let the way be blocked.

"We'll dig there," I said. "We can trench across it before the main stream of the tourists arrive."

Ahmed was watching me obliquely. Clearly he doubted my sanity. I said, "Well? Do you want to work for me?"

"As you wish, Carter." He turned away from me; his shrug was eloquent.

I went back to Luxor and got on the telephone to the Department of Antiquities in Cairo. Unfortunately it was Conway, the assistant curator, who took my call. He refused outright to let me dig across the route to Rameses' tomb.

"I'll have all the fill dirt lugged off out of the way," I said. "I'll leave the site by January. Just—"

Out of the black telephone receiver came the smooth voice of the assistant curator. "I'm sorry. We simply can't allow—"

"I'll leave a path up to the tomb past the dig."

"Now, Carter, please don't shout at me. I am not responsible—"

"I'll personally carry every tourist through the dig on my back. Please—"

"I'm sorry, Carter."

"Let me talk to the curator."

"I'm sorry, Carter."

The sound died out of the receiver; he had hung up his end of the line.

I put the phone down. My hand was wet. I sat down on the camp stool behind me; I was in the local office of tourism, in the back room. Around me were banks of files and stacks of papers. Putting my head down in my hands, I dragged in a deep breath.

There were other places to dig. Near the tomb of Amenhotep there was a very likely site for a tomb. I had trenched through it in 1920 and found nothing, but still—I might have turned the wrong way—dug in the wrong direction —not dug deep enough—

I shut my eyes. In the next room, a door clicked, a bell chimed, a foreign voice called for service.

For a few moments I could not find the will and the strength to get up. I thought of phoning Cairo again, but I knew those people: having said no once, they considered the word sacred.

Dig in another place. I raised myself up from the camp stool and left the office building.

When I reached my house in Luxor, Ahmed was sitting in front of the steps with a clutch of other men: he had gone out and gathered up all those people still living in Luxor who had dug with us the year before. They looked at me with eyes bright as bullets. Ahmed strode forward through their midst.

"I have the job book, Carter. They have all been signed into it. We can begin tomorrow."

"Tomorrow," I said, surprised.

"Or this afternoon, if you wish."

"No, no." I laughed; his eager efficiency buoyed me, and I felt better. "Tomorrow will be soon enough."

"Shall we meet you there?" he said. "At Rameses VI?"

The answer came as easily from me as a lie ought. "Yes." We could start digging. It might be days before the department caught on. Weeks. I wiped my moist palms on my trousers legs. Going up the steps, I went into the security of my house.

At dawn we all gathered together in the valley. The digging crew had brought their own tools and baskets, and we set to work at once. The ground where we began to dig was loose fill from Rameses' tomb and all we had to do was shovel it up into baskets and cart it away.

I laid out the trench on a line running straight away from the tomb. That cut across the tourists' route, but as long as I was defying the department, I might as well do it with a whole heart. Every time a stone fell on the valley wall, every time a shadow crossed the yellow rock floor, I started with guilt, sure that they had discovered me.

Just after noon, the front team of diggers began to uncover the walls of an ancient hut. Within an hour they had cleared half a dozen of these structures. They were barren little huts, packed close together; the fill piled on top of them had preserved them from the wind and kept them mostly intact. Some of them were no larger than large baskets. Probably they had been built to shelter the workmen on Rameses' tomb.

The tomb itself was large enough to house an entire

village; in the end it had sheltered a single splendid carcass.

Nothing gave me quite as vivid an impression of the way the common Egyptian lived than these huts. Rough as caves, cramped and rude, they were like kennels. I mapped them and made sketches of a number of them, and then my crew dug through them, and after thousands of years of existence they were gone.

Three feet under the ground level of the huts, we reached the flinty, ungiving bedrock. By then, the evening had come, and we left off work and went home.

The crew was all staying in Kurna. I dreaded returning to Luxor. The department could find me there at will; if they discovered what I was doing, they had only to wait at my house to arrest me. On an impulse I took Ahmed aside.

"I want a place to stay, in Kurna. Do you know of one?"

"A house?" he said. He blinked at me. "What do you need a house in Kurna for?"

I saw that he would not be satisfied with a simple request. I would have to confide in him. I turned aside from him and moved on down the path, put off. He trailed after me. His shadow reached ahead of me down the path. Half a mile away, the lights of Luxor pricked through the gloom.

"Carter," he said. "There is a house near mine that is empty. The old woman lives with her son now."

My breath hissed away between my teeth. Relieved, I said, "I will pay her a good rent."

"I will help you bring your goods," he said.

That made me suspicious. I remembered that he was a robber—I remembered what I had forgotten, that he had a good reason to wish me ill. I would have to keep a closer watch on him, henceforth.

I moved what I needed to live into the little house in Kurna; by day I worked in the valley and by night I stayed in Kurna, isolated from modern Luxor. I began to feel safe from the department. Then on the next morning, the fourth of November, I came up to the valley from

Kurna and found the crew there on the site, but not working.

They were sitting in a cluster on the ground, watching me expectantly. Among them, Ahmed got to his feet.

"Carter," he said, "you are a genius."

"What?"

"We have found something."

I went after him up the gentle slope toward the site. The trench was about ten feet deep and twenty-five feet long. The huts we had been digging out stood in the bottom. At one end, the hut and the ground under it had been removed. In the deep blue morning shadow pooled at this end of the trench, I saw a ledge in the bedrock.

I jumped down into the trench and bent to touch it. It was hand-hewn, much like the edge Lady Evelyn had found two years before.

"Ahmed, bring some shovels. And a basket." I pulled off my jacket.

Ahmed sprang into the trench, two shovels held high in his hands like weapons. He and I dug carefully around the ledge, shoveling the dirt into the basket. I was clearing away one side of the ledge, hoping to find a corner, but my shovel grated on something hard below the loose earth, and I scraped away the rubble and found another, lower ledge.

"A step."

I straightened. This was not like Evelyn's find. I pointed past the second, lower edge.

"There," I said to Ahmed. "Dig there. I'll bet fifty pounds there's another."

Ahmed yanked up the hem of his robe, tucked it into his belt out of the way, and thrust his shovel into the loose ground. He grunted with effort. The shovel grated on the stony earth. I knelt and scooped the dirt away with my hands.

"Yes. I was right. See?"

Another straight edge showed under the dirt, a third step

down into the hillside. I stood up. Ahmed smiled at me, and I nodded, like an idiot trying to stay calm.

"Yes, yes. It's an—well, it's something, anyway." I shook his hand, and he kept on smiling at me and nodding. "Let's get organized here," I said, and we climbed out of the ditch.

The crew was gathered there, but they were not looking at us. They were staring off down the valley. I shaded my eyes with my hand to see where they were looking.

A large motorcar was bumping and bouncing up the valley toward us. Puffs of jet black smoke burst from its exhaust. I swore. It was the department's notorious old motorcar.

I swore again. The crew was watching me, anxious; they gathered around Ahmed, looking to him for answers, but he said nothing. His gaze was pinned to my face. I stamped away from the trench, ready to meet the men in the oncoming motorcar. The suspicion took root in my mind that Ahmed had tipped off the department that I was digging here. Before I could think about that, the car stopped, and from all four doors there issued forth the minions of the Department of Antiquities.

Their leader was Conway, the assistant curator with whom I had discussed the issue over the phone. He came straight at me, and he didn't mince any words. The first thing he said to me was, "We should run you out of Egypt."

There seemed no adequate response to that. I kept still. There had to be some way through this.

The four men—they were all Englishmen—confronted me in a mass. Only Conway spoke, but the others emphasized what he said with nods and thunderous frowns, rather like a Greek drama.

"Have you found anything?" the assistant curator said.

I went by instinct. My conscious mind was still searching for an answer when my instinct answered, "No."

"I did not expect this of you, Carter. This is the most

unprofessional, disrespectful, childish, egotistical conduct I have ever encountered in an Egyptologist."

Through the corner of my eye, I saw the Egyptian crew watching us all. The look on Ahmed's face was one of anxious disbelief. Had he told them of the dig? I did not speak to the assistant, who was characterizing my behavior in very strong terms. My hands clasped behind my back, I tried to look chastened. My mouth was dry. It seemed as if I could still feel the edge of the step in the nerve ends of my fingers.

"I'm sorry," I said, when the assistant's diatribe slackened.

"Sorry," he said, contemptuously.

"I expected to find something extraordinary," I said. "I thought my goals justified it."

"And you found nothing. Appropriately enough. Well, this is the end of your dig, Carter. Immediately I return to Cairo, I will do what is necessary to cancel your licenses."

"Yes, sir."

Conway swelled. I could actually see him swell up. The other men murmured and looked from him to me. I was desperate; I had to get him to agree to one more thing—one last thing.

He said, "I warn you, I shall not be mollified by all this repentance, Carter."

"No, sir."

"Very well, then."

"I'll begin filling in the trench today, sir."

He was nodding at me. He was one of those big men who do so poorly in tropical countries: too much flesh, too much appetite. Below his eyes and along his nose his cheeks were raddled with tiny red lines. He said, "See that you do," in a voice smooth as a fluid.

"I shall, sir. If you'd care to stay, I'll have my men rig up some kind of shade for you. The heat can be vicious out here."

That gave him pause. He looked up into the sky, cast a

gaze all around us at the barren sun-washed hillsides, and said, "No—I have urgent business in Luxor. Riordon here will stay to supervise."

Riordon said, "I, sir," in a voice of pain.

Turning my head slightly, I met Ahmed's gaze, and a look of triumph passed between us: he understood what I intended. So, then, he had not turned me in to the department, after all.

"We'll fill in the trench," I said to him.

"Yes, sir. Shall we start there, sir?" He indicated the far end of the trench—the end opposite the steps.

I nodded. My crew started energetically toward the trench, and I followed them.

We set to work pouring dirt back into the trench. The big motorcar roared away, leaving a foul trail of smoke behind, and Riordon, deserted, walked up and down a few moments, his hands in his pockets. Then he went to the side of the valley, where there was still some shade. I carried a basket or two of dirt and let it trickle down into the hole we had made in the desert.

A few moments later, Riordon came up to me. "Now, Carter," he said, "you're going to do this, aren't you? I mean, here you are doing it."

"Yes," I said.

He was an associate or something to the department. Associates do not deserve "sir."

"Then I think it would be a slur on your word for me to remain here and watch," he said. "I trust you. I know you'll do as you promised."

"Thank you," I said.

"Especially in front of the wogs," he said earnestly. "One must stick up for another Englishman."

"The wogs clearly won't," I said.

"May I use one of your donkeys?"

"Oh, certainly," I said. "I can walk back to Kurna with the others."

"Thanks."

He took the donkey and started away down the valley. When he went out of sight around the bend, Ahmed and the other Egyptians and I moved as one man toward the shovels.

We worked without a single break through the rest of the day and into the night. The grit in my shoes rubbed my feet raw. When the dark made work impossible, I limped with the others into Kurna.

We had uncovered eight more steps, leading straight down into the bedrock of the valley. So far there was no indication of what lay at the end of the stairway. I was too exhausted for sleep; in my bed in the little house in Kurna, I lay staring into the dark and wondering what I had found. An unfinished tomb, a plundered tomb, a treasurehouse—one or two artifacts would be enough to justify me. A failure would ruin me. Just before dawn, steeped like an insomniac in the weird hopes and terrors that normal people lose in dreams, I fell uneasily asleep for a few minutes, only to be awakened by a tremendous crash.

I sat bolt upright in my bed. My hackles rose. Another crash sounded directly above my head, over the roof. I scrambled out of bed and into my clothes. I could hear people screaming, outside in the street, and I considered crawling under my bed but rejected that; the bed was too flimsy. I dashed into the front room of the house just as another deafening explosion echoed through the sky.

This time, fully awake, I noticed the flicker of light that accompanied it. I stopped, my arms falling to my sides. It was only a thunderstorm.

Rain is almost unheard of in the Nile Valley. In the intervals of silence between the claps of thunder, I could hear the wailing and shrieking of the terrified villagers. I went to the door. Now the rain struck. In a sluicing downpour it swept over the village, drenching in an instant the entire area. Muddy droplets began to fall from the ceiling over my head. A few moments later the drops were solid brown streams.

I realized that there was a good chance of my roof caving in, and I rushed back through the two tiny rooms of the dwelling, gathering my notes, my books, and my clothes and packing them into the boxes I had brought them in. I stowed them all under the bed and went back to the door.

The fickle airs that had made the storm were already disassembling it. A last racketing, rambling thunderclap sounded in the west, and the fitful lightning picked out the cliffs in the distance, the flat roofs of the village close by, in a lemony light. The rainfall lessened. It stopped entirely, and the sky grew swiftly lighter. The sun was rising.

The villagers were running aimlessly up and down through the alleys and lanes around their houses. They splashed through the runoff; they held their hands over their heads as if to shield themselves from something terrible in the sky. Directly opposite me was the house of a widow. The deluge had reduced it to a heap of mud, and as I watched, the roof collapsed inward with a sucking, plopping noise.

I ran to help. Fortunately no one was inside except the family's goat. The widow and her children gathered around me, sobbing, and I took them back to my house and made them all tea. Perhaps I had acquired that from Evelyn, the efficacy of tea.

In the first bleaching rays of the sun, the village lay like a smoking ruin. Plumes of steam rose from the soaked buildings and streets. A long cocoon of mist lay along the foot of the cliffs, obscuring all but the very tops, floating like gilded islands in the fresh sunlight. I helped my visitors back to their hut; they began to dig their belongings out of the mud.

I had to go back to the valley. Strangely, I had forgotten it during the storm, and it rushed back in on my consciousness like a flood. While I was taking my notebooks out of the box under my bed, Ahmed came.

"Carter," he said, "are you safe?"

"Yes."

I went into the front room, where he was standing. His head nearly grazed the ceiling, which was now decorated with feathery stalactites of dried mud.

"Interesting episode," I said. "How often does it rain here?"

His shoulders moved in an uneasy shrug. "I cannot remember the last time. You don't . . ." He gave an embarrassed laugh. "You don't think it means anything?" he said, in a sheepish voice.

"It scared me half under the bed, at first," I said. "Let's get going."

He laughed again, this time at me. We went out into a village now like a steambath.

I walked quickly back toward the cliffs. I had gotten almost no sleep; I was charged with restless nervous energy. Ahmed walked along beside me.

"I have never heard of such a storm," Ahmed said.

"Yes, it was a freak. It was interesting—I can see something more in stories like the biblical flood."

We climbed the path through the desert, past Deir el-Medina, where the ruins of an ancient village had been laid bare in a recent dig. I thought of those people, what such a flood would have meant, so chained as they were to the processes of nature. In the aftermath of the rain, the desert was magnificent, the air washed clear, every gaunt line of cliff and boulder sharply drawn, and the whole scene shimmering with the already blistering heat of the sun.

We went down the steep slope into the Valley of the Kings. My thoughts raced ahead of me to the steps leading down into the earth.

"Some people say it was an augury," Ahmed said.

"What?" I said, startled.

"The storm. Augury? Is that the proper word?"

He was coming just after me on the trail. I glanced at him. Because of the steepness of the hillside, his head was at the level of my shoulder. I said, "Yes, that's the right word."

"I don't believe it," he said. "I would have, before. But now I don't believe things like that. Because of you, Carter."

"Because of me."

"You sent me into the army," he said. "I did not thank you then, but I thank you now. I learned very much in the army, about Egyptians, about Englishmen."

"Always glad to help out," I said. I smelled something rotten in all his gratitude. He was up to something. I went between two boulders and down the short steep slope into the valley. Here the rain had not fallen; the soil was fine and dry as flour. Ahead, the dig came in sight. Ahmed was behind me still; he said no more about the army and my role in his entrance into it, which relieved me. I had to sort out what he had said and done, try to get some grip on his motives and intentions, and figure out what he was up to.

The rest of the digging crew came up behind us to the digging site. We all set to work at once. I kept half of them digging away at the stairway into the earth; the others went on filling up the other end of the trench.

I worked with the diggers. Every time I straightened up over my shovel I glanced out of the trench toward the east, looking for the assistant curator. The other men worked without even lifting their eyes from the spectacle that was slowly opening up at our feet.

We were lifting the earth of thirty centuries from a flight of steps that took us downward in space and backward in time. When we reached the end, what would we find? There were moments—long moments—during that day when I imagined we would go on forever clearing away the dirt from step after step: Sisyphus as Egyptologist.

At sundown we reached the twelfth step. Just beyond that we found a door.

Ahmed's yell of triumph echoed through the valley. I scrambled down the steps, pushing the workmen out of my way. My first instinct—I don't know why—was to press myself against the door.

The upper half only had been cleared. Rubble still masked the bottom. I felt rapidly over the door with my hands. The door was made of blocks of stone set one on the other and plastered over.

My fingertips grazed a regular ridge in the plaster. I grunted. The sun was going down and the area at the foot of the steps was darkening. I stooped to put my face up to the marking I had found.

"It's sealed," I said. I straightened, dusting my hands over my thighs. "Where's a light?"

Ahmed stood just above me on the steps. His face was shadowed. He held out my electric torch to me; when I turned, I still felt his presence there acutely, the faceless tomb robber. I switched on the light and shone it over the wall.

It was now quite dark. The beam of light was like a white blade. The rough-scored plastering cast little shadows around the doorway, so that it was hard to make out the features. I pointed to the oblong indentation the seal had made when the plaster was wet.

"Allah 'kbar," Ahmed murmured, behind me.

He recognized them, the figures on the seals. There was Anubis, the dog that led souls through the underworld, lying with his paws outstretched, and beneath him the nine bound men, symbols of the races of man, all bound by death. It was the royal necropolis seal.

I was breathing short. My hands were shaking so that I had to hold the torch with both hands. The beam of light showed me the top of the door, where the mask of plaster had fallen away. With one forefinger I poked a hole in the space at the corners of the blocks, right at the top of the door. The ancient mortar rained down. I widened the hole so that I could shine my light through, and saw the thin pale gleam shining on stones and earth beyond the wall. The room inside was filled with rubble.

Then it was almost certainly a corridor. My heart was hammering so hard and fast that it hurt me.

"What is it?" Ahmed said. "Shall I call for shovels?"

I was twisting and turning my head, trying to see more of the passageway beyond the door. The light of the torch glanced off the mass of dirt and small stones. More plaster crumbled away under my efforts, falling in a silky rain around me.

"Call for shovels, Carter," Ahmed said. His voice was breathy.

I drew back, warned by his tone. Why was he so madly intent on reaching whatever lay at the far side of that plug of earth? He would steal anything he could, steal everything we found.

With that realization a whole new sense of the problem rushed in on me. My skin cooled, and my heart seemed to find its normal rhythm again. I had a lot to do before I could go any further. I had to protect my find, prepare for it, prepare myself to deal with it. There was the Department of Antiquities, for example. It was time to get Carnarvon into the scene.

"No," I said. "It's too dark." Stooping, I gathered a handful of dust, spat on it, and plugged the hole I had made in the wall. "Let's cover it up again, before anybody else finds it."

6

We had shoveled the dirt back into the stairway, burying my find up to the brim. We worked until midnight at it. By the time we had done, I was at the edge of my strength, my hands bleeding, my shoes full of sand. With the Egyptians, I stood around the water jars draining dipper after dipper of cold water.

No one spoke. We stood close together, like a gang of thieves. We went back to the site and rolled stones over it and trampled over the earth.

The moon rose, and the valley grew perceptibly lighter. I stood at the mouth of Tomb Number 55, looking across the valley. It was like a landscape from the moon, waterless and windless. The cold blue-white light of the moon picked out the tumbled surfaces of rock and earth against pits of black shadow. The tomb had disappeared as if a tide of rubble had rolled in over it. I played with my imagination, pretending that it had been a dream; it might have been, for all the evidence we had left. I called Ahmed.

"Mount a guard over it. Discreetly, d'you understand? I have to go to Cairo for supplies."

"How long will you be gone?" he asked.

"A day and a half," I said.

Actually I intended to be gone three days.

He smiled at me in the darkness. "You trust me, Carter."

"That's right," I said. I trusted him to know that it would take longer than thirty-six hours to clear the passageway beyond the door.

He bowed to me. "I will do as you say." He would wait for a better moment.

I sent this cable to Carnarvon in England.

> At last have made wonderful discovery in valley; a magnificent tomb with seals intact; re-covered same for your arrival; congratulations.

There was no need to inform him prematurely of my little difficulty with the department.

I also sent a telegram to the museum in New York. I could use Carnarvon to manage Conway, and the Americans to manage Carnarvon.

When both messages were off, I went out on a minor buying spree. The main thing was to do this carefully, because if the department learned that I was buying, as an example, eight hundred packages of surgical gauze, they would know that I was planning to wrap something up, probably not wounds. Yet I had little time. Perhaps that helped: it takes time for rumors to filter from the Egyptian quarters of the city, where I was careful to remain, into the cloistered offices of the English. I was back in Luxor two days after the day we uncovered the doorway at the foot of the stairs.

The doorway was constantly in my mind. I saw it before me at every moment. That was what was real for me: that alone.

When I got back to Luxor, I went to see Conway, who was visiting an officially financed dig at the temple on the east bank.

"I've been out to look at your handiwork again, Carter," he said to me, smiling. "You seem to have repaired the damage done."

"Yes, sir," I said.

We were standing practically in the shadow of the Ninth Pylon. Before us loomed the tremendous columns of the temple. The sun shone through in slanted bars, foggy with dust. In that dust, who knows but that Pharaoh passed once more through the sanctuary of the god? Conway's coarse, fleshy face was before me.

"Sir," I said, "I've come to ask you a favor."

His eyes narrowed. "Now, Carter, let me—"

"I repaired it, as you said," I said quickly, trying to run him into my way of thinking. "Please, just let me keep my licenses. If you take them away, I'll be publicly ruined. We're giving up digging at the end of this year, anyway. Less than two months. Please."

He stared at me, frowning, his eyes like bullets. His jowls were wet with sweat.

"Please, sir," I said. "I'm begging this of you."

"It's against my better judgment," he said loftily.

"Oh, sir, please."

"Very well," he said. "I'll consider the matter ended."

"Oh, sir," I said, "thank you."

He smiled, puffing a little. Feeding on it. What power does to a man. I thanked him several times more and promised him to sign my inadequate report the very first time I was back in Cairo. Then I went back across the river to Kurna, to wait for Carnarvon to come.

A few days later I was at the river, but not to meet Carnarvon. The Americans had responded to my telegram by dispatching the young American photographer directly to me. Laden with bags and strung with cameras, he stepped off the ferry onto the quay at Luxor, put down his suitcases, and said, "I need a hat. My head is getting sunburned." With a smile he put out his hand to me.

Under the thin prickle of his close-clipped hair, his scalp was turning red. I reached for one of his bags. "Come and get indoors, then."

"I'd rather go directly to your dig."

I led him off the brick quay and onto the road to Kurna. He could put up with me; Americans were supposed to be egalitarian. He hurried along until he caught up with me.

"Where are you digging? Let's go there."

"There's nothing to see, yet," I said.

"What do you mean? You cabled us—"

"I know what I cabled you." I gave him the swiftest of oblique looks. "I've covered it back up again. Thieves abound here. When Carnarvon comes we'll set to work again."

"Oh," he said, his thin face settling a little. But he did not look as if he believed me.

Eighteen days after we had uncovered the first step, I stood at the ferry stage watching Carnarvon approach in a small boat. Evelyn was beside him. Lady Evelyn. When she saw me she waved and smiled. She wore one of her odd straw hats and a plain white dress; she looked lovely. Beside her sat her father, expressionless, his hands on his knees.

"Well, Carter," he said to me. "What have you found?" His voice was tight. Although he managed to keep his tone even, his handshake was long and warm and excited.

"I don't know yet," I said. "Come and look."

Evelyn was surveying the far bank of the Nile, littered with ruins, the columns of the temple like piles holding up the sky. She turned her level blue gaze on me. "You've waited for us, Howard? How extraordinary. I should think you'd have dug it all up by now."

"We're all part of it," I said.

I did not dare even approach the site until Carnarvon was there to use his influence with the government.

We went down the ferry stage to the tether line, where an array of shaggy gray donkeys was tied up. Ahmed had saddled four of them for us. There was a new service available to the valley, an old and smoky lorry, but the ride was slow and often unpleasant. Carnarvon was walking along beside me, his hands in his pockets.

"Very honorable of you," he said to me. "Waiting until we got here. I hope you haven't dragged me away at the height of the bird season to witness another of your flashy false alarms."

I kept my mouth shut. Let the old bastard see for himself. On his far side, Evelyn hooked her arm through his and lengthened her stride.

"Evie," Carnarvon said, "the thing's been there donkey's years, no need to run. Carter, how long has it been there?"

"If it's Eighteenth Dynasty," I said, "at least thirty-two hundred years."

Evelyn detached herself from her father. Ahmed held out the reins of a donkey to her, and she slid them over the beast's head. Across the broken cavalry saddle, she said, "Is it Eighteenth Dynasty, Howard?"

"Yes, I think so," I said. "Some ruins from the Nineteenth Dynasty were on top of it."

Athletically she climbed onto the donkey and reined his head around toward the yellow cliffs. I mounted. My donkey took me after her at a trot. Evelyn—Lady Evelyn—tucked her riding whip under her arm.

"I can't wait to see," she called.

"Was it a hard trip down from England?"

Her swift glance told me as much as a paragraph. Carnarvon and Ahmed were clattering after us, the Earl sitting well back in his saddle, his stirrups let down straight as a hussar's. Ahead, the notched terraces of the cliff were coming clearer as we approached. I urged my donkey toward the trail to the valley.

Ahmed had sent the crew out to the valley, but they had orders to wait until we appeared before they did any digging, and so when Carnarvon and I approached, the site was invisible. This part of the valley looked no different than any other, its honey-colored stone walls capped by the brassy blue archway of the sky. To the left was Tomb Number 55, with a little cairn of blue mineral-water bottles beside it. Directly before us as we approached, the gaping door to the tomb of Rameses VI opened in the cliff.

The American photographer was there, burdened with cameras. I introduced him to Lord Carnarvon and Lady Evelyn. The American was subdued. In the moment's polite conversation that ensued, he tried to say "my lord," but stumbled. Carnarvon was sweeping the area with his gaze.

"Well, Carter?" he said.

I had taken precise measurements, and while Carnarvon and Evelyn and the crew watched, I paced off the distances from the sides of the valley to the place where we would start digging.

Then we picked up the shovels.

It had taken us only a few days to dig it up before, including the long trenching across the floor of the valley. Now, knowing precisely where to dig, removing dirt and stones already loosened, we reached the first step within a matter of a few hours.

We dug furiously, madly through the day. I stopped a few times, trying to make talk with Carnarvon and his daughter, but the words always dribbled away: after a few moments of awkward socializing we all fell into staring at the hole in the ground, silent again. I kept a watch on the trail down the valley, where my enemies in the department would first appear.

Just before sunset we cleared the last step. Carnarvon and I went down to the bottom of the staircase to look over the door. I switched on my electric torch; I had never seen the bottom half before, only the top.

At once I saw that the plaster that had covered the top was different than the plaster on the bottom.

"Damn," I said. "It's been opened. Someone's got into it."

Carnarvon crouched down, squinting at the door. Evelyn was behind him; she said, "What? How can you tell?"

"See, the top half of the door was plastered over again, after the bottom half. And the seals are different." With my torch I picked out the necropolis seal for her. "This is the regular seal of the necropolis. This—" I stooped to show her the seals at the bottom of the door.

The light glinted on the plaster. The oblong imprint of the seal was set across the doorframe. At first I thought I was misreading the pictographs in the bad light; they were so familiar that I did not trust my eyes.

"These are Tutankhamun's seals," I said.

I stood up in the cramped space. Then it was. It really was. All this time, after all this hunting, it was here before me. Carnarvon was smiling wide at me.

"That's the fellow we were looking for, wasn't it?"

"Someone's got into it ahead of us," I said. I raised my head. The patch of sky at the top of the staircase was still blue. A dark head appeared against it, leaning over the head of the trench, its shape distorted in a headcloth.

Evelyn was saying, "But the ruins on top of it—they were so old—"

"The robbers got into it just after it was sealed," I said. "And the priests found out and sealed it again." I raised my voice. "Ahmed, what?"

"That man is coming," Ahmed said. "That man in his motorcar."

Conway was here. I swallowed with difficulty. Carnarvon was watching me, smiling.

"Well: congratulations," he said.

"There may be nothing left in it. Besides, there's this fellow." I started up the staircase.

"What fellow?" Carnarvon was coming after me.

We reached the top of the staircase in time to see the

department motorcar chugging to a stop a hundred feet away. The assistant curator burst out of the passenger seat door. His great long strides galloped across the valley. His arms swung, ending in fists, and his face was clenched like a fist. He strode up to me and shouted into my face.

"Damn you, Carter—I trusted you! You made a fool out of me! Get off the valley! Now—you'll leave Egypt within the week!"

"Now, what's this, Carter?" Carnarvon asked.

I said nothing; I had no chance to say anything. The assistant curator swiveled his beet-red face toward Carnarvon and gave the Earl a volley at close range.

"This is the rankest, most disrespectful action I've ever heard of, in all my life as an Egyptologist. You'll all be broken, I promise you that."

Carnarvon's calm was impressively stony. He said, "May I ask who you are?"

The assistant faltered. He glanced at me and back to Carnarvon, and he realized that he was taking on a different beast; he said, "I beg your pardon. Allow me to introduce myself. Conway, the Department of Antiquities at Cairo."

"I am Carnarvon," the Earl said. "What exactly is the difficulty? We have the permits to dig in the valley, do we not, Carter?"

"Yes," I said.

"Carter was told without ambiguity not to block the access to the tomb of Rameses VI," the assistant said. "Then when I found him digging here . . ." As he talked, his tone turned starchy again; he realized that he was right, if common. "He promised me to repair the damage and leave the site alone, and now look! He's dug it all up again!"

Carnarvon shot a look at me. "Quite," he said.

"It must be restored to its proper condition at once. And this time I shall insist on rescinding your licenses, and probably fine you as well."

The Earl looked slowly all around us. The sun was setting and the dark was filling up the valley. Finally Carnarvon returned his attention to the assistant.

"We have made a marvelous discovery here," he said. "We intend to—"

"No, no," the assistant said. "I don't want to hear about it. Don't tell me any more lies."

Carnarvon frowned at him. "Did you interrupt me?"

"No more tricks!" Conway cried. "I won't listen to—"

"Don't shout at me," Carnarvon said, and the assistant curator ran out of words. They stared at one another, the bureaucrat very red in the face, and the Earl monstrously calm. At last Conway took a step backwards and lowered his eyes. I warmed with triumph. Another class war won.

"We have found something here," the Earl said, "which will eclipse poor old Rameses up there for quite some time. Now, I'm sure you will want your name mentioned, somewhere in the reports. We will be happy to do so, considering the help you've given us."

The assistant curator's chest was heaving; eventually he marshaled the breath to say, "This is blackmail."

Carnarvon was already turning his back on him. "Damn bloody fool," he said. "Blackmail is entirely different. Go look it up." He strolled off toward the hole in the earth. Across the space he had occupied, I faced Conway, who gave me an unloving look. He and I both knew he could only accept what I had done. He went back to the motorcar, black as a beetle in the last sunshine.

The American was watching from the side of the dig, where Ahmed's men were already filling sandbags to make a wall. He gave me an intent look. I wondered how much of our exchange with Conway he had heard. He lifted his camera again and aimed it at the top of the staircase.

Carnarvon was there at the first step, looking down into the darkness. When I came up beside him, he said, "Now, Carter. So that's why you covered it up until we got here."

"Not at all," I said.

He lifted his head to smile at me. "Never mind. I'm pleased to be of use."

"Yes, sir," I said. "You're always that."

"And this American camera buff, here. How did you arrange that?"

"Oh," I said, "I just thought it would be a good idea to have a photographic record of everything, from the very first."

Carnarvon grunted. I could see he understood that I'd gone behind his back to the Americans.

"He's the very best, sir," I said.

"I'm sure he is," Carnarvon said. He turned to look down the steps again at the door. "Just the same, whatever you've found here, it had better be good."

The next morning we broke down the doorway to the tomb.

I was determined to preserve everything—not simply the materials in the tomb, if indeed we found anything, but the whole setting. That meant photographing and diagraming every inch we uncovered. Fortunately my young American photographer was on hand, and in the first light of morning we took pictures of the seals in the plaster, and of the whole doorway before we tore it down.

Beyond it lay the corridor packed with rubble, mostly a light-colored stone that I recognized as the chip of its own excavation. Through the top left-hand edge of the mass was a vein of darker stone, where whoever had broken through the door in ancient times had tunneled through the stuffing. The necropolis officials must have filled the tunnel up again with this dark detritus.

A single glance around the site was enough to show where it had come from. The whole far wall of the valley was half-buried in talus of the same rock. In fact, the pit where Davis had found the bits of gold had been dug out of that rock.

All that day we removed tons of rubble. I kept busy. I

was afraid to consider what that tunnel might mean. The priests would not have sealed the tomb again if it had been completely looted.

"You don't put a cork in an empty jug," I said to the American photographer. "As somebody said to Alexander the Great's mother."

We kept finding scraps of things in the fill we removed from the corridor. I had him photograph them: a piece of a vase, a waterskin, a broken seal. He had taken to snapping shots of the workmen—not of their toil, but of the workmen themselves. Thinking perhaps he was bored, I tried to involve him in the anxious waiting.

Every time I looked for him, I found him off among the workmen again, shooting closeups. That irritated me. Typically of an American, he could not keep his mind on the important things.

Steadily we dug away the interior of the corridor. Six feet wide, as wide as the door, it was at least seven feet from floor to ceiling. It slanted down under the first gentle slope of the wall of the valley. Within, it was so dark that we had to use electric torches even in the height of the day. At first, with each yard we cleared, I expected to find another door.

Night stopped our work. We had emptied twenty feet of rubble from a blank corridor. When the last workmen had come up to the surface I went down again and walked to the end. That far under the ground, the air was moist and cold. I put my hand on the wall of rubble. It had to end somewhere. It had to be going somewhere. I remembered the tunnel where I had met Ahmed. Ancient dust, empty jars.

Two carpenters in Luxor had built me a wooden grating to keep out thieves. With Ahmed's help, I hung it on hinges across the first doorway, and we locked it fast and went back to Kurna for the night. I was dead tired.

That night a gray mood seized me. I dined with Carnarvon and Evelyn, but none of us spoke; one glance into

Evelyn's face showed me that she was full of wild speculations. Thereafter I avoided looking at her. Whatever we found at the end of the tunnel, it was only sport for her, but for me it was the making or the breaking of my life.

I could not sleep that night. I lay in a paralysis of dread. The sounds of the village penetrated my room, so that whenever I drifted toward sleep, some racket teased me back to wakefulness—the crowing of a cock, or footsteps in the street. Before dawn, I was up, brewing tea, dressing, putting my notes together. The rising sun found me halfway to the valley.

The crew came out earlier also. They set to work at once. They did not sing as they worked. Carnarvon sat in the shade near Rameses' tomb, his hands on his widespread knees. He no longer tried to seem calm. Whenever I approached him his eyes gleamed with unspoken questions. Beside him, Evelyn took notes for me on the bits of pottery and alabaster and glass we sifted out of the tunnel stuffing.

We found another door.

It was the same size as the first, blocked, plastered, and sealed. Again the plaster at the top had been patched. My enemy had been here ahead of me. I sent for Carnarvon.

Standing on a box, I made a hole through the top of the door. Ahmed held the torch for me. I dusted my hands off; I could hear his lordship's footsteps clattering down the stairway thirty feet behind me. My knees were wobbling and I felt sick to my stomach. Suddenly the whole thing was totally unreal to me. I was dreaming this.

Ahmed held a slender iron bar up to me. I poked it through the hole I had made in the door.

Nothing. I stabbed the unresisting air.

"Light the candle," I said to Ahmed.

Jabbing the iron bar here and there into the vacant space beyond the door, I encountered nothing, no objects, no rubble, no wall. In my mind I saw it already, an empty room heavy with dust. A question with no answer.

Carnarvon said, breathless, "What have you found?"

"There seems to be a chamber here," I said.

Ahmed lit a match. The diffuse light showed me Carnarvon's face, pitted and lined with shadows, shockingly aged.

I took the lit candle and put it through the hole in the wall and held it at arm's length into the room. Sometimes there were poisonous fumes in rooms shut off for so long from the atmosphere. The malevolence of the ancients. Of course, there's no volition about it. The candle flickered in the rush of air escaping through the new hole. I put my eye to the opening and felt that flow of air on my cheek.

For a moment all I could see through the opening was the little wavering candle flame. I stretched my arm out and moved it here and there. My eye, pressed to the opening above my arm, became used to the darkness. Gradually other lights appeared. They winked and gleamed here and there in the black depth beyond my candle. I jerked, startled, and all the other lights jerked too.

There were reflections of my candle flame. Scores of them danced there in the darkness. Perhaps there were hundreds. My eye grew more accustomed to the light, and saw more lights, and more, flickering images gleaming back at me from surfaces of gold.

Then my eye began to divine forms in the dark. Opposite me the head of a great cat took shape. To my left, ten feet away, was a man with a lance. The round top of a chest appeared nearby. There were stacks of boxes to my right. That was a chair, there, and a couch or a bed. The room was packed full with furniture, piled to the ceiling. Everywhere, over everything, was cast the soft seductive glow of gold.

"Do you see anything?" Carnarvon said, behind me.

"Wonderful things," I blurted. "Wonderful things."

I drew my candle out and gave it to Ahmed. Widening the hole in the door, I moved to one side so that Carnarvon could look in.

# 7

After the blocking had been removed from the door I entered the tomb for the first time. The excitement had transfigured me. I felt like another man; I felt immortal. Holding an electric lantern out before me, I went into a magical realm where I was king, putting my feet down with such care I did not disturb even the dust.

A little alabaster cup lay on the floor just inside the threshold. Beside it was a heap of what looked at first like brown paper. Stooping, I saw that a garland of flowers lay there, so dry the petals were turning to dust in the wash of air through the open door.

The mourners had dropped that wreath behind them as they left, fifty lifetimes ago.

Yesterday. To the tomb the intervening centuries were only a moment of silence. I was standing in the tracks of the ancient Egyptians. I was entering a place modern to them, breathing the air they had breathed, bringing with me the first light to pierce this darkness since before Moses led the Israelites away to Sinai.

Here at least I could strip myself of those years and return to the world where I had always felt spiritually more at home than my own home. This was where I belonged.

The room was small, about the size of an English parlor, and so crowded with furniture and boxes that Carnarvon, Evelyn, and I had to pick our steps single file down the middle. Everything I saw was made of gold. Before me were the great heads of beasts that I had first noticed when I looked into the tomb through the hole in the doorway. The lamp painted the wall beyond with their monstrous shadows. Their elongated and flattened bodies formed the beds of couches. He must have lain there when he was alive, daydreaming, waiting for sleep to come.

"Howard, look!"

I spun around. Evelyn was squatting down before a casket-shaped box, marvelously painted in black, white, and shades of red-gold with an archer in a chariot. The wild rush of beasts he drove before him filled the whole right side of the scene. I started toward Evelyn, and my gaze went beyond her and I let out a low cry.

Against the far wall stood two life-size figures, facing each other. They were men, painted black, the color of the dead, and dressed in gold. Between them the wall had been plastered and sealed. The two figures carried lances.

They were guards. They were standing watch over a doorway beyond which could only lie the body of the King. Rags of their sacred funeral shawls still hung from their shoulders, their arms, like tendrils of moss. He was still here.

I stood frozen in my tracks. The enormity of what we were seeing was at first beyond my mind's grasp. Slowly I was understanding that we had come on a tomb virtually intact from the greatest and richest dynasty of the New

Kingdom. Where before we had made do with fragments, two or three pieces out of thousands, now we had the thing complete.

This would begin a new epoch in Egyptology.

Carnarvon's hoarse voice broke the silence. Evelyn and I went high-stepping like storks across the jumbled treasure to his side. He was bent to look under the hippopotamus couch, where there were boxes, gloriously painted. Evelyn gave a soft murmur, sensuous, and knelt beside her father to look.

There was another murmur behind me. I turned my head to see Ahmed, standing at the mouth of the corridor. His black eyes moved over the room. One hand braced him against the side of the door, as if he might have fallen down with awe at what he saw.

I stooped beside Evelyn. Ahmed would have to be dealt with.

"Howard, what are these?"

The boxes piled up before me were familiar, although I had seen them before only in pieces or in pictures. I said, "They hold food. For the mummy." I was looking past these boxes. A golden wing had caught my eye.

There were a pair of wings, vulture's wings, extended, forming the arms of a chair. I raised the lantern, and the light swept up across a gilt and glass-paste picture on the chair's back.

Two royal Egyptians were molded there in low relief. The man sat in a chair, one arm crooked on its back; his wife leaned toward him, one hand extended, to anoint him with oil from a little pot she held in her other hand. The work was exquisite. They were so naturally posed that I half expected them to move.

That was he, in the chair; it had to be.

Carnarvon and Evelyn were chattering beside me. I put the lantern down. There were scores of things here. Everywhere I looked, I saw something new. The casket Evelyn had noticed first was slightly ajar; my hand moved toward it, longing. I yearned to open it.

First I had to make diagrams, take notes, number everything, photograph everything. And this was only the beginning. Behind that plastered wall was at least one more chamber. I imagined several, a chain of rooms, each packed with grave goods. I had a lot of work before me.

First there was Ahmed. He was still in the doorway, feasting his robber's eyes on my treasure. I kept my back to him. I knew just the way to keep him off.

"Now, look here," I said, in a theatrically loud voice. "What's this?"

"What?" Carnarvon and Evelyn said, together.

"Writing," I said. I reached for the lantern and stuck it under the couch, to light the wall beyond, as if I were reading something written there. "It says something about a curse."

"What?" Evelyn said, in a voice high with skepticism.

"It says that Osiris will avenge Tutankhamun on anyone who violates this tomb." I straightened out from under the couch and looked her in the face. Through the corner of my eye I kept track of Ahmed behind me. I wiggled my face at Carnarvon and Evelyn to keep them quiet. "Osiris," I said, "was the god of death."

"Ridiculous," Carnarvon said.

Evelyn put her head to one side. "Really, Howard. How quaint."

"A curse against anyone who takes anything from this tomb," I said solemnly. "We ought to think about that. Make clear in our minds exactly what risk we are running."

"Rubbish," Carnarvon exploded.

He was getting angry. Did he half believe it himself?

I turned casually to the door. Ahmed was gone. The corridor looked empty. Satisfied, I rose to my feet and reached for my lantern.

"We have a lot of work to do," I said, and started toward the door.

A few days later, my stratagem got an unexpected boost: one of the workmen, an elderly relative of Ahmed's, died in the night. Thereafter none of the workmen would go near the tomb. There was plenty for them to do on the surface, building the wall around the entrance. I did not need them below anymore.

From my notes: objects found in the first days of opening the tomb.

1. The head of a child, six inches high, made of wood painted and sculpted in stucco. The head of the child emerges from the petals of a lotus flower: an emblem of rebirth.

2. A small shrine made of wood plated over entirely with sheets of gold, and mounted on a silver-plated sledge. The shrine is in the shape of a miniature building, approximately twenty inches tall and ten inches deep. The gold is embossed with pictures of the King and his wife, Ankhesenamun. The front doors, bolted with a tiny ebony bolt, open to disclose a chamber where there must have been an image of the King: the pedestal with his name remains. Obviously the robbers took the statue.

3. The golden throne I noticed on the first visit to the tomb. This is only one of several thrones we found in the tomb. It stands forty-five inches at the back and is twenty-five inches deep. The back and legs are covered with gold and the arms are made of gold in the shape of vultures' extended wings. The legs are fashioned like lions' legs, topped with the heads of lions. Around the legs of the chair are the remains of what was once an openwork design depicting the lily and the papyrus plants, symbols of the Upper and Lower kingdoms of Egypt.

The scene on the back of this throne is riveting. I have sat staring at it for many hours, taken by the charm of the young faces, the grace and naturalness of their poses. It is like a window into that past time. I feel I know him, I would recognize him in the street among crowds, I could talk to him as easily as to Evelyn, say, or Carnarvon.

His wife bends over him affectionately. I am jealous of him; she is beautiful.

4. A box used to hold sacred oil, made in the shape of the double cartouche in which the King's names customarily are written. In place of the name of the King there appears his image in each cartouche. The box is made of wood plated with gold. Blue, green, and red glass-paste pick out the details of the pictures. On top of each of the oblong cartouches are a round solar disk and two towering ostrich feathers. The box is six inches tall.

5. The cup we found at the doorway to the tomb was made of calcite sculpted in the form of an opening lotus flower. The individual petals are delicately traced in low relief. The two handles of the cup are in the shape of lotus flowers on which rides a manlike figure in a boat, bearing in each hand the symbol of life. Probably this cup was used in the funeral ceremony, as part of the rite conferring immortality on the King. It is seven inches high.

We were keeping the things we removed from the tomb in the spacious vacant rooms of the tomb of Rameses VI, on the slope above Tutankhamun's tomb. A heavy grate covered the door, and only I and Carnarvon had the keys.

I loaned my key to the young American photographer, thinking he wanted to take more photographs of the treasure. When I went up to the tomb the next morning, he was in there, in among my treasure, with a dozen Kurnite villagers, showing them around, just as if he were the curator.

They were bunched together before the long table on which several small items were standing. I could imagine those small things disappearing into the villagers' heavy drooping sleeves. I rushed in between them and the table.

"Please," I said, pushing them away. "Please—" I had to

lie; I would win their hatred if I accused them. The excuse sprang to my lips. "These things have been untouched for thousands of years. They are delicate. One careless touch could crumble them—even your breath might damage them. Do you understand?"

They goggled at me. The light was dim; their faces were hidden in masks of shadow. The American in his few words of Arabic joined in with me, and we steered the Kurnites out.

On the threshold, the American caught my arm. We stood there, on the lip of the tomb, watching the villagers walk away from us. When they were out of earshot, I turned to the young man beside me.

"What did you mean by that?" he said. "What rubbish!"

"Don't you ever bring people into this storeroom again," I said. I kept my voice down. "You, and I, and Carnarvon and Evelyn can come in here, no one else!"

His eyes widened. He flung out one arm to point after the villagers, now far down the valley. "But it's theirs! The treasure belongs to them. The tomb—"

"To them," I said, amazed. "To them."

He slid his hands down into the pockets of his trousers. "It's their history," he said.

"It's their history," I said, "but it's my find. Give me back my key."

Silently he took the key out of his pocket and handed it to me. I turned and pulled the grate shut. One hand on the bars, I shook it, to make certain that the latch was fastened.

"Go ask Carnarvon who owns it," I said. With the grate fastened, I could smile at him. "Go tell him that it belongs to the fellahin. He'll think you're a Bolshevik." I laughed and went down toward the tomb.

"Four chambers, you said." The American journalist was scribbling in his notebook.

"Yes. The antechamber, the chamber off to the side we call the annex—"

"Where did you find the throne?" This was a woman, a Frenchwoman; she attached herself to my arm like a bird hooking its feet around a branch.

"The throne was in the antechamber," I said. "If you please—"

"Would you mind repeating what you said before?"

"I beg your pardon?"

It had been like this since the first photographs reached the world's newspapers. Suddenly the Valley of the Kings was the haunt of newsmen. They crowded Kurna like a great migrating swarm. Whenever I left my house, I had to fight my way through their midst.

It did not satisfy them to answer their questions because that only incited them to think up new ones.

"You said that the throne was the greatest piece of art so far discovered in Egypt."

That had already won me the active hatred of the German Egyptologists, who had discovered the previus champion, the great limestone bust of Nefertiti that every schoolboy knows. I pushed at the massed bodies blocking my way. "Please, let me through. I have a lot to do today."

"Now, just a moment, Mr. Carter, just a few more questions."

"Who was Tutankhamun, anyway?" the American journalist said brightly.

"He was a man who died," I said. A very young man, on the evidence of our findings so far. Of course, we had not yet opened the sarcophagus. I bullied my way forward, now careless of trampling on people.

Behind me, someone murmured, "Isn't he perfect? So natural, so unaffected."

"But what did he do as King? This Tutankhamun."

"Nothing."

I forced a passage through the thicket of the press. Reluctantly they gave way and let me go by. Ahead of me was the tomb. The wall we had built stood straight-edged and modern around the entrance. "The most important thing

Tutankhamun did was die and be buried," I said. I hoped that was unaffected enough.

I reached the gate through the wall and plunged down the stairway into the shelter of the dark corridor, where no one could follow me. There, in the tomb, I was safe: I could do what I was meant to do, which was to record the treasure and remove it to a safe place.

We were still working in the first room of the tomb complex, although by now I had discovered that there were actually four rooms, each packed with grave goods. In fact I had only cleared half of the first of these chambers. Already I had found at least one fabulous object: the throne. I had never actually said so—I had said that the throne was the finest piece of art yet discovered *in this tomb*—but I did believe it to be the finest thing ever found in Egypt. And I had found it. I had discovered this wonderful object. The panel on the back was like a window into the past for me. I could imagine the life of that smiling young man, crowned with the elaborate headdress of a King of Egypt, his adoring pretty wife caressing him with oil. Above them the solar emblem shone, showering them with its blessing of life. Pictographs on the panel named the couple Tutank- hamun and Ankhesenamun.

I loved it. That single picture told me more about the occupant of my tomb than anything else we had found or were likely to find until we reached the mummy. Given the amount of material between me and the burial chamber, which all had to be sorted and identified and preserved, we would not set eyes on the mummy for quite some time. But the throne was there, clear and irrefutable evidence.

They were young, that couple, and they were in love. Probably they still worshiped Aten in private—in their hearts. So young, they would have been innocent of the problems and power of rule. They must have lived in a close little paradise, where everything they could remotely wish for was provided for them at once, while the officers of their court schemed and connived around them.

97

Sometimes, looking at that appealing little scene on the throne, I was filled with a curious wishfulness, as if I had been there once and longed to go back again.

"Carter, are you in there?"

"Yes," I said, short. I had just got to work again. Kneeling by a box, I was picking out the beads of a necklace with tweezers. The string had rotted to dust and the beads had to be removed one by one and their relative positions marked to preserve the design. It was difficult work, especially in the glaring lights we had installed. Each interruption strained my powers of concentration.

Carnarvon came down the passageway into the chamber behind me. "Carter, these news people want another photograph."

"I'm in the middle of this," I said.

"We'll just keep you away from your work for a few minutes, sir," said the photographer. It was not my American friend, who kept out of my way. Three cameras hung around his neck, and he carried a valise and a three-legged stand in his hand.

"Do it without me," I said. All this modernity offended me.

"Howard," Carnarvon said. "The nobility obliges."

"I have work—no! Not there—" I lunged at the photographer, who was putting his valise down on a shrine. I snatched the valise out of his hands. The photographer gave me the look reserved for madmen.

Carnarvon burst out laughing. "Come along, Howard—the sooner you yield, the quicker we'll be gone."

While we were posing stiffly among the relics, Evelyn came down.

She had been working above, taking notes; there was a pencil stuck behind her ear. Her short, trim hairdo was covered by a flat scarf.

"Lord Allenby has arrived, Father," she said.

"Excellent," Carnarvon said. "You'll have tea with us, Carter."

I grunted. I saw the day draining away from me. The photographer was hunched over his tripod. The barrel lens of the camera swung up and down. Over the flat back of the man taking the picture, Evelyn smiled at me. She caught her father's eye and fingered her cheek, and he touched his own cheek. There was a tiny bit of sticking plaster on his skin; he had cut himself shaving. He picked it off.

"Hold still, please," the photographer said, and made a gesture like a conductor with his right hand, but nothing happened.

"Damn."

"Father," Evelyn said. "Lord Allenby—"

"I beg your pardon," Carnarvon said to the photographer. I was holding still, my eyes were sore, and a stubborn ache was clamping a hold on the back of my skull. One of the lamps, suspended directly over me, was cooking me lightly in my own juices.

"The flash failed," the photographer said.

"Lord Allenby is waiting," Evelyn said.

The photographer was rummaging madly in his valise. "Just a minute—just a minute—" He plucked the offending lamp out of its socket. "Just a minute—"

Carnarvon was already moving toward the door. Smiling, leisurely, he brushed by the photographer. "I beg your pardon."

"My lord!"

The Earl switched on the arrow beam of his torch. "Take your picture of Carter. After all, he found it." He went into the passageway.

The photographer swore again. He glared at me obliquely and took his camera off the tripod. Evelyn and I watched him pack away the pieces in his valise. Little straps with snaps held everything in place inside the leather compartments. At his every move, I twitched, my hands leaping out, to shield the precious things in the room from his blundering, stupid ignorance. With one last oath he followed Carnarvon out.

"Poor Howard," Lady Evelyn said. "You didn't realize this would happen, did you?"

I knelt down again by the box with the loose necklace beads. "Do you know how much mail I've received? I didn't know there were so many cranks in the world."

She laughed. Taking the pencil from her soft hair, she put it into the flapped pocket of her jacket. "You deserve it. Not the cranks, the recognition. Are you coming to tea?"

I closed the lid of the box. "One man wrote to ask if I'd found any connection between the tomb and the Belgian murders in the Congo. And someone else in America was furious at me because—he says—the world will end now that I've found the tomb."

"I'll answer them for you," she said serenely.

I collected my notebook and straightened. We stood alone in the room, among the artifacts. I had tagged each with a number on a white card. The place looked like a museum. She raised her face to me, soft and warm and alive. Her eyes were clear and steady as a hunter's.

"Lady Evelyn," I said. "Evelyn." I reached for her hand. I was ready to tell her how I felt about her, how tender, how kind, and how I wanted her, now that I was worthy of her.

She backed away from me. "Howard," she said, "no." She shook her head, unruffled. "No." Turning away from me, she went into the darkness of the corridor. I stood gaping at the place where she had been. My hand was still stretched out. I felt like a dupe. I stayed down there, unable to work, my head pounding, until it was time to go home.

My house in Kurna was near the north end of the village. Three or four little steps led up from the street. As I went up to the door, a woman rose from the top step.

"Mr. Carter?" She strolled toward me in a sinuous walk like a film star. "I've been waiting for you all day."

"What do you want?" I asked.

The twilight veiled her face. A long, white hand reached for my shirt front. "Shall we go inside?"

Her hand fingered my shirt buttons. The fabric of her skirt rustled like snakes in a pit. I went on past her toward my house. She followed me, saying, plaintively, "Mr. Carter?" I slammed the door shut in her face.

My headache had taken over my whole head. My stomach churned. I sat on the chair in the front room for fifteen minutes before I could summon myself up to light the lamp. I heard the woman prowling around outside; once I saw her at the window, peering in.

When I was sure she had gone, I trimmed the lamps. The light shone feebly around the room, burnishing the bare walls. There was no furniture here. I was only here to be closer to the tomb. I had never missed having furniture before; now I did. My head hurt. I poured a shot of whiskey into the cup I had drunk my tea from that morning.

There was a knock at the door. Thinking it was the strange woman, I swore and strode across the room to yank the door open, determined to drive her away. But it was Lady Evelyn.

"Well," I said.

"I'm sorry to bother you, Howard. It's my father. He's ill."

Just the sight of her added to my anger. The serenity that had charmed me now was an affront. How dare she be so unmoved by me. I put my hand to the back of my throbbing head.

"Ill," I said.

"Did he seem well to you this morning?"

I stepped back into the room, so that she could pass by me through the door. "Come in. No, I didn't notice him to be out of sorts. What is bothering him?"

She stood in the middle of the little room, her hands clasped tight before her. "He cut himself while he was shaving. He felt strange in the afternoon, so he went back to Luxor, and now he has a fever. He won't let me call the doctor in."

The teacup of whiskey was sitting on the low table by the lamp. I drained it and poured another. "You should. This is Upper Egypt, not Surrey."

"I'm sorry to bother you," she said, her voice stiff. Disapproving.

"So am I. I have a filthy headache." I drank my whiskey.

"Oh. I am sorry, then. You think I should call the doctor for my father."

I put the whiskey bottle on the shelf. "How high is his fever?"

"One hundred and two."

"He cut himself? I think you ought to take him to Cairo. It sounds to me like a good case of blood poisoning."

Suddenly her face was very white. "Yes," she said. "Come help me."

Carnarvon was sitting in the parlor of their suite, his chin on his fist. He looked sick. His cheeks were papery with fever and he was obviously in some pain, although he refused to admit it.

When Evelyn told him that we were taking him to Cairo, he said, "Don't be ridiculous."

"Howard is here," she said, "and the motorcar is outside."

"Carter?" he said. "Tell my daughter she's a goose."

He took his chin off his fist. His eyes were shining, and he gave me a look desperate with fear. I cleared my throat.

"No, she's being wise. Evelyn, have you packed?"

"No," she said, behind me.

"Then put some things in a bag. Night things, his toilet gear."

I went to help Carnarvon out of his chair. At first I thought he was resisting, but he really needed my support. He was almost too weak to walk.

The motorcar took us down the thread of road, from one silent, darkened village to the next. We were seldom out of sight of the Nile, glossy in the moonlight. For a while the canal ran beside us on the other side of the road. The tiny villages stood like outposts among the wide orderly fields of cotton, the towering stands of palm trees. The slender stalks of the trees rose from clumps of exposed and tangled roots, like stage scenery whose feet, being out of the audience's sight, need not be papered over. Here and there, a canal cut through the landscape, straight as a rule.

I drove. In the back seat Evelyn sat beside her father.

"He's asleep," she said, presently.

"Good."

Probably he was unconscious.

"Howard, what happened today, between us—"

"Let's not talk about it."

The open road was bordered by eucalyptus, planted there for wood for the railroad ties. The pavement was littered with droppings of leaves and bark. The old moon was rising. It was a long way to Cairo; she would have to drive part of the way. I wondered if she knew how. I was sure she did. Like the short hairdo and the independence of mind, driving a car would be a mark of her citizenship in the postwar world.

"Howard," she said, "what does it all mean to you? The tomb. Why is it so important?"

"It's the greatest find ever made in Egypt," I said.

"Yes, I know, but why was it so necessary that you find it?"

I shifted my back against the leather seat. My ankles were already stiff from driving. "Someone had to."

"Why?"

"Don't be foolish, Evelyn. Ignorance is not bliss. Or don't you believe in the pursuit of knowledge for its own sake?"

"Knowledge," she said, in a dreamy voice, "is an elusive quantity. How can we know anything about the past? Especially a past as remote as pharaonic Egypt?"

"There's evidence. The tomb is evidence. The more such we uncover, the more we know."

"The more we think we know."

"Evelyn, what are you driving at?"

"Well, it seems to me that the only reality about any time in history is the sort that never leaves a trace. I mean the way people felt about their lives."

She was making me angry. She was trying to tell me everything I did was for nothing. I said loudly, "Rubbish."

She was still. In the rearview mirror I could see her watching me.

"The trained mind can infer something of people's attitudes from the evidence," I said. "We piece together this idea and that one—"

"The trained mind interprets," she said. "In the end one can interpret only by reference to one's own experience. It's a circle, Howard, isn't it? You may look into the past, but it's only a mirror, it can show you only yourself."

I drove on a long while down the empty road before I could even try to answer. Finally all I could say was, "If I accept that, dear, I'm pitching out my whole life."

"Why?" she said, passionately. "Is it so useless to understand yourself?"

"You're being melodramatic, Evelyn, calm yourself down."

"Oh, I'm sorry."

She did not sound sorry; she sounded sarcastic. We did not speak for several hours after that.

Later, when she was driving, and the sun was up, she said, "What are you thinking about?"

"I should have sent someone out to guard the tomb."

"Ahmed will watch over it."

"Ahmed! He's the one I want the tomb guarded from."

She threw me a look of startled amazement. "What?"

"Ahmed is from Kurna. He's a tomb robber. His people

have robbed the tombs of the Valley of the Kings for centuries."

Ahead of us a man was driving a water buffalo down the road. She braked and steered the car around the beast. On its withers, between the broad backswept horns, a child lay asleep. We flew on into the morning.

"I think you're wrong," she said, when she had the car up to speed again. "Ahmed is dedicated and hardworking, and, besides, he's devoted to you."

That made me laugh. I did not bother to explain Ahmed's reasons for giving me trouble.

"Well, not to you, exactly," she said. "But to the work. He loves the work, he's always right there where the hardest and most productive work is—"

"Watching," I said, "for something to steal."

"Really, Howard," she said. "You aren't just single-minded. You're immovable."

After that we did not speak until we reached Cairo.

We arrived just after noon. Lord Carnarvon was quite unconscious. Lady Evelyn went for a French doctor, and I got the sick Earl settled into a suite in the Continental Hotel. The menials and serving people closed in on him, and I was freed of the responsibility.

From the window of the second bedroom in the suite, I looked over the city's twisted streets and straight Parisian boulevards, blunt white Egyptian houses with iron scrollwork grilles over the windows, the spires of mosques, the grotesque modern buildings sprouting like mushrooms after the rain, all strung precariously with the wiring for the electricity that was Cairo's proudest monument. In the streets water buffaloes and donkeys competed successfully for space with the few blundering motorcars.

The Nile Corniche was almost below my window. On the benches facing the slow-moving filthy water sat the ubiquitous boys, their arms languidly extended across the seatbacks, and their pretty faces turned toward the water.

Pigeons crowded the pavement. A sheet of newsprint had wrapped itself around the base of a palm tree near the river. I turned away from it all. Lack of sleep, the sick man in the bed, being here instead of where I belonged; all my troubles were laying siege to me. I felt all grinding edges.

Evelyn did not come back for hours. When she did, there were nurses in gray uniforms, and doctors with rubber tubing hung around their necks, and the sick man. Evelyn and I were never alone, we could not talk—there was no way to pick up the tear in our night's conversation and sew it together again. She seemed to be drawing further away from me.

She had notified her mother. Lady Carnarvon flew from England with the family doctor, hopping in a small plane from one city to the next, until at last she arrived in Cairo. Evelyn was busy at her father's bedside until her mother came. The doctor took over with the Earl, who seemed to be rallying.

Evelyn's time was absorbed in caring for her mother. I could not reach her.

I thought of returning to Luxor, but there was no use in that. I certainly could not work with Carnarvon ill, not while the attention of the entire world was fixed on us. I was jailed in Cairo. The Earl seemed to be improving. Soon, surely, we could return to the valley.

Then he sickened again. This time no one thought that he would get well. Evelyn's brother, Lord Portchester, was summoned from India. The suite filled with doctors and nurses and telegrams and flowers. I stood unnoticed in one corner of the room and watched; or I went out entirely and walked and tried to organize my thoughts.

Evelyn, caring for her mother, overseeing the care of her father, directing what now amounted to an entire household, never tired, never looked frightened or upset. I never saw her sit down, much less sleep. Once I came into the room and found her at a window, staring off across the city. Her chin was set. I went up behind her.

"What an odd place," she said, under her breath. "It's as if it's struggling to be born."

"Let me help you," I said. "Let me do something for you."

She lifted her face to me. "You could make me a cup of tea."

"I will."

"Thank you." She put her hand on my arm and pressed with her fingers an instant. Comforting me: I intended to comfort her. Or perhaps with her it was all automatic. She went off toward the door. I looked out the window, wondering what had elicited from her that odd remark about being born, but there was nothing, only the broad street clogged with a throng of donkeys and strollers, an open touring car honking and inching its way through. When I looked around, Evelyn had left the room.

Portchester arrived late that night, a young, bland, baby-ish face quite lost above his splendid Hussar's uniform. He saw his father, who was delirious then, and went off to bed. Then at two in the morning, people rushed down the hall past my room, which was only a few doors from Portches-ter's. I jumped out of bed and went to the threshold.

The corridor was brilliantly lit by electric lamps on the walls. The nurse was babbling through the next door to someone I could not see.

"It's his lordship, your lordship—he's just now passed on. Your lady mother is with him."

In the midst of her words, the light of the hall lamps dimmed. The nurse screamed. I reached for the light switch and flicked it stupidly off and on again, to no avail. The light was dimming out, the filament a dull red curl inside the glass. The corridor sank into utter darkness.

I went back into my own room and tried the lamp by my bed. It was out too. I went to the window. Out there in the city, not a light glowed.

"Now, damn it, shut up," a man barked in the hall. "I want to see my father."

The nurse sobbed. I wheeled around and through the open door of my room saw Lord Portchester march down the hall, an electric torch in his hand, and the nurse tagging after.

A few moments later, the lights came on again all over Cairo. I went to bed but I could not sleep.

The morning newspaper was sensational with headlines.

CARNARVON IS CURSED! DIES OF ANCIENT EVIL!
AT THE MOMENT OF DEATH, CAIRO IS SWEPT INTO DARKNESS!

Of course, that was nonsense. The lights had gone out several moments after the death. I sipped my Turkish coffee; I was sitting on the terrace of the hotel, trying to keep the flies away from my breakfast. I folded up the newspaper to a manageable size and read through the article as I ate.

The headline told the whole story; some feature writer for the local papers had seized on the wild notion that Carnarvon had somehow violated an ancient taboo in opening the tomb—as if Carnarvon *had* opened the tomb—and so had been struck down by the long arm of the past. The malice of Pharaoh had reached down through thirty centuries to destroy him who had dared to burst in on the peaceful sleep of Tutankhamun.

Halfway through the article, it began to sound familiar to me. That was when the writer mentioned in passing the general terror of the workmen at the tomb. I thought of Ahmed. A cold tingle of my nerves warned me. I had been in Cairo too long; I had better get back to Luxor and protect what was mine.

I went to find Evelyn, to tell her I was going.

She was sitting in the parlor of the suite, her hands in her lap, her shoulders rounded. I stopped in the doorway. She looked so young, suddenly, so frail. She turned and saw me there, but she said nothing, as if we were strangers. The dried tracks of tears lay matte on her cheeks.

"I'm going back up to Luxor," I said.

"Good-bye, Howard," she said. She swiveled her face away from me; her clasped hands opened, the fingers parting, and then twined shut again. I should have said something, but that gesture of her head shut me out. She did not need me, and so I left her there.

On the stairs down to the lobby, I met the young American photographer, going up as I was going down.

We stopped face to face. His mouth was tucked up primly into a little frown. He said, "I'm sorry to hear of Carnarvon's death."

"Yes," I said, "it's a loss. What are you doing in Cairo?"

"I heard he was going," he said.

"And you wanted to remind me that your people have the first call to take over the dig?"

"No. Oddly enough, that isn't why I'm here." He snapped the words out; he looked angry. I'd have looked angry if I were accused of such a thing. I didn't believe him for a moment: of course he wanted the tomb. He glared at me.

"That's why I was here," he said. "As a counterweight. You used me."

"Don't be a schoolboy," I said. "You're acting naïve. The world is more complicated than that."

"It looks simple enough to me," he said. His broad Yankee accent was more pronounced than ever. "We aren't actually real to you, are we, Carter—the people around you. Just tools for you."

I grunted at him, unamused, and started down the stairs. His voice rang after me.

"Tutankhamun isn't real to you, either, Carter—he can't be! You can't live in his world, and you won't pay attention to your own!"

The people on the lobby were turning to look. I felt the

heat climb in my face. I reached the foot of the stairs and walked out across the black-patterned red carpeting.

"You're caught out of time, Carter!"

A bright haze of sunlight marked the open doors to the street. I strode toward them as fast as I could walk.

# 8

I drove the motorcar back to Luxor. The road was straight and wide; I made good speed most of the time, although I had to slow down through the villages. It was a hot day, and the heat climbed as the sun climbed across the sky. In the broad fields, graded to a perfect slope by millennia of floods, the fellahin tilled the rows of cotton, the buffalo trudged around the track of the pump that raised water to the fields, the Nile gushed over the land.

The road came down suddenly into a twisting alley through the outskirts of Luxor. A crowd of boys blocked my way. I held down the button of the car's horn, but the boys only grinned over their shoulders and sauntered down the middle of the street. The white brick walls came down flush to the edge of the pavement. The city closed around me. The air was thick with the fighting odors of beans, fish, sewage, and incense.

I left the car on the ferry stage. The barge was in the slip, but the crew was hosing the deck down, and it would be a few minutes before I could cross the river. I stalked up and down across the road. Down the river, the tufted heads of palm trees peeked up above the tops of the columns and gates of the great temple, but directly opposite me, standing above the roofs of the city, was the spire of a mosque.

Of course, there were obelisks in the Imperial Temple, too—the golden needles of Hatshepsut and Thothmes, symbolizing the rays of the sun. I tramped up and down the apron of the ferry stage, my eyes shifting from the mosque to the temple. Those old spires were gone now. The Greeks had nicknamed them obelisks, meaning "spits for roasting meat"; the various conquerors of Egypt had carted them off. To Karkamesh, to Rome, to London and New York. My eyes returned to the mosque.

The horn blasted, announcing that the passengers for the far side of the river could board the ferry. I got on with a crowd of tourists.

The broad boat nosed its way across the Nile. A flat island had risen in the center of the stream; there were farmers on it, cultivating tomatoes there. I glanced back at the scene behind me. As we got out into the middle of the Nile, my view of the Imperial Temple widened. There was something random about it, something secretive, in the close-packed columns, the heavy space-absorbing cross-beamed gates. It reminded me of Evelyn's theory of history, or should I say theory of ahistory. I turned toward the bow of the barge, my head throbbing in the first stages of headache.

The tourists disembarked in a swarm, all headed for the dragomen and the horse-and-buggy service to the valley. There was yet another addition to the clutter, now, a large truck, and several ugly painted signs advertising guided trips to THE TOMB OF KING TUT.

They were charging twice the price for tours at this season. I rented a donkey from the string at Kurna and rode back into the valley, to see what effect all this was having on my dig.

From the mouth of the ravine I looked back and saw the tourists in their herd being led toward the two colossi of Amenhotep III on the bank of the river. The dragoman guides would see that the European visitors saw everything in proper order.

I kept my donkey trotting at top pace through the valley. Now that I was here, I yearned to see the tomb again. That at least was permanent and real. Everything else had gone exactly contrary to what I had hoped, since we had opened the tomb. The donkey began to snort, a warning that it intended to quit soon, and I kicked it hard in the ribs. My sort of warning. I resolved not to think any more about Lady Evelyn Herbert.

We rounded the bend in the ravine that brought me before the tomb. The panoramic cliff spread out before me. The sky above it was a perfect infinite blue. A small crowd of people stood around the mud-brick wall that surrounded the tomb. Above it, the tomb of Rameses VI was deserted. Gratified, I reined the donkey in, to approach at a dignified pace.

Two armed Egyptians in military uniforms stood guard over the gate through the wall. I left my donkey near the wall and went around to the gate, and the guards turned their rifles toward me.

"No one goes in," said the soldier on the left of the gate.

"I'm Howard Carter," I said. "I'm just here to make sure that everything is in order."

"Nobody goes in."

"You don't understand," I said. "I am Howard Carter."

The soldier on the left shrugged and turned one hand palm up. The soldier on the right said, "This place is under the command of the government of Egypt. Nobody goes in."

I did not understand. I stared from one face to the other, wondering why they were not letting me into the tomb. The government of Egypt. What did he mean by that? Those were my people.

"Carter!"

Ahmed was coming across the narrow part of the valley toward me. He slipped between me and the gate.

"This place belongs to the people of Egypt," he said. "Even the British Commissioner admits that. You will have to apply through the Cairo Museum—"

"The Cairo Museum!"

"—The museum has taken control of it," he said.

I backed up one step from him. Behind him the soldiers stood impassively gripping their rifles. At first I could not collect myself enough even to face Ahmed. I got my control back and sputtered at him, "You! You damned tomb robber — You've been plotting this all along! You and the department—I'll wager they were very happy to do this to me—"

"Carter, quiet down." He put out his hand to me. "Let me explain."

"Explain!" I cried. All around me, heads were turning; in the crowd of tourists, people murmured. I shouted at Ahmed, "What will you explain—how you can steal a man's life work—" That thought stopped me; I stood with my mouth open, realizing that he was doing just that.

"No," he said. "I am not stealing anything, Carter. This is my past. This belongs to Egypt, the tomb and everything in it, and everything that it means. You taught me that. I tried to tell you that, how you taught me the value of that. I am grateful to you for it."

I did not answer him. I could not gather myself together enough to talk. In the background, near the line of the yellow cliffs, was a gaggle of motorcars. Among them a man stood watching me. It was Conway, the assistant curator in charge of catalogs. A sense of the order of my loss rushed in on me.

I would apply to the Cairo Museum for the permission to work on the tomb, and perhaps it would be granted. But still I had lost. My whole life had been devoted to my search, and now that the search was over it was all anticlimax and disappointment. I would never recover the moment when I looked through the hole in the wall and saw the glittering reflections of my candle flame on the treasure of the King. That was the curse on the tomb. I would never be happy again.

The people standing around the tomb were watching me, talking to one another about me. Stiffly I walked away from the tomb of Tutankhamun.

# 9

Sunset. The lotus flower closed. The sun god Ra grew old, and his power dwindled, until all that was left was his red swollen eye, watching Egypt from the western rim of the world, and the least beggar could look on him with impunity.

Hapure the mason thought with longing of his village, where now his daughter would be stirring the dinner in the pot, and the aroma of beans and bread would welcome the workmen home. Hapure was not going home. A stocky man, short and strong, he carried his tools in a sack over his shoulder. As he walked along the road, he kept watch around him. In this troubled reign, thieves and murderers were common on the roads after dark.

Behind him lay the river Nile, bearing on its breast the reflected lights of the great city sprawled along its eastern bank. Hapure was walking into the west, putting each foot higher than the other. The road was climbing up from the valley into the desert; he was leaving the place of living men and entering the realm of death. He kept his fingers on the amulets that he wore around his neck. He thought of his wife, sick and sleeping in their house in the village. For her sake he had given his name to the overseer for the work that waited at the end of his journey.

The path twisted and turned along the uneven ground of the desert. Hapure glanced over his shoulder. The valley of the Nile was out of sight behind him. The desert had shut him in. Like a sudden gust of wind a gust of loneliness came over him. He gulped; he thought of his wife.

In the night sky the first stars shone. He went on toward the west.

At last he reached the rim of a narrow gorge, running like a knife slash across the body of the desert. With his sandaled feet, he felt out the thread of the path that led down the steep side.

He knew this gorge. He had been here often enough, nearly every day of his working life, at some task or another. This was the Royal Valley, where the eternal houses of the kings of Egypt were built. Hapure was a mason in the crew that made those houses. But he had never come out here before at night.

Halfway down the side of the gorge he paused to catch his breath. Below him the narrow bed of the valley was drowned in darkness. Ahead the sharp edge of the clifftop cut across the starry night sky. He blinked his eyes. The darkness was growing lighter; the moon was rising behind him in the east.

He went down into the valley and paused, wondering which way to go. A low voice called, "Hapure."

His hair stood on end. He spun around, the amulets gripped in his fist. A man in a white garment stood on the path a few yards away from him.

"I am Hapure," the mason said, in a low voice.

"Then come," said the stranger, and gestured that he should follow.

Hapure went after the stranger, keeping hold of his amulets. He tried to calm himself. Diligently he forced his gaze straight ahead. But his mouth was dry with fear, and the moonlight tricked his eyes. A shadow crossed over him, and he flinched and threw back his head, staring wild-eyed at the moon, but the sky was clear.

The stranger in the white garment stopped to let him catch up. They walked side by side along the floor of the Royal Gorge. The stranger said nothing. Hapure's mind teemed with questions, yet he was afraid to speak.

The path followed the curve of the valley, and they came into a place where the floor widened out between steep cliffs fluted and worn by the wind. The moonlight gleamed on the stone. At the widest part of the valley were two doorways cut into the rock, one on either side of the path.

Hapure's shoulders settled an inch, and he drew air deep into his lungs. This place he knew. He had worked on these two tombs; he felt at home here, even in the night.

The stranger turned to him. "You are here to do work in secret," he said. "You were chosen because you are known to be trustworthy. Will you swear to keep the secret of this place?"

Hapure glanced around him again, puzzled. As far as he could see, only he and the stranger were in the valley. "Yes," he said. "Of course."

"Then it will not be necessary to seal up the secrets in you with a knife," said the stranger. "Go there, and wait." He pointed to the doorway on the left.

Hapure hitched up his sack of tools on his shoulder and climbed the short path to the opening in the rock. A corridor led back into the hillside. Letting down his sack at the threshold, he went a little way down the passageway, until the darkness closed around him and made it impossible to go farther. He turned and went back and sat down in the threshold of the doorway.

He had brought a loaf of millet bread and a little jar of beer; he made his dinner of them. The moon had risen high in the sky. Ra's pale afterbirth, it symbolized the mysteri-

ous cycle that united all truth. Hapure was fond of the
moon; he liked to consider its meanings of surge and ebb,
life and death, power and weakness. He munched the millet bread and drank his beer and told himself that as long
as the cycle was uninterrupted Egypt and he would remain.

A faint silvery jingling reached his ears.

He lifted his head, his mouth still full of bread, and
strained to hear. It was the wind. A stone falling. No. He
heard it more clearly: the music of sistra and flute.

He got to his feet and drew back into the doorway, trying
to keep out of sight. He put his head around the corner of
the doorway to see. The music seemed stronger now. It
came from down the valley, and it was approaching him.

A low cry escaped him. Around the curve in the valley
a procession was winding.

Three by three, musicians circled around the bend in the
trail and walked down toward the two tombs. Some held
sistra in their hands, the branches hung with tiny silver and
gold leaves that shivered together when they were shaken.
Some carried flutes, and some played on little drums. Their
feet kept time. Their song was sweet. Women followed
after them with urns and boxes. As they marched, the
women chanted ancient laments for the dead; they bent to
scoop up dust from the road and scattered it over their
garments.

Hapure flattened his body to the inner wall of the passageway; he craned his neck to see. The first of the musicians had reached the doorway across from the one where
Hapure was hiding, and still the procession wound back
out of sight around the bend in the valley, with more people rounding it every moment.

The musicians surrounded the doorway. Bending from
side to side, they combined the delicate voices of their instruments into music as sad and various as the wind. As
each group of women reached the tomb, they drew up to

one side or the other. Their voices keened. Their bodies swayed from side to side.

Hapure shivered in the passageway, his arms wrapped around himself. His breath had stopped in his throat.

Six oxen trudged into sight down the valley. They dragged behind them a sled hung with the trappings of Osiris, god of the dead. On the sled lay a body. Behind him more women walked, lamenting, their white garments rent and stained with dust, and their arms raised in mourning.

Slow-pacing, the oxen drew the dead man on his bier down to a stop on the path, midway between Hapure's hiding place and the tomb entrance on the opposite hillside. The men came forward to remove the dead Osiris and bear him into his house of eternal life.

One of the women behind the sled rushed forward. She threw herself on the breast of Osiris and cried out in anguish. Hapure wrung his hands together. Her grief stirred him to the tenderest pity. The men lifted her up; they bore off her dead husband into his grave.

Singing and sighing, the women followed into the dark passageway. Hapure shook himself out of his daze. His heart was pounding. He understood now what secret he was to carry in his heart.

The stranger in the white robe who had brought him here was climbing the slope toward him. Hapure collected his wits. He rubbed his sweating palms together.

"Come," the stranger said.

Hapure took his sack of tools on his shoulder and went after him down to the trail and past the oxen and up the steep rise to the other tomb. The moonlight seemed cold. He shivered a little when the wind touched him. He walked between the rows of musicians whose sistra and flutes graced the air with song. The stranger led him into the tomb.

At the far end of the long, sloping corridor was a lamp, lighting a square-cut doorway. Hapure lowered his eyes.

He was afraid of what he knew. The stranger guided him down to the lamplit door and into a wide empty room hollowed in the rock.

Two doorways led from this chamber into other chambers. The stranger took Hapure across the room to the farther of the doors.

"You will stop up this doorway. Here are the bricks." The guide indicated a stack of bricks with his hand.

Hapure fell to work. He kept his eyes lowered. He tried to seem ignorant, as if his knowledge did not burn in him.

But he saw, almost against his will, into the chamber he was blocking up; he saw the great sarcophagus there, hewn of stone as old as the world, which now contained the body of Osiris.

He laid brick on brick evenly across the doorway, spacing them with an expert eye so that they filled the door exactly. They had mortar ready, and an urn of water, and he mixed the water into the mortar and layered it onto the bricks. Gradually he became aware that another person had come up behind him and stood there beside his guide, watching.

He set the last brick in place, and from behind him came a sigh, so soft he scarcely heard it.

Adding more water to the mortar, he stirred it well with his stick and began to spread it over the face of the bricks. He worked as fast as he could. The only sound now was the sound of his trowel dipping into the wet slip and slopping across the brick wall. He covered the whole of the brickwork, smoothed the edges, and stepped back. Already the slip was drying.

A slight, tall figure stepped past him, knelt, and pressed a seal to the drying plaster. It was a woman. She rose to seal the door again at eye level. Her only garment was of sheer linen, torn and stained with mourning. Hapure licked his lips, his eyes upon her. She wore no sign of her rank, but he knew her, as all Egypt knew her, for Nefertiti the Beautiful One Who Comes.

She turned, the seal in her hand, and her eyes met his. For an instant, his whole attention fixed by her beauty, he could not look away.

"Thank you," she said.

He went down on his knees, his head bent.

A hoarse voice spoke softly behind him. "Shall we bring in the furnishings, O Lotus of the God?"

"Let it be done," she said.

Then the servants of Osiris began to file into the chamber, and each of them brought some object for the comfort of him in his life beyond the grave. Hapure, on his knees, bit his tongue to keep from gasping. He saw them stack up chairs and couches as if they were fuel for the fire—priceless things, gleaming with gold and jewels in the light of the lamps. They brought in jars of food for Osiris, and little statues of themselves, to serve the god in his eternal life as they had served him in this. They brought in little boats that he might sail on the eternal river, and nets to catch his fish, and fowling nets; they brought caskets of jewels and piles of clothing, and laid it all down and left. The room that had seemed so large when empty shrank with each new offering until at last there was no space left save that where Hapure knelt and Nefertiti stood.

They went out, and Hapure shut up this chamber in its turn with bricks, and Nefertiti sealed it.

On the surface the musicians still played their timeless song. Hapure stood off to one side, his hands clasped together. One by one, the women knelt down at the doorway to the tomb and kissed the threshold, taking leave of him who now dwelled in eternity. They rose. They moved around Hapure as if he were a stone; they took no heed of him at all. The musicians went off down the valley. Their music grew fainter. The women followed with empty arms. The oxen dragged away the sled.

Hapure stood watching until they had gone. He passed his gaze once more around the valley. Nothing moved. It was as lonely as before. At the threshold of his hearing, the last whisper of the music played, and then was gone.

The stranger came to him. "You may go," he said. He gave him a sack of money. "Speak of this to no one."

Hapure closed his fingers around the purse. He knew he would not be able to keep secret the knowledge that burned in his heart. On quick feet he hurried away down the path that led to his village.

"The Queen," said Sennahet, derisive.

"It was Nefertiti herself whom I saw! Oh, she is beautiful —more beautiful than her images, alive, and warm—" as he spoke, Hapure laid his hand over his breast.

They had met in the crowded street at the foot of the ferry stage. Every few moments a passerby brushed against Sennahet, or trod on his foot; he stood braced against the swarming people around him. Hapure was facing him, his expression intense. Sennahet scratched his chin. Hapure was usually a truthful man, but this story was fantastic, that he had spoken with the Queen Regent.

"Come to the beer yard," Sennahet said. "Tell me the whole story."

They walked single-file through the crowd. Hapure went first. Over his shoulder, he said, "I shall only drink one jar with you—my wife is still very sick."

"In the hands of Isis let her lie," Sennahet said.

Ahead two palm trees held their tasseled heads above the crowd, their slender trunks bracketing the gate. The two men went between them into the alehouse. The stone benches that lined the yard were all sat upon, and Hapure and Sennahet took their jars of beer to a corner of the wall and stood in the shade there.

"Now tell me your story," Sennahet said.

"But you—am I keeping you from something?" Hapure stroked his chin with thumb and forefinger, his eyes shrewd.

"No, of course not," Sennahet said. "I am looking for

work. There is no work. Therefore I shall go to the temple and beg for beans and bread. Tell the story, my uncle, and take my mind from my unpleasant future."

"Well, then," Hapure said.

He told of being hired for extra work—of going by himself into a desert valley, to an old, unused tomb. Then a funeral procession came, which carried a dead man into the tomb, and laid it down with great ceremony.

"And I stopped the door and plastered it, and she who sealed the tomb was Nefertiti. It was the Queen Regent. No other could be so radiant. Her greatness and power shine forth from her face."

With his hand Hapure imitated the effulgence of the Queen's features. Sennahet grunted, his mouth full of Theban beer. In this place it was like speaking of dreams to talk of the Queen Regent. The beer yard was hot with the bodies that crowded it. Here and there a man had fallen asleep on a bench, and the yardmen went along and knocked him to the ground. Those who did not wake were dragged out of the yard. Sennahet's back itched. A trickle of sweat ran down his spine. He longed to spend the afternoon in the public bath, but he had no money for that. He swallowed the beer.

"Well?" Hapure said. "Do you believe me?"

"I think you grow a little strange, you folk in Kalala," said Sennahet.

He was speaking of Hapure's village, isolated from the rest of Thebes, where lived those who labored in the royal necropolis.

Hapure's face settled. "I knew I should never have spoken of it."

"And who of recent has died in the palace?" Sennahet drained his jar. "Whom was the Queen burying?"

Hapure took the jar from his hand. "Think on that." He went across the beer yard toward the vats, where six men with clubs were standing, to see that everyone paid for what he took out.

Sennahet stayed in the shelter of the wall. He did not think of princes. His own life weighed on him. He should not have paid out his money for the beer; he owed money to the man with whom he lodged. The thought of the bathhouse crossed his mind again. He wondered if Hapure would give him the small money for a few hours in the sweat room. Hapure returned, smiling, with full jars.

"Well? Have you thought it over?"

Sennahet put his lip into the foam. "It takes seventy days to justify a man's corpse for Osiris. No one in the royal family died seventy days ago." He drank deep of the free beer.

"Exactly." Hapure beamed at him. He was shorter than Sennahet. He still had most of his teeth, white in his dark face, polishing his smile. "No one has died—not for three years."

"Then whom was she burying? But—" Sennahet caught back his words. He stared hard at Hapure. "Three years? You mean since Pharaoh died. What are you saying?"

Hapure bounced a little, pleased. "It was no one newly dead whom she buried. It was an old friend of the earth."

"Akhenaten?"

"Who else could it be?"

"You are mad! Pharaoh is buried in the north, in his own city."

"And so Nefertiti stayed there, in the north. But now the priests have forced her to return to Thebes. Would she leave him there, alone? Would she leave him where his enemies might find him? No." Hapure gulped beer and wiped the foam from his mouth with a hasty hand. "No indeed. She brought him here, to Thebes, and buried him in secret."

"It cannot be."

Their voices had risen. Two or three men nearby had turned to look. Sennahet licked his lips. He raised his beer; his hand was trembling with excitement. Hapure was grinning broad as the summer Nile.

"Damn him!" Sennahet said, and the grin vanished from the other man's face.

"Yes, damn him." Sennahet threw the jar down empty. "I say damn Akhenaten. He made war on the gods, and so they have ruined him, and us with him."

Half the faces in the yard watched him. He lowered his eyes, ashamed of his outburst. A fat man nearby raised his fist.

"Liar! Akhenaten tried to bring us to the truth!"

The man beside the fat man turned and struck him in the belly. His mouth was working, but Sennahet could not hear what he said; his voice was lost in the general outcry. All around the beer yard, men were shouting at one another. Someone crashed hard into Sennahet from behind, and he staggered; the men around him were fighting.

Hapure gripped Sennahet by the arm and pushed him toward the door. They circled two men who stood screaming insults at one another. After each torrent of abuse, they slapped one another. With Hapure just behind him, Sennahet strode out to the street.

He paused, drawing a deep breath. Hapure was shaking his head.

"Three years he has been dead, and yet mention of his name starts a brawl."

The shouts and sounds of blows from the beerhouse were drawing the attention of people passing by in the street, and a small crowd was gathering near the door. Sennahet and Hapure walked away.

Sennahet wiped his hand over his neck. The sun was high in the sky. Thebes baked in the furnace heat of noon. On the corner a line of people waited before a public scribe, cross-legged on his mat. Sennahet and Hapure separated to go around them. The crowd beyond was full of priests and harlots. Hapure caught up with Sennahet, who was still walking at top speed.

"Akhenaten was a curse on Egypt," Sennahet said. "Did

I not have my own farm—a rich man's daughter to marry me—then Akhenaten smote the gods."

"It was your brother's farm, not yours."

"It would have been mine, when he died." Sennahet clenched his fists. He went along with his head down; people swerved to avoid bumping into him. Abruptly he stopped and faced Hapure, his eyes burning with a new idea.

"When they buried him, was there gold?"

Hapure's face grew long. He stepped back away from his uncle. "What do you mean?"

"Could you find the tomb again?"

"What are you saying? What sacrilege!"

"We could be rich!" Sennahet cried.

Hapure turned on his heel and walked away through the crowd. Sennahet swore at his disappearing back. The beer was making him bilious. The heat of the sun was attacking him. He stared after Hapure until he lost him in the swarm of hurrying people. Aimless, he walked away down the street. A man passed him on a donkey, another donkey pattering after on a lead line. Sennahet dodged out of the way of the led beast. He hunched his shoulders. Even the beasts thought him less than they.

He tramped along past the stalls of the leatherworkers, the racks of pottery. The stink of the tanning vats reached his nostrils. A priest began to chant in the next street. He walked along, his head down, unwilling to go to the temple and beg for bread, unwilling to return to his hired room and face his landlord, and as he walked, he thought with envy of Pharaoh's gold.

# 10

The Queen Regent had a waiting woman, whose name was Meryat. Although this girl was not of royal blood, Nefertiti loved her like a daughter. The girl cared for the Queen's cats and took her messages about within the palace, and when Nefertiti was ill, which was often now, Meryat sat next to her with a fan and cooled her face.

So she was there when the Vizier came to Nefertiti and said, "Radiant One, there is evil news from the south of the land of Egypt. The Nile is not coming to flood. The famine will not be broken this year."

Meryat made as if to go, but Nefertiti called to her and bade her stay. "All Egypt will know of this within three days, anyway."

The Vizier spoke ritual phrases of consolation and reassurance. They were in the Queen Regent's enclosed garden. The openwork of the alabaster walls caught the breeze and kept the sun at bay; a boy sitting in the corner played on a flute. Meryat with her fan of heron feathers wafted the breeze toward the Queen.

Nefertiti was pale as winding linen. Her eyes shone with fever.

"Another year of the famine. It is I who shall be blamed —I and my God."

"My Queen," the Vizier said. "I have sent for the diviners—"

"More auguries! Last year they said that if I returned the court of Pharaoh to Thebes, the old gods would smile on Egypt again. Next they will say that I must give an ox and an oxload of gold to all soothsayers!"

The Vizier was bowing up and down, murmuring, "Radiant One, Radiant One." The braided tresses of his old-fashioned northern wig swung over his shoulders.

"Meryat," the Queen said fretfully. "Bring my slippers."

Meryat put the fan down and went to the foot of Nefertiti's couch. The slippers were under the cushion. The Vizier talked of messages to be sent around Egypt, to explain the failure of the Nile. Meryat wished he would leave; the Queen was very pale. The maid knelt to put the royal slippers on Nefertiti's narrow feet.

"Enough," said the Queen to the Vizier. "I will consider this later." She rose from the couch, her hands to her temples. "Meryat, my pomander."

Meryat hurried across the room for the pomander, in the cedar chest below the window. While she knelt by the chest, the drapery over the door to the terrace billowed out on a gust of wind, and through the fluttering curtains the young Queen Ankhesenamun came into the room.

"Mother, I need your advice."

Her voice was clear as the note of a tuned string. Her black, unpainted eyes were direct. Tall and slim, scorning ornaments, she looked more like a boy than a young woman; least of all, she looked the Great Wife of Pharaoh. On her left forearm was a leather bow guard. The tail of a lion hung from her belt. She loved to hunt. Meryat admired her and was afraid of her. The Vizier bowed deep to her.

"Welcome, Favored of Isis."

Nefertiti had walked across the room to Meryat's side. She took the pomander, a puff of spicy scent, and touched it to her nostrils.

"My advice, daughter, is to shun my advice. Everything I do seems poisoned, everything I touch."

Ankhesenamun said calmly, "Is that a riddle? What has happened now, Mother?"

"The Nile has not grown great—there will be no flood to nurture Egypt."

Ankhesenamun gave a visible start, as if she had been struck. She turned her head to stare at the old Vizier. "Well, then, perhaps we made a mistake, when we abandoned our God, the Aten."

The Vizier's face toughened. He stood squarely on his wide-spaced feet. "We are suffering now for the evil-doing of the Atenists! The gods avenge themselves on us for degrading them, who kept us all these generations."

"Bah," said Ankhesenamun, turning away.

The Vizier thrust out his jaw. "The Beloved of Egypt does ill to speak of the faults of others, for how can the Nile swell, or any good come, when the Strong Bull of Egypt is a virgin King?"

Meryat saw the quick bright color stain the cheeks of Ankhesenamun, but the young Queen said nothing; she kept her back to the Vizier. Nefertiti lowered her pomander.

"You exceed yourself," she said to the Vizier. "The King is a boy—you want miracles. Please. My head is throbbing. We shall discuss it all later, when we have time." She turned to Ankhesenamun and reached out her hand sadly to her, reproachful.

"My dear one, daughter, the grand audience begins in one quarter of an hour. You cannot sit beside Pharaoh dressed like a herdsman's wife."

"I am not sitting with Pharaoh," Ankhesenamun said.

"Meryat, attend her. Let her be made beautiful."

"I will not sit down with Pharaoh!"

As she spoke the last words, two men in gold-embroidered skirts strode into the room. They stepped to one side and with a flourish clapped their hands together. Two more men appeared, shaking sistra with both hands; the sistra were shaped like faces, with bells for their eyes and tongues, and their silvery ringing was like the purr of a cat. The smell of incense was rich in the air. Meryat dropped down on her knees and put her face to the ground between her hands.

Preceded by children with flowers, Pharaoh entered the room. Meryat watched through the corner of one eye. It seemed to her that the air of the room was gilded by his presence. Tutankhamun was gorgeously dressed; not even the statues of the gods were adorned as he, the living god. Bracelets of gold clasped his arms, and the feathered crown towered on his head. A collar of jewels hung around his neck and down over his bare chest; in the center of the ornament was a great Eye of Ra made of lapis lazuli and ivory.

His wife and the Queen Regent had knelt to him. Pharaoh thrust out his chest and strutted up and down before them. He was fourteen, still narrowly built, still beardless. During the highest ceremonies, there hung a false beard with wires from his chin.

"My audience begins in a few moments," he said. "Are you ready? I insist that you sit beside me, my wife. There is gossip if you do not."

Nefertiti began to rise. "We have—"

"Don't stand! You cannot stand without my permission."

Ankhesenamun grunted a vulgar, humorous noise. She got supplely to her feet and stalked out of the room.

"Go," Tutankhamun said to her back. He waved his hand at Nefertiti and said in a lofty voice, "You may rise."

The Queen Regent was already standing. Meryat on her hands and knees crossed the painted floor to take up her place just behind Nefertiti.

Tutankhamun spoke peevishly of his lessons. "All they do is recite homilies for me to copy down. I think I shall spend my mornings henceforth in the garden. I need no lessons. My fellow gods will instruct me."

"We shall find you a more engaging tutor," Nefertiti said. "Now, Your Majesty, we have very bad news. The word has come from Edfu, at the head of the Nile. This year when Sothis the Great Star rises, the river will not flood, and the famine will not be broken."

Tutankhamun shrugged his shoulders. He looked down at the sacred Eye on his chest. "Isn't this splendid? Horemheb gave it to me. I shall give him a thousand chariots. He has only asked for five hundred."

The Queen Regent's voice sharpened. "Your Majesty, this is grave news. You must pay heed."

He swung around, his elbows jutting out. Heavy with gold, his skirt clanked when he moved. He said, "The Nile floods when I call it—I, Pharaoh. If it does not, then I must have some reason for holding it back. It is your task to find out. I am not interested in *how grave* the news is."

Meryat lifted her head. Nefertiti stood directly before her; the Queen's fist was clenched at her side. Meryat heard the strain in her mistress's voice.

"Pharaoh, the audience will soon begin. But we shall speak later of this frivolous outburst."

"I want Ankhesenamun there."

"You will be courteous, or you will sit alone."

"Courteous," he said. "I am Pharaoh. All of you are my servants. What claim have you on my courtesy?"

The Queen's hand relaxed. Her voice was calm again. "Do you want to sit alone at the audience?"

The King shut his lips tight together. His large, expressive eyes, outlined in kohl, looked angrily at the Queen Regent. The silence grew taut between them. Finally the boy lowered his eyes. He put his fingers to the Sun's Eye on his chest.

"Why do you always treat me so badly? Why did Ankhesenamun go?"

"You told her to go, my King." Nefertiti put her hands together. "We shall go together to the Chamber of the Jubilation of Ra. Meryat, bring my fan."

Meryat went on hands and knees to fetch the heron-feather fan. The Queen spoke, and Pharaoh obediently went ahead of her out the door. Meryat put her feet under her. Nefertiti could always master Pharaoh; she knew what to say to him when it seemed that all others were baffled by him. Everything would yet be well. Raising the spread feathers in her hand, she pattered after her mistress into the audience hall.

Sometimes at night the young Queen Ankhesenamun hunted lions in the desert. One evening, as she was leaving her chamber in the palace to join her companions in the stableyard, Nefertiti met her in the hallway.

"Where are you going?" asked the Queen Regent.

Ankhesenamun did not answer. Indeed, her clothes answered; she wore a short skirt of linen belted with leather, and high laced boots, and bow guards on her arms. She saw that her mother, Nefertiti, was unattended. Three of Ankhesenamun's own women were waiting on their mistress, but with a motion of her hand the young Queen sent them away.

"Do you wish to speak with me?" Ankhesenamun asked.

Nefertiti inclined her head. "Yes."

"Come to my private room, then, if it please you."

"Thank you, daughter."

The two Queens returned down the hallway toward the younger woman's quarters. Ankhesenamun shortened her stride so that her mother could keep up. The hallway was lit with oil lamps. The soft light was kind to Nefertiti's face; she seemed young again, beautiful again.

They went into Ankhesenamun's bedchamber. There the light was brighter; Nefertiti again looked old and worn and sick.

She sat down on the low couch at one end of the room, away from the window. A fine fringed shawl, thrown carelessly down on the couch, slid to the floor, and Nefertiti lifted it up and put it on her lap, stroking the soft fabric. Ankhesenamun watched her from the far side of the room. Even in her age and decline, Nefertiti was more beautiful than Ankhesenamun in her prime of youth.

"What do you wish to say to me, Mother?" Ankhesenamun said.

Nefertiti lifted her eyes from the fringed shawl. "You have a husband, my daughter. Why, then, do you go abroad at night to hunt lions and leave me without a grandchild?"

"Bah," Ankhesenamun said. She put her hands behind her on the cool marble chest and bounded smoothly up to sit on it. "You sound like Ay, the old Vizier. You cannot expect me to join my flesh with the flesh of a beardless, mindless whelp like Tutankhamun."

"It is your duty," said Nefertiti.

"I cannot do my duty, then. I will not endure him."

"Do not think of it as union of the flesh. It is a sacred act —a sacrament—"

Ankhesenamun said roughly, "Do you think I do not know how sacred and how magnificent it is? I, the daughter of Pharaoh, who in Pharaoh's bed made the circle complete?"

Her mother faced her, eyes bright, and no longer calm. Nefertiti was canted stiffly forward. Her fists were buried in the shawl in her lap. She and Ankhesenamun stared at one another, the old rivalry broken open again. Ankhesenamun's chesks burned. She felt afresh how she had gloated when she took her mother's place beside Pharaoh, and Nefertiti had been forced to bow to her.

"You were not enough for him," she said to her mother. "He needed a wife of royal breeding."

Nefertiti lifted her head. The black paint around her eyes made her lids gleam. Her teeth showed against her lip. Then she shook her head; she looked away and, raising her hand, shielded herself from Ankhesenamun.

"No—we have hurt each other too much. You are my own child, and I your mother, and that should be how we treat each other."

For a moment neither of them spoke. Ankhesenamun was determined not to look away and show weakness. Yet her mother's words moved her, and she had to struggle to keep still.

Nefertiti spoke again, her eyes still averted. Now she was cool again, remote, and old. "It was different with each of us, of course. With you, he performed the sacrament. But with me—it was a union of the flesh."

"Mother—"

"We were not gods to each other, Akhenaten and I," Nefertiti said. "That was for the others—that was the false life. We put on those lives together with our gold clothing and our crowns. What we were to each other was true. Every moment."

She gripped her hands together. Her voice fell to a whisper.

"Then he came to want to be the god, and for that, you are right, I was not enough."

Impulsively, Ankhesenamun slid down from the marble chest. She knelt beside her mother and took her hand. "I am sorry."

"Sorry!" Nefertiti wheeled toward her again. "I am sorry for you, child. Because you have no such love as I."

That reminded Ankhesenamun of Pharaoh, her husband. She rose and paced away from her mother into the shadows, away from the lamp. She felt betrayed in her sympathy.

"Give me a grandson," Nefertiti said. "Give me a child of the lineage of Akhenaten, and I will teach him to be Pharaoh."

"Meanwhile, Tutankhamun is Pharaoh."

"Only give me another male of the blood."

"Of his blood? A child of his?"

"Your father's grandson!"

Ankhesenamun kept her back to her mother. She would not be tricked again by sentiment. She paced along the room, passing a window; she turned her eyes longingly on the boundless night. The moon was rising. The desert cliff was sharply set against the black sky.

"I am late. I must go." She strode toward the door.

"Wait," Nefertiti said.

At the door, Ankhesenamun turned her head; her gaze crossed her mother's one more time. "I am sorry," the daughter said to the mother. She went out and left Nefertiti there alone.

Plague stalked Egypt like a lioness, taking victims at her will, and everywhere was famine. Still, when the temple of the Aten at Thebes was complete, Nefertiti chose to go herself to consecrate it.

The temple stood on the east bank, close by the Temple of Amun. Thus the Aten challenged the dread god of fear in his very sanctuaries. The Temple of Amun was close and dark, buzzing with the flies that fed on the blood of sacrifices; the new Temple of Aten enclosed wide courtyards open to the sun. Amun was served only by men; the new temple was dedicated to women. On all faces of the columns of the temple were painted images of women, worshiping the Disk of the Sun, whose rays streamed down around them, each ray ending in a hand that caressed them with love.

Amun kept his people miserable with fear. The Aten loved all people. This was the difference between them, and it was this difference that Nefertiti thought would save Egypt, even as famine and plague ate up the people, even as terror of things to come ate up their hearts.

The Queen Regent was passing by along the Avenue of the Sphinxes that led to the temple. Above the massed heads and shoulders of the crowd in front of him, Sennahet could see the golden tassels swaying from the awning of her chair; he saw the high plumes of her fans, white as wool against the brilliant sky.

No one cheered her. Her chair, which six men bore, was surrounded by rings of armed soldiers.

Sennahet lowered his gaze to the backs of the people before him. He was sweating; his eyes shifted back and forth, looking to see if anyone was watching him. As far as he could see along the Avenue of the Sphinxes, people stood packed together to watch the procession. They stood on tiptoe; they held their children up to look. No one was paying any heed to Sennahet.

Directly in front of him was the broad back of a young man with heavy gold rings in his ears and a purse dangling from his belt. Sennahet's fingers curled when he looked at the purse. The muscles tensed in his thighs.

A great cry went up from the crowd. The King was coming. First came men swinging censers, turning the air peppery with the smoke of the incense; flute boys followed, piping and dancing. In their wake the King appeared.

His chair was made all of gold, worked in the images of lions and giraffes, the sacred beasts of his house. He sat on the skins of lions and he wore the towering double crown of Egypt. The people could not watch him in silence as they had the Queen Regent. His appearance drew gasps and sighs from every throat. He was laden down with jewels like a savage bride; his arms were armored in bracelets; amulets hung about his neck; on his breast was a great Eye of Ra made of glass paste and gold. Inside the casing of his royalty, the face of a weakling boy looked out, with pouting lips and a beardless chin. In his hands he carried crossed over his breast the authority of Egypt, the crook and flail of Osiris.

So richly adorned was Tutankhamun that to Sennahet it seemed his very flesh was made of gold.

Now the King was passing before him. The back of the youth jumped with muscle as the young man flung his arms up and shouted in amazement at the god passing. Here and there people knelt and pressed their faces to the dirt. Most of the men and women in the crowd simply stood awestruck. Sennahet's hand shot forward; he plucked the purse from the belt of the youth.

"Thief!"

The cry was like a sword in his ears. He whirled and fled.

"Thief! Stop him!"

Before him was the solid mass of the crowd. He slithered between two bodies and dodged around a fat woman with a child and shoved and pushed at the family behind her. A hand gripped him. He jerked his arm free. He could not run, there was no room to run.

Right behind him someone shouted, "Stop him—he's a thief!"

He blundered into an old man and knocked him down. That taught him the way. He began to seek out weaklings —old people, children. He charged at these weaker people. Knocked them aside, trampled them. A man seized hold of his skirt and the skirt tore and Sennahet ran on naked.

"Thief!"

The cry was fainter, farther behind him now. He threaded his way through the mob. Here, back from the street, people were scattered. He walked in among them, one hand over his nakedness. They were all watching the King. No one gave him more than a curious glance.

In the shadow of one of the great sphinxes that lined the road, he stopped and opened the purse. It was empty. He swore and shook it upside down, but it was empty. He cast it into the dirt and went away, cursing the youth who wore his wealth all in his ears.

Hapure had been standing in line before the new temple for two hours, since before dawn. His legs hurt.

The line curved across the broad apron of the rear court-yard of the temple. There were young palms growing in jars around the sides of the courtyard, and people were sitting on the edges of the jars to rest; people sat on the lip of the little lily pond in the center of the court. The head of the line stopped at the rear entry to the temple, and there it had stood for hours, since before Hapure had taken his place at the tail, and no one yet had come to attend to the suppliants.

At noon, when the sun was at its height, the Queen Regent and the young King made their magnificent proces-sion down the Avenue of the Sphinxes to the temple. Ha-pure was still standing in the line behind the temple. The ceremony of dedication took place on the far side, and he did not see the Queen. He heard the roar of the crowd and knew what had occurred and he began to despair, because the line had not advanced one inch since before dawn.

The people before him grumbled and spoke evilly against the priests of the temple. Hapure shut his ears to them. He looked around the courtyard at the tall columns of the temple. They were so newly painted that the colors seemed to shine forth with their own light. It was a beauti-ful temple, if a little strange, with its broad expanses, its airy vistas. The sunlight shone down through the columns all the way to the ground. Idle, musing, Hapure let himself imagine that the columns of the temple and the rays of the sun twined like the fingers of two hands clasping.

At last a scribe came down the line, beginning at the head, and asked each person waiting there what his pur-pose was. Hapure saw him, and he stood on his toes to watch the scribe's progress.

Many of the people to whom the scribe spoke left the line and went off. Hapure wondered what sent them away; puzzled and uncertain, he felt in the rolled top of his skirt for the coins he had brought and fingered them out to his palm.

The scribe came to the man and woman in line before Hapure.

"We have come to ask a share of the sacrifice," the man said. "When the Queen Regent consecrates the temple. May she live forever! We are hungry, and to share the sacrifice is the right of the hungry."

The scribe looked sympathetic, but he wagged his head from side to side.

"There is nothing to share, unless you can fill your stomachs with flowers. The Aten asks no blood sacrifice, no flesh of lamb or oxen, only gifts of flowers. The Queen Regent will give him lilies; and the King, hyacinths."

The man and woman cried out in one voice. "Shame! For shame! We are hungry. What manner of god is this, who denies food to the hungry?"

"Go to Amun," said the scribe. "Today eighteen prime oxen will be slain for his pleasure, and he takes only the flesh of the left thigh."

The man and woman moved away, talking in angry voices. The scribe turned to Hapure.

"What do you wish of the Aten?"

Hapure said, "I have money, and my wife is sick with the plague. I want some priest to speak her name during the ceremonies, so that the God will favor her and make her well again."

The scribe was shaking his head. "I am sorry. The priests of the Aten do not take bribes."

"Alas," said Hapure.

"And they will tell you that the Aten looks on all of us the same, and will heal your wife if it is his will."

The scribe went on to the next in line. Hapure stared after him, gloomy. In his fist were the precious coins with which he might have bought his wife's health. Now the scribe had told him that her health was beyond any price.

"I will go to Amun, then," he said.

Without turning, the scribe said, "Surely Amun will take your money."

Hapure went away.

Meryat knelt at the left hand of the Queen Regent. The great words of the prayer sounded over her, and she was half in tears with the memories it wakened in her.

> Thy dawning is beautiful in the horizon of heaven,
> O living Aten, beginning of life!
> When thou risest in the eastern horizon of heaven,
> Thou fillest every land with thy beauty!

Pharaoh himself had composed this song, the hymn of Akhenaten to his God. Meryat had heard him sing it countless times, in his New City, away to the north. There every day had passed in contemplation of the Aten. There, where no enemy came, and no adverse word was spoken, Meryat had believed that the triumph of the Aten was complete. How could she have guessed that everywhere else in Egypt, people did not understand the Aten and clung secretly to their ancient gods?

> When the chicken crieth in the eggshell,
> Thou givest him breath therein to preserve him alive;
> When thou hast perfected him that he may pierce the egg
> He cometh forth. . . .

When the King had spoken thus of his God, none could listen without yielding to his vision. But Akhenaten was dead.

And here in Thebes the old gods were vigorously alive. Meryat prayed that the Aten would protect her; she trembled with dread even as she rejoiced in the great hymn. The sacred columns around her would protect her in the temple. The images on them would protect her when she imitated them, doing her daily work. Yet she was afraid.

Before her, Nefertiti stood at the foot of the high pillar. As she spoke the words her husband had taught to them all, her body swayed, and Meryat too began to sway. Many in the crowd began to speak with the Queen Regent. They locked arms and their bodies moved from side to side.

Meryat closed her eyes. Surely while Nefertiti lived, the Aten would protect his people. She put away her fear and gave herself up to the welling joy of communion with the God, her arms locked fast with those of the rest of the worshipers, her tongue speaking in unison with them and once more with Akhenaten.

Akhenaten's face was ugly: his jaw like a plow blade, his eyes slanted above high, slanting cheekbones. He looked down on his daughter Ankhesenamun with a faint unreadable smile on his lips.

Rather, six stone images of him looked down on her, and she bowed deep before him.

"Greetings, my father. I have offerings for you, for the delight of your ka."

She set the little dish of millet and honey at the foot of the first statue.

The six images were set around the sides of a courtyard at one end of the Temple of the Aten. They were fashioned in the extreme style that her father had encouraged toward the end of his reign, in which the grace of the Aten in him showed itself in a swelling of his loins, and his special powers of life and death were represented by female breasts, so that he seemed both man and woman together in the same body.

Once every courtier in Egypt had hastened to have himself depicted in painting and statue in this same style. Now, of course, they ordered that the artists show them thin and frail, like Tutankhamun.

Nefertiti had come here this afternoon to consecrate the courtyard to the immortal ka of her husband. Then the courtyard had rung with the strong voices of men loudly worshiping the dead King. Ankhesenamun had not been able to bear it; she had gone away. She knew none of them still loved the King. They loved Tutankhamun now. The Grand Vizier and the General Horemheb put on whatever face and manner would keep them in the favor of Tutankhamun and Nefertiti.

So Ankhesenamun had waited to pray alone, sincerely, before her father. But she did not pray. She brooded on the failures of her mother.

Tutankhamun had looked on as Nefertiti consecrated her temple. He had not led the prayer, or even joined in it, although Nefertiti had pleaded with him to show that favor to the Aten. He had toyed with his rings as the Queen Regent sang the hymn to the God. Akhenaten meant nothing to Tutankhamun. Daily Nefertiti's influence waned over him. Soon even she would mean nothing to him.

"My father," the young Queen Ankhesenamun said, "he does not honor you, but I shall."

She clasped her hands together, looking up at the face of the statue, and fell into a dreamy reverie of times she had sat so at his knee, and heard him tell of the Aten. He had had such a fire in him, such a spellbinder's gift of words, that she had listened to him for hours, even as a tiny child.

Now, of course, she saw how much he had failed—even though she adored him, she saw that he had failed. The old gods were still masters over Egypt, and the Aten was a lonely god who wandered in the desert and called out, but none came. In Egypt things were done the old way, or not at all. Ankhesenamun saw the virtue in that: otherwise, the whole world would fly apart.

Her mother was not so sensible. Her mother was a fool. Even today, Nefertiti had pointed to the presence of the high officers of the court as proof that this ceremony would reunite Egypt. Ankhesenamun, remembering, frowned and clenched her fist. She had seen how the Grand Vizier and the General Horemheb murmured together when Nefertiti's back was turned.

And Tutankhamun had not taken part in the ceremony; he had not come to this courtyard at all. That was the worst.

Ankhesenamun rose to her feet. She bowed down again before each image of her father; she knew that each bow would gladden his ka, wherever it should be, even all the way north in the New City where he was buried.

As for Tutankhamun, that brat, although he and she were married, she had not yet endured his embrace, and she vowed she never would.

She waited in the courtyard, thinking more of her father, until Meryat came. In the distance she heard the sounding of the ram's horns. The sun was setting. The courtyard was already dark. Ankhesenamun blinked, surprised, at the shadows around her. With Meryat, she left the little courtyard and returned to her mother's side.

In her bedchamber in the palace, Nefertiti sent Meryat off to bed. Alone, the Queen Regent sat before the golden mirror.

She had expected joy of this day, and she knew no joy. She had expected at least to recover some of her failing control over the people. Certainly the royal procession had brought the people of Thebes into the street by the thousands. Yet few of them had followed her into the temple.

In the golden mirror the familiar face of the Queen returned her gaze: the face of the woman Nefertiti hid within. Her beauty belonged not to her but to the people who looked on her. Her overt serenity was won at such a cost of nerve and will that she was left, now, not so much calm as exhausted. Behind this face of painted eyes and mouth, composed expression, and grave intelligence an old woman lived.

She touched her cheeks with her fingers. In the golden

mirror her skin seemed flawless, but her fingertips touched the lines, the drying, flaking skin, the sagging flesh. She put her arms down and laid her head on them.

There was so much to be done, and she had no strength left. She thought of Tutankhamun. He was a silly boy, but that was not her fault; unjust, then, that she should bear the consequences of his spoiling. The child of his mother's age, he had grown up at her knee, toyed with, petted, and pampered. No one ever guessed that he would rule, with three brothers ahead of him in the succession.

She raised herself up again on her elbows and stared at herself in the mirror. The gold cast a haze around her. She seemed so young, in the mirror. When she had been young, her energy and will were boundless.

She would be strong again. She would shape Tutankhamun into a proper man, or if not, then she would take a son of his and Ankhesenamun's and make a King of him. Ankhesenamun was fecund; she had borne a child to her own father, a rarely beautiful little girl, dead now, alas. She would have stronger children by Tutankhamun. Boys. Kings.

Nefertiti's eyelids were heavy; her head ached. Tomorrow she knew she would shake off this lassitude that burdened her like an invisible demon, riding on her back and wrapping its wings over her arms. The Aten would restore her. The God needed her; none other would take his cause in Egypt. They had an agreement, the Aten and Nefertiti, never to desert one another.

She was so tired. She laid her head down again to rest. She fell asleep there, before the golden mirror.

# 11

The river sank to a muddy trickle along the bottom of its bed. It ran red with dust, like the blood of Osiris when his brother Set hacked him. The stubble of the millet stood in the fields along the banks, dead as Osiris. Far inland from the edge of the water, the one-armed water hoists hung useless in their frames. The red sand of the desert blew down across the black tilled land of Egypt.

In Thebes, Sennahet's landlord had thrown him into the street for not paying his rent. Now he lived with a dozen other outcasts in an abandoned building on the west bank of the Nile. He no longer went about the city seeking work. Once a day he and thousands like him swarmed into the Temple of Amun to be fed. Afterward, he gambled in the street for sips of beer. He daydreamed, skulked about looking for something to steal. He sat on the cracked mud of the dead river, flapping his hands to swat away the stinging flies. Then, in the cool evening, he crossed the river and walked into the desert.

Since the mason Hapure had told him of the secret burial of Akhenaten in the desert, Sennahet had thought endlessly of the gold that Nefertiti must have buried with her lord.

Every evening he went into the desert gorge where kings were buried and walked along the narrow valley, searching for the tomb. Often he slept there, in the desert, with the desert wind around him and the jackals barking in the distance.

He found old rooms there, deserted tombs, robbed and empty, and long corridors that led back into the earth and stopped there, stopped at nowhere. The place was haunted. His dreams were troubled. At night, as he shivered in the wind, as he sat surrounded by the weird moonlit beauty of the desert, strange mad thoughts came into his head. He imagined himself rich with Pharaoh's gold, rich beyond dreams, rich and mighty, as if here where so many kings were buried he put on a little of their splendor.

One night he went along the gorge, kicking at stones as he walked. The light of the full moon painted the walls of the gorge. Every now and then Sennahet swore aloud, and often he swore against Akhenaten, whose war against the gods of Egypt had ruined Sennahet, and whose gold would save Sennahet, if he could but find it.

The jackals yapped and prowled along the top of the cliff. A rock bounced down the rutted wall. Sennahet dragged his feet. His eyes ranged back and forth across the gorge and his mind brooded on his wrongs. He knew nothing of any danger until the lion growled.

He stopped. All over his scalp his hair prickled painfully erect. He was looking forward down the gorge; here the walls pinched close together and a fresh slide of rock half hid the path.

Now his ears caught the far-off shout and the beating of a drum, just loud enough for him to hear. Someone was hunting lions.

In the moonlit gulch ahead there was the low throaty mutter of an alerted lion. Somehow Sennahet had walked into the field of the hunt. He was between the lion and its way of escape from the beaters.

He swore in a shaky voice. Casting around him, he sought some weapon, a stick, or even a large rock. The drums were getting louder. In the distance, beyond the lion, a horse whinnied. When he faced the gulch again, the lion was walking into view down the narrow throat of the gorge.

Sennahet let out a scream of terror. He spun around and ran the other way down the gorge.

His breath sawed back and forth through his lungs. He flung a hasty look over his shoulder. The lion was trotting after him. Its mane shook with each step. Its broad face was intent on him. He screamed again and his legs churned and he sprinted over the stony ground.

The lion's roar deafened him. The beast was right behind him. On the slope ahead of him was the doorway of an empty tomb. He lunged toward it. On hands and knees he scrambled up the loose hillside of rubble toward this refuge. The ground gave way beneath him and began to slide, and he clawed up through the moving slope to the mouth of the tomb and flung himself down across the threshold.

The lion roared below him. Panting, his arms and knees bleeding, Sennahet staggered to his feet. At the base of the slope the lion was pacing back and forth, its head reared back and its yellow eyes glowing on its prey.

Higher in the gorge, the sound of galloping horses racketed off the walls and chariot wheels ground over the earth. The lion's tail twitched. Sennahet was trembling. He pawed at his face. The doorway where he stood was the only foothold on the whole sheer slope behind him. He was trapped here; he had caged himself up for the lion. A trumpet blew, just around the bend, and the drums thundered. The lion crouched. So might Sekhmet crouch, goddess of revenge, stalking her victims. Sennahet shrank back, wondering which god he had offended, and the lion sprang.

He screamed again. The great beast bounded up the slope in three great leaps. Sennahet fell to his knees. Prayers poured forth from his lips.

Down the gorge two horses charged, a chariot flying at their heels. The lion had reached the doorway; it wheeled, so close that its lashing tail brushed across Sennahet's shoulder, and its roar rolled forth across the gorge. Sennahet covered his head with his arms. He prayed for a quick death. The lion stank of blood and musk. Below, a voice cried out in command. The lion crashed into Sennahet and knocked him down.

Sennahet whimpered. He lay still on the cold earth, waiting for the pain to begin. The beast was sprawled over him; his mouth and nose were stuffed with its rough hair. Then Sennahet heard voices, and hands touched him.

"Are you hurt? Ah, fellow, look at me!"

His ribs ached. He gasped; he had never felt so alive, so real. The lion lay dead beside him, an arrow in its ribs. The hands on his shoulders tightened. The musical, unmasculine voice above him spoke again: "Are you hurt? Tell me that I may tend you."

He raised his head. A young woman stood before him, her brows drawn together. Her bow was still in her hand. It was she who had slain the lion. On her head was a crown. Sennahet fell forward again and, bending, made his bow to Ankhesenamun.

The Queen Ankhesenamun, who has rescued Sennahet from the lion, took him back with her to the great palace of Pharaoh, on the west bank of the Nile across from the city of Thebes. There she ordered that Sennahet's name be entered into the lists of her servants.

Of these there were hundreds, and Sennahet, being unskilled, was given menial tasks to do. Yet the Queen noticed him often. Now and then she gave him a coin, or a sweet; whenever she saw him, she smiled.

In the isolated village of Kalala, Hapure woke before dawn. He was ill with the plague that had taken his wife. His teeth chattered, and he wrapped the bedclothes around himself and turned his face to the wall.

He was afraid and alone. His wife was buried and his daughter had deserted him when he fell ill. He lay shivering in the dark. His stomach heaved and his bowels burned.

He would not foul his own bed. He dragged himself out to the privy. The sun was rising, a pitiless fire that scorched the sky itself, hazy with the dry dust of Egypt. Hapure knelt down in the yard behind his house and gave thanks that Ra had survived the fearful night.

He anointed himself with a palmful of oil and dressed. From a niche in the wall of his house he took coins. He set forth to walk down to Thebes.

Kalala was set deep in a dry gorge, in the desert above the fertile plain of Thebes. There was no water there, no place to grow food; the families who lived there served Pharaoh in the Valley of the Dead, and Pharaoh had always fed them. But now Pharaoh had forgotten them. Hapure walked along the narrow street, rock-hard under his feet, past house after house that stood open and deserted. Nearly everyone had fled.

Hapure reached the edge of the village and walked down the thread of the path that would take him to the plain. As he walked he saw before him the whole of Thebes. He saw the naked fields turning to dust in the wind and the deserted villages crumbling on the high ground. He saw the palace of Pharaoh, covering enough land to support a whole city, and surrounded now with soldiers to keep the desperate poor from stealing what was the King's. He saw the gleaming needles of Amun standing above the Imperial Temple to the south, just beyond the dead river.

The ferry was tied up to its landing stage. Under its keel was dry mud. The river had retreated down into the lowest part of its bed and left the ferry on dry land. Hapure needed no boat to cross the Nile into Thebes. The river at its deepest ran only knee-high. He waded across it and went up the slope on the far side.

People slept there, on the dry mud along the river. The flies buzzed busily around them. Only the flies were lively; only the flies moved. As if they were already dead, the people there sat and stared into nothing. Hapure wound his way through them. He did not look at them. Especially he did not look at the children. There were few children left, few old people, now that even the strongest suffered.

He trudged into the dusty street of Thebes. His coin tight in his fist, he started his search. He coughed to clear his throat of the dust. His legs were weak and his knees hurt. He went first to the shop where three days before he had found bread for sale. Then they had sold each loaf for its weight in gold. Now the shop was empty, and the bake ovens behind it were cold. Hapure went on to the next shop.

The temple granaries had given up the last of Amun's grain many long weeks before. Whatever bread was baked now was made of grain from private hoarding, and those caches were also emptying. Hapure went from shop to shop and found none selling bread.

Exhausted, he sank down on the threshold of an empty house and stared into the street. The sun turned the dust-filled sky a brazen red. Down at the end of the street, where the houses stood wall to wall and flush with the street, a woman put her head out through the door and saw him and hastily withdrew again. Hapure looked away. He had learned to avoid other people, who begged and stole and made him unhappy.

The fever was working in Hapure's blood. He put his face down on his hands. The dust and the heat made his head pound. He started up onto his feet again, to go on, and his knees gave way and dumped him down in the street.

His eyes itched. He hacked out a cough, trying to scrape the dust from his throat.

He did not try to stand again, but only dragged himself

on his arms back to the shelter of the wall. He tipped his head back against the wall. He felt emptied and finished. The shuttered houses around him were like blank faces, turned away from him. In an hour, he might be a corpse in the street, eaten by flies.

He considered that dispassionately at first. But as he thought of his death, his passion returned, and he staggered to his feet and went on through Thebes in his search for food.

Red dust had drifted into the corner of the balcony outside the Queen Regent's window. Meryat put her hand on the railing. Her skin was prickly with sweat. She felt dirty. She stood looking across the courtyard, her weary mind a blank.

Four date palms shaded this side of the building. Their great fronds stirred and rustled in the wind. From the brick courtyard below came the scratch-scratch of a broom. It was the lout Sennahet, whom Ankhesenamun had taken in, sweeping the walk. Meryat sighed.

From the room behind her came the fretful voice of Nefertiti, calling to her. Meryat went back through the curtains.

Three girls sat by the head of Nefertiti's couch, stirring the sullen air with ostrich-feather fans. The Queen Regent lay on her back. An ivory rest supported her head. Fever burned like hateful blossoms in her cheeks. Her lips were the color of ash.

"Meryat, bring me wine—I am so parched."

Meryat went to the chest by the door. On it was painted a scene of the Queen's married life. The servant took her eyes from that. She wished that Nefertiti would let her remove such things from the royal rooms. She poured wine into a cup figured with sacred words and signs.

Glancing over her shoulder, she saw that no one was watching her, and she sipped a mouthful of the Queen's wine. Since Nefertiti had fallen ill, Meryat had tasted all her food.

"Meryat, where is my daughter? You said that she was coming. Where is she?"

At that moment the Queen Ankhesenamun entered the room. The servants knelt and put their foreheads to the floor, Meryat among them.

"Mother, I am here."

At the sound of her daughter's voice, Nefertiti started up from her couch. On her knees, Meryat crossed the room and gave her the cup and pressed her, unresisting, back onto the bed. Ankhesenamun sat on the foot of the couch. It was shaped like a great lotus blossom; the curled tips of the petals framed the young Queen's shoulders.

"Where have you been?" Nefertiti said to her. "And dressed like a—I know not what. My child, there are things required of Egypt's Queen—"

"Not now, Mother," said Ankhesenamun.

Nefertiti's mouth curved into a weak smile. Meryat dipped a linen napkin into water scented with jasmine and bathed the face of the Queen Regent. The fan girls had returned quietly to their work.

"You could be beautiful, you know," Nefertiti said.

"I have no wish to be," Ankhesenamun said. She stroked her hands down her knees. The tendons in her wrists were like bowstrings. Her long legs were sheathed in charioteer's boots. She took Nefertiti's hand in hers.

"Ah, you are so warm!"

"I am too dry even to breathe," Nefertiti said. "Meryat, another cup of wine. Yet I cannot help but think how many of my people suffer this same sickness, without a Meryat to tend them and wine to dull the pain."

Meryat took the cup back to the chest where the ewers of wine were kept. Furtively, again she tasted the wine.

"Where is His Majesty?" the Queen Regent asked. "Have you not sent for him?"

Meryat turned, the cup in her hand, and for an instant her gaze met Ankhesenamun's. She lowered her eyes. On her knees she returned to the Queen Regent.

"Rise, Meryat," Ankhesenamun said. "You go about naturally in my mother's presence, you may always do so in mine."

Meryat stood. She gave the cup into Nefertiti's hand. The Queen Regent lifted it, and it wobbled in her grip; Meryat took the cup and the hand of the Queen and helped her to hold the wine and drink.

"I feel so weak," Nefertiti said. She lay back again on the ivory headstand. "I know I shall die soon. Ankhesenamun! When I am dead, you must care for Meryat. Take her among your own women—let her be to you as she has been to me."

Meryat put her hand over her face. These words filled her with pain and sorrow and gratitude for the Queen.

"Mother, Mother, you shall not die," Ankhesenamun said. "Not if you truly wish to live."

"I will die, and soon," Nefertiti said. "I am failing, so weak, so tired, and yet I cannot sleep, and the most fearful thoughts come into my mind. —where is Tutankhamun? Did I ask that he be sent for?"

"He has been called, Mother," Ankhesenamun said. "But do not talk of dying. You will put yourself into such a cast of mind that the grave will seem more home to you than your own bed."

Nefertiti shook her head from side to side. "That is your father in you—ever he believed that the mind ruled the body—dragged the flesh around itself like a garment, to wear as it willed."

Ankhesenamun's smile was false and taut. She said, "Perhaps, then, he did not really die, but only put off his garment for another."

"I loved him," Nefertiti said. "Even when he became what I did not understand." In a lower voice, she said, "I love him yet."

154

"May I ask your advice, Mother?"

The Queen smiled, and her eyes opened a little. "Of course."

"Someone—a soothsayer—it has been said that if we make sacrifice to Isis, the goddess will heal Egypt." Ankhesenamun held her mother's hand. "Should we give heed to such talk?"

"It is an offense to the Aten."

"But if we are wrong . . ." Ankhesenamun held her mother's hand to her cheek. "Every day I see more—how they suffer—the people cannot follow the Aten. What if we are wrong?"

"The Aten is God. No other is God. He alone is the truth. If Egypt must die to serve the Aten, then let Egypt die."

"How they suffer," Ankhesenamun said. She was biting on her lip.

"Think of the Aten," Nefertiti said. "It is the Aten who matters, and not the people—they are only shadows of his will." Her voice began to carry a fretful, whining edge. "But where is Tutankhamun?"

Ankhesenamun leaned forward, intense. "All this suffering began when the Aten and my father drove away the old gods."

"How dare you say so?" Nefertiti cried. "He is God! He can do with us as he wishes."

Ankhesenamun said nothing. She looked deep into her mother's face. Meryat dampened a cloth to bathe the sick Queen's face. Ankhesenamun took it from her and touched the cool linen to her mother's brow.

"We failed him," Nefertiti said. "When Akhenaten died, we let that foul rat of Amun back into his nest."

"Otherwise we could not keep power. Was that not the bargain?"

"It was then that the evil came upon us."

Ankhesenamun held her mother's hand. "I will not argue with you now."

Nefertiti's head rolled from side to side. "Where is Tutankhamun? Why is he not with me now?"

Ankhesenamun made herself busy with the damp cloth. Meryat turned away to fill the basin of water.

"Answer me! Why has he not come to me?"

"Mother—"

"Answer me!"

The Queen Regent started up from her couch. Ankhesenamun pushed her gently down. "Meryat! Bring her wine. Mother, please, be calm."

"Where is he? Is he ill? Is the King ill? O Aten, my hope, let it not be."

Meryat was at the chest pouring the wine. She glanced over her shoulder at the two Queens, surrounded by the fan girls like people in a frieze.

Ankhesenamun said, "Mother, lie still. Tutankhamun is well. He is healthy as the crocodiles. He has gone. He went to Istufti, to escape the plague." Istufti was the King's great palace near Saïs, in the Delta.

Nefertiti lay still. Her face was white. At last she said, "He has fled? He has left me?" Her tongue slid over her lips. "I am so dry. Meryat, the wine."

Meryat brought the chased cup. The Queen Regent drank deep of the wine. She lay back; Ankhesenamun put her hand behind her mother's neck to cushion her.

"He ran away," Nefertiti said. "Where is the king in him? Hiding, like a rat, in the little finger of his soul."

"Mother."

"I shall not speak of him again."

She did not. Thereafter they spoke of minor things, their clothes, their friends, and the wine. The night gathered outside the windows. Meryat had a meal brought for Ankhesenamun: duck's eggs and bread and honey. Untouched, it drew the flies into the corner by the balcony.

Nefertiti was failing. Meryat imagined the sickness as a bird that struggled to be free, that carried Nefertiti's soul in its golden beak. The Queen Regent's mind was unquiet, and she spoke as if this were her wedding day. Her face blotched with fever, her wide eyes glazed, she spoke with delight of the robe of embroidered linen that she considered herself to be wearing, and said that she heard music. Apprehensively she asked her women of her bridegroom, whom she had never seen.

"Is he ugly? I cannot bear ugliness—"

"Mother," Ankhesenamun said and, putting her hands on Nefertiti's shoulders, tried to push her down again on the couch. "Calm yourself, you will exhaust yourself—"

"Sister." Nefertiti resisted the pushing; one hand gripped Ankhesenamun's wrist. Her nails were broken. Her eyes were as wide open as they would go, so that a ring of white encircled her pupils. "Sister," she said, "call for my father. I will stop the wedding."

"Mother, please listen to me. Oh, she hears no word I say."

"I have heard that he is ugly," Nefertiti said. Meryat started forward with the wine; Ankhesenamun waved her back. The Queen Regent raised herself wobbling on her elbows.

"Is this what it means to be beautiful—to marry an ugly man? Bear ugly children?"

"Mother!"

Nefertiti sank back. She had worn herself out. Meryat crept nearer and helped Ankhesenamun care for her. Before dawn, Nefertiti died in her daughter's arms.

Meryat pressed her hands over her face. She longed with all her heart to return to an earlier day, before the troubles, when she had been a child and Nefertiti laughed and played whimsical games with her.

In the morning the red dust had drifted in under the Queen Regent's bed. Meryat swept it out again with a broom of rushes.

Some days after the death of Queen Nefertiti, Hapure left his village for the last time. He wandered along the edge of the dead Nile.

There, as if in extremity to be there was some comfort, clumps of people sat beside the river, their knees drawn up, and their eyes turned on the thread of murky water that lay in the bed of the Nile. No one spoke. No one took notice of the other people there. At the very lip of the water, green slime was growing, like the putrescence of death on Egypt. Hapure sat down at the rim of the water and covered his head with his garment and mourned.

It was not for Nefertiti that he wept, nor even the Nile that was slain in the battle of the gods for Egypt. He could not really say whom or what he mourned. He thought of Tutankhamun, but that was just a name: he had no Pharaoh in his heart.

"Hapure!"

The voice roused him; he lifted his head. A man crouched beside him. With a shudder, Hapure recoiled from the other man.

"Hapure! Look at me—it is Sennahet."

Hapure's lips shaped the name. He looked into the face of the man beside him, and an old interest awoke in him. He said, "Sennahet. Are you alive, then?"

He looked around them. The bodies of the folk of Thebes were clotted here and there on the bank of the river. Clouds of flies buzzed over them. The sky was yellow with dust.

He began to shake violently, and his head snapped painfully on his neck. It was Sennahet shaking him.

"Hapure, heed me. I have a place in the palace now. I will bring you bread. I will save your life," Sennahet whispered into his ear. "Only tell me where the gold is hidden!"

Hapure coughed and could not stop coughing; his throat was raw and swollen. He had no notion what gold Sennahet was speaking of. The only word that found his ears was the word *bread*, and he put out his hand. His body was torn with coughing. He held out his hand to Sennahet.

"Bread—" Between coughs he spoke the word. "Bread—"

"Only tell me where is the gold!"

"Bread—"

"Aiyyiih!"

The scream turned them both around. Hapure blinked. His eyelashes were coated with dust and he saw everything through a red haze.

Down the river someone was jumping and shouting.

The people near Hapure began to groan. One scrawny man stood up, his limbs like birds' limbs, bone swathed in horny skin. All along the riverbank, folk stirred, and a general whimper rose, as if now even to move hurt them. Hapure leaned forward to see what they had seen, what had brought them to this effort.

"Aiyyiih!"

Startled, Hapure scrambled to his knees. He rubbed his burning eyes. Beside him, Sennahet muttered an oath. They looked where all were looking. Egypt, dead save for its eyes, looked on the Nile.

There a little boat was sailing, drawn along by one with a rope. In the boat was the Goddess Isis.

Hapure filled his lungs. He put out his hand to Isis as he had to Sennahet. He saw the face of the goddess turn, her eyes shining with tears. Tears wet her cheeks. Bedecked with her sacred crown, with the lily and the spindle in her hands, all glistening with her golden robes, she sailed slowly down the Nile, turning her head from one side to the other. Her gaze of pity fell upon the people, and everyone cried out.

"It is Ankhesenamun," Sennahet murmured, beside Hapure. "She has brought Isis into the world again."

Hapure gave a glad cry. He stumbled down toward the river. In the green slime along the edge of the water he fell on hands and knees and worshiped the goddess.

"Isis, save us!" His voice was lost in the thousands of voices that took up the cry. "Isis, save us, save us. . . ." He pressed his face to the barren mud, the stink of the dead river in his nostrils, and wept for joy.

Every day thereafter, Isis traveled on the Nile, and the people worshiped her. Then at last the dead one began to live again. The river swelled. The ripening waters rose and spread across the land of Egypt, and her people were restored to hope.

# 12

The Queen sat upon her throne and called the High Priest of Amun to her.

"The flood has come," she said. "Now the crops will grow again, and if the gods are kind all Egypt will eat and grow strong. But we must have seed, and the people must be fed and cared for until they can plant and bring in the harvest."

The priest stood erect before her, the privilege of his office. He wore no wig and no black kohl about his eyes, only a white cloth about his loins. Under his fingernails was the stale blood of sacrifices to his god, the god of fear, Amun, Lord of the City.

He said, "What you say is all true, my Queen."

"Then you will help me from your secret stores."

"Ah," the priest said, "but what can we do? The times have stripped us of everything."

"I see no starving priests," the Queen said. She gripped

the right arm of her throne and leaned over the priest, her will strong against him.

He said, "And I see the palace, all covered with gold."

She looked awhile on him without saying anything. Her fingers gripped the arm of the throne. There were torches on the wall behind her, casting her shadow over him who stood before her. She yearned to crush him for his impudence. Yet she needed his help.

At last she said, "I had hoped to find you generous, recalling on whose goodwill your very life depends."

"Yes, now you love mercy, Daughter of Akhenaten. But when your father set upon my god, then you hated mercy."

She started up from her place. The priest flung out his hand to hold her.

"Destroy me if you wish! Every day I see the black scorch on the pillars of the temple where Pharaoh set fire to the house of my god. I will not relent, nor will I help you, until I see the walls of Pharaoh humiliated as well."

He departed. The Queen sat rigid in her chair. Her blood was hot against the priest. She thought of sending forth her soldiers to take her vengeance. Slowly her hot temper cooled. Deep in thought, she sat there a long while, considering where else she might find the seed to plant the fields and the grain to keep the people alive until the crop ripened. In the end she called the priest back again.

"I shall make naked the walls of my palace," she said, "if you will give of your secret hoardings."

The priest bowed before her. "The will of the Queen is my command."

A long look passed between them. Ankhesenamun was thinking in her heart that in time to come she would have some opportunity for vengeance. On the face of the priest, she read the same thought, that when the chance came he would strike at her again. So it was truce, not peace. She raised her hand to him.

"Go."

*

Sennahet dreamed that the sun fell to earth and rolled into a hole in the earth and was covered up. This dream he took to refer to the secret burial of Pharaoh Akhenaten. He went into the desert west of Thebes, and there he came on a place that seemed like the place of his dream. He dug there.

Every day another place seemed to be significant, and he dug another hole in the desert. He did no work. Soon his absence from the palace was noticed. The overseer of laborers warned him to be more responsible.

Then Sennahet had another dream, and he went out into the desert and dug more holes in the ground, and found nothing. He stopped returning to the palace, except for food and water, which he took out in sufficient supply for two or three days. He slept in the desert. Every day he dug holes.

One day when he came to the royal pantry for bread the overseer of laborers caught him and drove him away from the palace with stones.

Sennahet's feet were sore; his belly was empty. He trudged off down the Avenue of the Sphinxes of the Jubilee until he came to the river. The sun struck him with its blades of heat and light. He could not return to the desert without food and water, and he had no money. Yet he longed with his complete soul to dig holes in the sand.

The savior flood had recently ebbed. All around Thebes, people worked in the fields. As the waters subsided, a long, silty island had appeared in the river above the Imperial Temple; on it men planted and hoed, and some tips of green already showed above the black surface of the land. Sennahet looked on all this with no interest. He thought only of digging up the dry sand of the desert.

He sat down on the ferry stage, at the edge of the bench where people waited to board the boat. Two or three people stood around the stage. Sennahet thrust out his hand.

"Have mercy on me . . . have mercy. . . ."

Someone threw him a handful of figs.

He crossed the river and went along the broad street that ran from the Common City in the north to the City of the Gods where the temple stood. At one end of the avenue was the highest of the Golden Rays of the Sun, a pillar sixteen cubits in height, plated over with gold and silver alloy. Sphinxes and statues of Pharaoh lined the street. Sennahet, trudging in their shadow, felt no greater than a speck of dust. His throat was raw. He begged a drink of water from a vendor.

At the temple a scribe of the priesthood of Amun heard him without pity.

"A measure of wheat," he said, "and half a measure of oil, and a small jar of beer, that is all we give. For that you must work a full day in the fields of the god."

"Work in the field," Sennahet said, angry. "But the Queen has ordered that all who are hungry should be fed from your stores! I was there—I heard her decree."

"The fields are fertile again," said the scribe. "Amun has restored Egypt. Can you plow?"

"I am no plowman," Sennahet cried. "Once I had my own fields—before Akhenaten brought the curse on Egypt—"

"It is sin to speak of the Criminal," said the scribe. He took a tablet from his workbox and a stylus from behind his ear. "In any case, all the fields around Thebes belong to the god, now. Your name?"

Sennahet shouted, "I had two plowmen in my fields, and I gave them each a full pot of beer, morning and evening!"

The scribe shrugged and stuck his stylus back behind his ear. He went away into the temple.

"All the beer they wished!" Sennahet shouted after him.

The scribe disappeared into the darkness and gloom of the temple. Sennahet raised his head; his temper was spent, and he felt short of breath. The giant columns around him were as thick around as three men. On the south-facing side was carved in low relief the image of the lotus, symbol of Upper Egypt. Sennahet put his hand into the rough stone.

The tremendous columns around him enclosed him in silence and solitude. From beyond, outside, the murmurings of other people reached him, the sighs and laughter. The past several days seemed like a dream to him. He shut his eyes.

He went back along the Imperial Street. Rows of men marched like soldiers past him, carrying hoes and rakes on their shoulders. They chanted as they walked. Sennahet was going in the opposite direction, and they forced him off to the side of the road, almost under the paws of the sphinx there. The many voices of the workmen were raised in a farmer's song. He waited until they passed by before he went on.

Sennahet sat down on the side of the road. He stretched out his hand to beg. He sat there for three days. The dust and the bright sun and the biting flies tormented him. His soul shrank until he was aware only of the sun and the flies.

Chariots with wheels of gold whirled by him in the road. He put out his hand, and his voice began its weary plea. The nearest chariot rolled on by him, with the sun gleaming on its wheels.

He looked up. The Queen held the reins of the high-stepping horses.

Sennahet bleated. He saw his only hope there, rattling away behind two trotting horses. On cramped legs he hurried after her, crying out to her in a croak at each step. His strength lasted only a dozen strides. The chariot was just beyond his reach. He flung himself at the shining wheel.

"Hold!"

He lay in the dust, panting, and the Queen stood above him.

"Who is this man? Why does he try to take hold of me?"

"Lady Queen," he cried, "it is I, your servant Sennahet."

She looked frowning down at him; she did not recognize him. Beside her in the chariot was another woman, her waiting woman Meryat. This woman leaned down suddenly and stared into Sennahet's face.

"It is Sennahet," she said to the Queen. "He whom you rescued from the lion."

"Then what does he here?" the Queen asked.

Sennahet got up, his hands locked on her chariot wheel. "O Great One, save me. I am fallen very low, for no fault of my own."

She recoiled from him. To Meryat she said, "See to him. Do what is necessary." Grasping her whip, she turned back to her horses.

Meryat stepped down from the chariot, and the horses jumped forward, tearing the wheel from Sennahet's hands. He fell in the dust and skinned his knees. Meryat stood before him. Her nose was wrinkled in distaste, perhaps at the dust.

He said to her, "Why does she flee from me?"

"You should have stayed saved," Meryat said. She beckoned to a chariot that waited nearby. "Come with me. We will return to the palace."

Three months after the Nile came to its flood, when the threat of plague was gone, Pharaoh returned to Thebes.

No one came to greet him. The shrilling of the flutes of his own musicians were the only cheers. Tutankhamun's golden barge sailed past the colossal gates and pillars of the temple, where the black scars still showed of the Fire of the Aten. Beneath the gently waving ostrich fans, Tutankhamun sat with his eyes turned forward. His fanbearers and flute boys stood around him, sleek with scented oils. But no one cheered at this spectacle.

The desolate city passed by on either side. Tutankhamun seemed not to look. He wore a chest ornament of gold and carnelian; he wore sandals of gold, with the names of his enemies written on the soles. His great city Thebes surrounded him, yet no cheers rang across the water to meet him.

The wharves of the city were rotting away. A pall of gray

smoke hung over the shabby buildings along the river. Nothing moved in the streets.

The oars of the King's barge rose dripping from the water and stroked forward. Tutankhamun stared forward, and without any effort he saw the turning panorama of Thebes as the barge swung toward the west bank.

At the edge of the Nile two gigantic seated images of Pharaoh greeted him. Looking between them, Tutankhamun saw the gold- and silver-plated walls of his palace. The sun blazed on them. The barge glided forward toward the mouth of the canal that led to the palace. Sitting motionless as the gigantic images, Tutankhamun was borne swiftly across the river and into the narrow waters.

As the blazing palace swept toward him, he saw that great patches of the precious metal adornment were missing. The report was true. She had peeled away the very walls of the palace to feed the rabble.

She was waiting on the wharf: Ankhesenamun. She was his niece, daughter of his elder brother Akhenaten, and for three years wife to her father, Akhenaten; she had mothered his daughter. Tutankhamun's fingers moved, stiff and heavy in their sacred rings. Strange feelings stirred in his breast. When he chose to speak to her, he would reproach her for what she had done, yet he would speak kindly to her, as well, because she was his wife.

His boatmen rowed the barge in to the quay. There the Queen stood, ajingle with her emblems and wearing her crown. Tutankhamun did not deign to look at her. He kept his gaze straight forward. The bearers approached him and lifted up his chair onto their shoulders. He moved forward to the ramp and down to the quay.

The Queen had knelt down. All her attendants had their faces in the dust. Tutankhamun signed that his bearers should stop. He hated to talk, to break the sacred silence around him, but he had not yet devised a way to make his wishes known without speech.

"Bid my royal wife attend me in my chambers."

Before she could demean him with argument he was carried away into the palace.

Here his servants surrounded him. They knew his will without having to be told. They brought him his favorite cup and a dish of sweets and anointed him with oil in the scents he liked. They removed his sandals and massaged his feet. They did all this on their hands and knees, as neat and swift as cats.

Ankhesenamun did not come.

In the evening, when he could bear no more of her indifference, Tutankhamun went himself to her apartments. He found her in her robing room, with two low women undressing her.

"You must obey me," he cried. He marched straight up to her. "I am Pharaoh!"

She pulled a robe over her own shoulders. She was lean and tall, taller than he; her elbows looked sharp.

"I will obey you," she said, "when you give commands that honor you to give and me to receive."

"And you took my gold—you robbed me."

"The people were starving," she said. "They needed seed for the fields." She moved away from him, walking on her long feet across the painted floor. "You deserted them. Someone had to help them."

"Them," he said scornfully. "They are dross. I am Egypt. I must be protected. Without me there would be no world."

As he spoke he saw himself as the whole world, bringing things into existence by looking at them, making men live by the beats of his heart.

Ankhesenamun was putting out the lamps set in recesses in the walls. The light flickered over her. Shadows formed under the high arch of her cheekbones. Her long throat was like a column of gold. Tutankhamun lifted his hands to his chest, where beat the drum of the god.

"You are my wife, Ankhesenamun."

She wheeled. Her eyes widened; yet she was not looking at him, but beyond him, above him.

"We must make Egypt fertile," he said. "We must show the land how to grow. Tonight I will come to you."

"No," she said.

He shouted at her, "You cannot deny me!"

"Tomorrow night."

"You would rob my palace to buy seed, but you will not do with me the ritual necessary to make it grow?"

Her lips were white. There was a long silence. He struggled to make her look at him rather than beyond him. With all his will he fought to lower her gaze to him.

"Very well," she said, almost in a whisper.

He touched his lips. His fingertips caressed his own cheek. His body was warm with new feelings.

"We shall make sons," he said. "I shall see that they are all sons."

He turned. The door was hung with tissue of gold; as he reached it a hand yanked it aside. His attendants closed around him and he went off through the palace to his own chambers.

Meryat went into the Queen's chamber and found Ankhesenamun all in tears.

"I cannot do it!" Ankhesenamun struck herself with her fists. "No!"

"What has happened?" Meryat cried. She took the Queen by the hand and led her to the couch and made her sit. "What can you not do? Oh, my dear one, there is nothing beyond your ability. Here, let me fetch you wine."

The Queen was shaken with weeping. Her voice was ragged. She said, "Pharaoh has commanded—commanded, as if I were a—something to be bought, a jar of ointment, or a doll—as if I were dung—oh! I will kill myself, Meryat —poison myself!"

Meryat brought her a cup of wine. She sat down beside

the Queen on her couch and slid one arm around the girl's shoulders.

"Tell me what he has ordered." Meryat stroked the Queen's cheek. Her breast was heavy with affection for Ankhesenamun. She used the gestures and the words that she had seen Nefertiti use a thousand times. "Tell me what is wrong, and we shall right it."

Ankhesenamun flung back her head. Her eyes gleamed like a beast's. "He wishes to lie with me."

Meryat startled from head to foot. Her arm lay heavy as harness over the shoulders of the Queen.

"Ay," Ankhesenamun said scornfully, "we shall not right that, shall we?"

She rose and stalked across the chamber. Meryat sat still.

"I will slay myself," the Queen said, "before I allow him to handle me."

The fine linen bedcover had slid down to the floor. Meryat bent and lifted it, folded it carefully, placed it on the bed. She passed her hand over her face.

"I shall not do it," Ankhesenamun said.

"It is Pharaoh's will," Meryat said.

"Bah! You are like all the others. Full of easy sympathy, but when I need help—when I am all alone—you shrink like the others." The Queen wheeled around; she strode down on Meryat, her fisted hands like hammers in the air. "You tell yourself you are my friend, my closest friend, but see what worth your friendship is! Behold, you are a servant, with a mouthful of bread and a heart of money."

Meryat flinched. In her throat a lump grew painfully hard and large.

Ankhesenamun gulped for breath. She flung her arm over her face. Restlessly she paced around the room again. Meryat sat still in her place, miserable. One of the other servants popped her head in the door, saw the Queen's mood, and rapidly withdrew. The curtain stirred a little and was quiet again.

"I have no choice," Ankhesenamun said. "You will prepare some potion for me."

"Oh, you must not," Meryat said.

"He comes tonight. He will find a cold bride in my bed, and a hot enemy in the world of the dead."

"But what of Egypt?" Meryat said. "Will you leave us all to his mercies? You saved us, my Queen—we need you to rule us."

"I will not be defiled."

Meryat bit her tongue. Her mind scurried from thought to thought. The Queen paced up and down through the room, beating her hands together.

"My father and I performed the ritual of fertility a hundred times together. With him it was as pure and blessed as the light of the sun, his mind was so elevated. But with Tutankhamun! I cannot believe he was my father's brother, they are so unalike. He will use my body as a potter beats and pounds the Nile mud."

"He is Pharaoh," Meryat said. "He must be satisfied."

The Queen strode the width of the room again. She passed the tall windows where the sun shone in; her body made the sunlight seem to wink.

"Perhaps there is a way. If you love me, Meryat—do you love me?"

"With my whole heart," Meryat said.

Ankhesenamun sat down beside her on the couch. Her eyes blazed. "Then we shall satisfy Pharaoh." She clasped Meryat's hand in hers. Meryat could not look away from the Queen's fierce eyes. Ankhesenamun said, "What I tell you now must never be spoken to anyone else. Do you swear to keep faith?"

"I swear," Meryat whispered, frightened by the look of the Queen.

Ankhesenamun put her mouth to Meryat's ear and whispered to her. "You shall take my place in Pharaoh's bed."

"I! But how?"

"Be still and listen to me. I will lie down beside him when the lights are bright. But then I will rise to put out the light, and you shall take my place."

Meryat could not speak. Her hands were slippery in Ankhesenamun's grasp.

"You must! If you love me—"

"I love you."

"Then you will do it."

Meryat closed her eyes. "No man has ever used me."

"We shall deal with that," Ankhesenamun said. "Meryat, I swear to you, do as I ask, and you and I shall be as sisters. If you swell with a new life, I shall raise him as my own child. Your son will become Pharaoh, and your daughter shall be the princess of the sun."

Meryat nodded her head, her eyes still closed. She was unable to speak.

Ankhesenamun kissed her, and said many other words to her, but Meryat's ears were stopped, her sight turned inward. Although the Queen pressed kisses on her and hugged her, yet Meryat felt distant from her; she felt a distance of the soul between them.

They set about preparing for the night. They sent all the other waiting women away on errands. Meryat lay down on the Queen's couch, and Ankhesenamun took a wand of ivory. With this stick she made a place for Pharaoh between Meryat's thighs; she broke into the chamber of her waiting woman, so that Pharaoh would not know he used a virgin. There was blood. They wiped it away. Meryat rose up again, ready for words of sympathy and gratitude. Ankhesenamun was turned away from her, disposing of the bloody clothes. Meryat shut her eyes again, angry.

In the evening the King joined his Royal Wife, Ankhesenamun, in her bedchamber. They lit incense and prayed together, so that the Queen might conceive. Tutankhamun was flushed. He could not keep the smile from his face. He looked no older than a boy. The Queen, older than he, taller, said little. Her wide eyes were painted larger with kohl. She hardly looked at her young bridegroom.

Their attendants placed them side by side in the bed under the canopy and put out the lamps on the wall; only one lamp burned, on a small round table by the door. The servants crept backwards out of the room.

"Turn out the light," the Queen said.

Tutankhamun turned his head toward her. "Don't talk to me that way. Tell me loving things." He lay beside her in the gloom; he made no move toward her.

"I will turn out the lamp," she said.

She went to the lamp beside the door and cupped her hand over it to snuff out the flame. The room fell dark. Ankhesenamun looked behind her at the bed, but she did not go there. Meryat came through the door and in silence lay down in the King's arms. Ankhesenamun stood beside the door, her fists clenched against her breast, and her gaze fixed on the wall beyond the bed, where groaning and sighing the two bodies thrashed together.

# 13

Sennahet was carrying jars of oil to the palace pantries; he crossed through the garden behind the apartments of the Queen. As he bore the heavy jar down a path of colored gravels, he heard the sound of weeping beyond a hedge and looked over it.

There sat a wretched-looking girl on a bench, her hands covering her eyes, and she wept. Sennahet put the jar down. He stood watching her curiously, but he made no move toward her, until with a start he realized that the crying woman was the Queen's favorite waiting woman, Meryat.

When he recognized her, a scheme came to him, and without even thinking it through he went around the hedge and sat down on the bench.

"Here, girl," he said, and pulled one hand down from her face and chafed it between his palms. "Do not cry. Such a pretty one, you will make even the gods unhappy, and we want the gods to go on smiling on Egypt, don't we?"

Her eyes were red and swollen, all the handsome paint washed away. She gave him a look of scorn and turned her face away.

"Go away," she said. "Leave me."

Her hand was still in his. He rubbed it vigorously. "Tell me what makes you cry, my child."

"Child!" Again she faced him. Her eyes were bright with fresh tears. "Whom do you take me for? A child!" She laughed a broken, unhappy laugh. "Child am I not, no, never again."

"Has someone mistreated you?"

He knew she was beloved of the Queen, tender and sheltered. He did not expect the wild look she gave him, the strength with which she pulled her hand free of him. She cried, "Leave me alone!" Twisting away from him on the bench, she set her back against him and, burying her face in her hands, wept in storms of tears.

Sennahet sat on the bench watching her, unnerved. The great folk led such certain lives, with plenty to eat and drink, and all their rights and duties assured, that it startled him that one of them could be genuinely unhappy. He put out his hand and touched her shoulder.

"Tell me, child."

"I cannot," she said. She put her hands in her lap. "It is doings of the Sun People." Turning her stained face away, she jammed her hands down between her thighs.

Sennahet put his face close to hers. "Do not let them make nothing of you, girl."

She blanched. He saw fear in her eyes. "I have said too much," she said. Biting her forefinger, she shut her eyes, and new tears slipped from beneath the lids.

"They care nothing for those under them," Sennahet said. "People like you and me—what are we to them but straw? They care more for their faceless gods than for us."

Meryat was staring off across the garden, her face slack. In a dull voice, she said, "No—Pharaoh knows nothing of us."

"Then why do you serve them?"

"It is my life to serve the Queen," she said, in the same listless voice.

"Meryat—" He clasped her arms. He spoke with heat to her. "You could be a queen. You could be rich and loved as the Queen—"

"What are you saying?"

"With the gold of Pharaoh! You served Nefertiti. You must know, then, that she buried her husband, Akhenaten, in the desert, and surrounded him with gold—"

She was rising, shrugging off his grip, her face set scornfully against him. "Don't tell me any of this." She marched away down the gravel path below the palm trees.

Sennahet pursued her, speaking into her ear as he followed her. "Pharaoh stole away my patrimony! My farm was the finest in the district. Three buffaloes had I, and a house with windows in every room, like the palace—"

"Shut your foolish mouth," she said. She wheeled around to confront him. Her eyes were narrowed. She looked much older. "There is no tomb," she said, "and if there were, how could treasure repair what he has done to me? Shall I make a new maidenhead of gold—"

She broke off. Sennahet goggled at her, his thoughts galloping after this bait. She struck at him.

"Go away! I don't need your comforts. And it is not what you think!" She was backing away, her voice rising with each word. "I am pure—go away! Leave me alone!" She raced away down the path and disappeared through a gap in the hedge.

Sennahet stood where she had left him. His mind whirled. Surely there would be some way to use what she had told him. Full of thoughts, he turned and went slowly back to take the jar of oil on to the pantry.

The corn ripened in the fields. Splendidly ornamented in gold and sacred stones, Tutankhamun was carried in a litter into the ceremonial field in the palace. All the court watched. The King took a gold scythe in his hand and cut one sheaf of the ripe grain.

Those watching lifted their voices in the ritual phrases, shaped in the ancient tongue, which no one understood anymore. Meryat knew what it meant, because someone had told her:

"Thanks to thee, Osiris, who has died that I may live."

Her voice trembled as she spoke. Her voice was only one among the hundreds that spoke the same words. She knelt behind Ankhesenamun, her head down, and her eyes on the figure of the King.

He was across the millet field from her; she saw him only as a gorgeous doll in his towering atef crown. Her palms knew the smoothness of his body beneath the gold-encrusted robes. She knew him unlike any other man, and no other woman knew him as she did. She could not take her gaze from him. All the hundreds of people around her, greater than she, took her for an ordinary woman, but they knew nothing of the King, and she did.

Now, in the distance, Tutankhamun was passing his scepter back and forth over the grain. The people watching recited formulas. Ankhesenamun knelt just before Meryat. The Queen's back was straight, her shoulder blades like little folded wings.

A man appeared unobtrusively and knelt near the Queen. Meryat recognized the Grand Vizier. While the court and the little gilded figure in the field spoke ritual words, the Queen and the Vizier whispered together.

Meryat watched Tutankhamun. Ankhesenamun was a fool; she thought she dealt in power. Meryat shifted on her knees. She felt much older than the Queen. Now she knew what power was.

With drums and twittering flutes, the ceremony ended. Tutankhamun was carried away. Meryat attended Ankhesenamun back across the open courts and passages of the official quarter of the palace. The Queen was excited; she walked with long strides, her arms swinging. Meryat followed her with her fan. Just as they reached the entrance to Ankhesenamun's private apartments, a man in armor approached them.

This was Horemheb, the King's favorite general. He greeted Ankhesenamun with flourishes of his hands, his head bobbing so that the silver-braided locks of his wig swayed. The Queen allowed him to come near, and they spoke.

Meryat watched them with concealed interest. Ankhesenamun was dealing much in private with the great men of the court. Meryat saw the Queen with new eyes, with the eyes of her own power. She guessed that Ankhesenamun was plotting against the King.

"Meryat," the Queen said. "Run and see that my dinner is ready."

Meryat backed down the steps. Almost she forgot to bow; she dipped down at the foot of the step instead of at the top, but no one noticed. She lingered a moment longer, her eyes on Ankhesenamun's face. The young Queen's cheeks glowed a fiery red. Her eyes blazed as she spoke. Meryat had seen her so when she was preparing for the hunt. The servant went away toward the Queen's kitchen.

The Queen's game now was Pharaoh. Of that she was sure. If Pharaoh were destroyed, then what would Meryat's power be? As she walked, she laid her hand over her womb. She would be an annoyance. A bringer of bad memories.

In the kitchens the cooks had laid out trays of bread and meat. The scullions hurried about, their faces shining with sweat, and their arms laden with jars of honey and wine. Curls of steam hung in the air. Meryat stood in the doorway. She saw that Ankhesenamun's meal was ready, and she took it away to the Queen with her own hands.

As she carried the tray across the courtyard, she took a sip of the wine, a bite of the bread, and a taste of the meat. It was the Queen's food, after all, and Meryat knew herself to be the true Queen.

178

In the evening, when the moon had risen, Ankhesenamun called Meryat into the garden. They walked
together near the foot of the lily pond.

"He is coming again tonight," Ankhesenamun said, low-
voiced.

Meryat twisted her fingers together in the thin stuff of
her dress. She could not bring words to her lips.

"You must do it," the Queen said to her. They spoke face
to face, like equals. "It shall not be for very long. Soon it
will be over."

"Do you mean to depose him?" Meryat asked.

The Queen put her hand over Meryat's mouth. They
stared at one another a moment. Finally Ankhesenamun
lowered her hand to her side. They both turned away. In
spite of the evening cool, Meryat's brow was damp with
sweat. She wound her fingers in her linen dress, around
and around.

"I shall repay you for all that you suffer," Ankhesenamun said. "In a little while."

There was no coin to repay Meryat. Yet she knew of a
way that Meryat could repay the Queen.

She said, loudly, "That Sennahet, you know—the man
whom you have saved, now, twice—"

"The wretch."

"He told me the oddest tale."

"Oh?"

"That your mother brought the king, your father, with
her, when she came back here from the New City."

"He was dead," Ankhesenamun said harshly.

Meryat gladdened at the strident note she heard in the
Queen's voice. She said, "Nefertiti brought the justified
body of Akhenaten here and buried him in secret in the
desert." Lifting her eyes, she looked into the fretted face of
Ankhesenamun. "Is that not a strange tale?"

Ankhesenamun did not speak.

"But of course, if she had done anything of the sort,"

Meryat said, "you would know." She started toward the door.

"Where are you going?"

"I will make myself ready for Pharaoh." Meryat went along the garden toward the doorway into the palace.

In the evening, when the moon shone in the eastern sky and the admiring waters of the Nile copied that image, the King caused himself to be taken to the bedchamber of the Queen. There he lay down on the bed, and the Queen came and lay down beside him. The stars looked in the window. The sweet breath of evening was scented with myrrh and royal incense. The King and the Queen lay side by side. After a few moments had passed, she turned and began to caress him.

His skin grew lively at her touch. He shut his eyes. Her fingers pressed and stroked his skin, awakening his senses. She said nothing to him, nor did he choose to speak.

She licked his throat. He lay stretched upon his couch with her crouched over him and touching him with reverence and grace, as the sky arched over the earth. She made him feel sacred and perfect. He tried not to move. He must draw the utmost effort from her as the land of Egypt demanded everything of the people. Her tongue and her lips toyed with his nipples. His fingertips curled. His stem was rising hot and erect from his loins.

Her soft weight rested on him. She groaned. Against his chest her breasts were warm and soft. Her lips were sweet against his. He opened his mouth; he breathed into her and claimed her.

She touched his staff and held in her fingers the eggs in which the whole world began. He pressed his lips together. He would not break silence. He would not turn this sacred act into the mating of brutes. He thought of the Eye of the Sun, and as she raised herself above him, he imagined that the Sun glowed forth from his forehead. She descended on him.

She caressed him with the secret places of her body. She made a whole world of him; through her touch he became rich and fertile. He felt the life in him swelling toward its fullness. Then she was sighing, her rich odors like incense in his nostrils, and her ecstasy drew from him the hot spurt of life.

His joy went forth to her in words. "Ankhesenamun, you have served me perfectly well. You have earned my favor. I grant you whatever you most desire."

She moved away from him. His skin was cold now, where she had warmed him, and he shivered. Her voice seemed to come from a distance.

"Find me the tomb of my father, Akhenaten," she said.

In the morning the King remembered what his Queen had asked of him. He summoned into the audience chamber the chief scribe of the Justification of Osiris, who supervised all work in the City of the Dead.

"Tell me," Pharaoh said to the scribe, who was prostrated before the throne. "Is it not true that on death every King becomes Osiris, and rules over the Blessed Land of the Dead?"

"He who is great over Egypt speaks ever the perfect truth."

"Then you must know where every King is buried, so that he may be preserved and protected."

"And honored with ceremonies, may you live forever."

"Tell me, then, where my predecessor and my brother, Akhenaten, is buried."

"Commonly it is supposed, source of all prosperity, that Akhenaten-Osiris is buried at his own city, the New City, in the north."

"Is this the truth?"

The scribe said, "Greatness of my fathers and their fathers, know that the Great Lady of Egypt Nefertiti brought her husband here and caused him to be buried in secret in the Royal Gorge. But that was years ago, and now none knows where. The Royal Lady did the rite far from all save the most necessary eyes."

"Whose?"

"I shall discover this for Pharaoh," the scribe said.

He went out, and later in that same day returned.

"The source of all that lives asks who could find the secret house of Akhenaten-Osiris. Be it known that I have searched the rolls. The Queen did what she did in secret. I have found record of only one who would know, a man of Thebes."

"Who?"

"Hapure. The mason."

Meryat burned; she considered that Ankhesenamun had stolen away the King's favor from her. She went into the garden where the cooks grew their herbs. Sennahet was there pitting dates. Meryat sat down beside him on the bench.

"You seek the tomb of King Akhenaten," she said.

"Yes," he said. He fastened his gaze on her, unblinking, so intent it frightened her, and she slid away from him on the bench.

"Keep watch on the Gorge of Royal Dead," she told him. "Someone will surely lead you to it within a few days."

He went away without even thanking her, without even taking away the bowl of pitted dates. She sat on the bench wondering if she had done ill. She could not collect herself. From the palm tree over her head, something fell into her lap.

She looked down and saw a great black spider on her skirt. Violently she brushed it off. She rose and went into the kitchen and washed her hands.

Hapure stood to his knees in the muddy Nile, filling his bucket with water. A staff across his shoulders supported the buckets. A few steps downstream several women were washing out linen; he took care not to roil the water. He straightened. A familiar pain pierced him in the small of the back and he gasped.

The weight of water pressed the staff down onto his shoulders. He walked up out of the Nile; the women with their laundry screamed at him for muddying the water. He trudged through the children playing on the bank and walked out along the top of the dike that ran between the fields.

The powdery dust puffed up between his toes. Holding the buckets steady with his hands, he walked up past the newly harvested fields. Only stubble stood there now; all the grain was safely gathered into the silos of the Temple of Amun. The priests had promised to keep everyone who had worked. Nobody else save the priests had any land anymore, therefore everyone had worked.

Hapure climbed steadily across the broad, sloping bank of the river, past the black fields of the farms. He came to the edge of the desert, where abruptly the black soil of Egypt became the red dust of the desert, and there he followed another trail that climbed and wound through the barren rock, until he came to his village, Kalala, high in the desert cliff.

He had come back to live in Kalala although he could have found a place in the valley to live, although he was almost alone here. The quiet of the village still dragged on his spirits at times. It was his home; he belonged here, like Pharaoh in his palace and Ra in the sky. He took the water through the still street to his house and filled the little cistern in the corner of his garden. Then, with a bowl, he watered the three rows of beans he was struggling to keep alive in the garden.

He took the buckets back down to the Nile again in the afternoon. A great lumbering barge was wallowing north along the river, and from the bank he watched it pass, curious. The men on the deck shaded their eyes to see him. They were light-skinned men, from the far north. He waved his hand to them and they answered. He stopped to fill his buckets, and the wake of the barge lapped around his knees.

"Mother and Father of Egypt, renew me and thee." He filled his buckets.

When he turned, there were five soldiers on the bank, watching him.

"Are you Hapure the mason?"

"I am," he said.

They took him off in a chariot toward the King's Road. They made him leave the buckets and the staff on the riverbank, although he protested that he would never see them again.

Dark had fallen when they reached the edge of the great sprawl of buildings that surrounded the palace. The soldiers led Hapure through the broad lanes between the buildings. He passed below a window and heard someone inside chanting the evening prayers.

He was afraid to talk to the soldiers, even to ask where they were taking him. He had done nothing wrong. They had not bound him or drawn their swords. Taking heart from that, he followed the men into a small room.

"Prostrate yourself," said a soldier.

Hapure lowered himself down. His back hurt again in the usual place. The soldiers stood along the wall. Their sandals rasped as they straightened to attention. Behind Hapure several people entered the room.

"You are Hapure, and you are a mason?"

An unknown voice. On his elbows and knees, his face against the painted floor, he said, "I am, master."

"Some few years ago, did you do the mason's work on a secret burial somewhere in the Royal Gorge?"

His breath hissed in his teeth. Should he lie? He could smell sandalwood. Courtiers, these men behind him. Nobles. Trust the great, as he would trust the Nile, because he had no choice.

"Yes, my lord."

"Could you find the spot again?"

"No," he said.

"Pharaoh commands your answer."

"May he live forever, the Strong Bull of Egypt."

"Let it be so. Can you find the tomb?"

"I will try."

Then he was taken in another chariot back across the plain. The horses' harness jingled. He held tight to the rail, wondering at the easy stance of the driver. Three other chariots accompanied them. They took the road that led through the temples and tombs that crowded the west bank of the river. The nightbirds twittered in the grass alongside the road. Ahead rose the desert cliff.

Hapure ran his hand over his forehead. He was tired; he had walked most of the day to and from the river. The chariots trotted into the cleft in the sheer escarpment of the desert, and the gorge enclosed them.

The moon sailed through the depth of the sky. It cast black shadows under the boulders, shadows that seemed more substantial than the rocks themselves. Hapure looked wildly around him. Everything seemed strange to him. He wondered how he would ever find the tomb. Yet if Pharaoh required it, he must find it, or they might slay him.

"Go more slowly," he cried.

The driver reined the horses to a walk.

They traveled through the gorge. A gentle river of wind was flowing along it. The moonlight was so bright it seemed like twilight. Hapure caught himself staring straight ahead into the pale ghostly light, his mind empty, drunk with the cool night. The cliffs loomed before him. A jackal barked. The moon sank in the sky. On its face the sacred words were written as clear as stele writing.

At last he said, "Stop the horses."

The driver pulled back on his reins. Hapure climbed down from the chariot. He walked forward a few strides. Here the gorge was narrow, and the feet of the sheer walls deeply buried in talus. On the slope to his left a black hole led back into the hillside. That was the open, unused tomb where on that long-past night he had waited to do his work, and looked out on Nefertiti's procession, lamenting with voices and flutes.

He pointed to the slope on the right. "There," he said. "They have shoveled rock over it, to hide the doorway, but it is there."

The driver dismounted from his chariot. "You are sure?"

"I will never forget this place," Hapure said.

The soldier's eyes glistened. The moon was bright on his face. He said, "Fool," and drew his sword, and struck Hapure down.

Sennahet had followed the chariots by the thundering echo of their wheels. He was too afraid to go within sight of them. When the racket stopped, he stopped, and hid behind a boulder.

The moon was setting. The sky glittered with stars. Sennahet clenched his teeth to keep them from chattering. He peered around the boulder. The gorge ahead was buried in the darkness. He leaned against the boulder, longing for morning to come.

A distant rattle reached his ears. The chariots were coming back.

He made himself small at the foot of the boulder, his arms around his knees. The chariots hurried down the gorge. The leading team approached the boulder, and suddenly the horses shied off. They had sensed the presence of Sennahet. The charioteer cursed; his whip cracked. He forced the prancing horses past Sennahet. Each of the other three teams shied at the same place and in the same way, but the drivers paid no heed. They whipped the horses on and galloped away down the gorge.

Something fell out of the last chariot. It lay motionless in the track.

When the horses were gone, Sennahet rose to his feet. Cautiously he drew near the object lying in the path. When he saw what it was, a cry escaped him. He ran forward and turned the body over onto its back.

It was his kinsman Hapure, covered with blood.

"Hapure," Sennahet said, several times. He shook his head. Laying his hands on Hapure's arms, he thought on the ways of the gods that had brought them both to this place.

The flesh under his hands was still warm. He leaned down over his cousin's face. Hapure's lips moved.

Sennahet's heart jumped in his chest. He gathered Hapure in his arms and took him off down the gorge.

When the sun appeared above the horizon every man in Egypt went to his household shrine and opened the doors and brought forth the image of the god. He anointed the god and dressed him for the day. He put food and drink before the god.

In the palace Pharaoh was anointed and dressed. He ate his breakfast.

Horemheb came into the presence of Tutankhamun. A general of light cavalry, he always wore a magnificent breastplate of bronze and gold. Whenever he sought the attention of Pharaoh, he brought such wonderful gifts that Tutankhamun could not help but give him everything he asked for.

Today Horemheb prostrated himself before the King's throne and his servants brought in a chest of painted wood. The servants held up the little box so that the King could admire the scenes on its sides. On one long side Tutankhamun himself was drawing his bow at the hunt; on the other he drove his chariot over his vanquished enemies.

"You have made your King glad, my general," the King said.

"That is the aim of my whole life," said Horemheb.

Tutankhamun watched his servants take the chest out of the room. He began to consider which of his possessions he would keep in it. The general was kneeling at his feet, his head between his hands. Tutankhamun cast about him for some substantial token of his favor.

"I have a special task for you," he said. "To you shall I entrust the well-being of the Queen herself, when she makes her progress to the tomb of her father Osiris."

"Your Majesty is most generous."

"You may rise."

Horemheb straightened. His armor was wonderfully decorated in gold with figures of animals. Tutankhamun let his gaze wander around the room. Horemheb fitted it well; he was another decoration here, among the gilded columns and the walls painted with images of the gods. Pharaoh laid his hands on his knees. He felt the pressure of the crown upon his brow.

"I have found the tomb of her father for her. She will be very grateful, I am sure of it."

"Your Majesty surrounds us all with his power. Even the Royal Wife is no more than a stone under the foot of Pharaoh."

Tutankhamun smiled to hear this. Horemheb was a great man and knew much of the world, and what he said was true.

"Yes," he said. "It is a great thing that I have done."

"A deed worthy of Pharaoh. I shall place myself at the Queen's beck. Shall she go by barge to the New City?"

Tutankhamun was already bored. He gave a slight shake of his head. "Nefertiti had the body of Akhenaten brought here to Thebes and secretly reburied."

"Ah. How very dutiful."

"She was devoted to my brother until the end." The King put his fingertips to his chin. He closed his eyes. "My Queen is as devoted to me. It is the proper way of women."

"Your Majesty understands everything."

The King sat still, his hands and knees together, studying his ringed fingers. He was trying to think of some new diversion for the afternoon.

"Nefertiti had the treasuries of Egypt in her power," Horemheb said. "She will have surrounded Akhenaten with every luxury."

"I am sure of it."

"Yes, half the gold of Egypt must be in that tomb."

The King's attention caught on those words. He lifted his gaze from the jewels. "Do you think so?"

"You yourself have said so, Your Majesty. It must be true."

"I did say so," Tutankhamun said.

"Then the conclusion follows that she must have beggared your treasury to furnish Akhenaten's eternal house. She was regent for you, in those days—it was not right to do it."

Tutankhamun sucked in his breath. "Yes," he exclaimed. "She stole it all from me."

Horemheb bowed down before him. "Magnificence of Egypt, command me. I am your servant. There is nothing you may not ask of me."

The King was angry. He remembered all the slights and injuries that Nefertiti had offered him, and now he saw that she had robbed him as well.

"Shall I restore your treasure to you, Pharaoh?"

"Do it," Tutankhamun said.

"Pharaoh's decision is my will."

"But Ankhesenamun must not know." He gnawed at that problem a moment. He wanted so much to please her, to solicit her caresses, her ardor. He shook his head, peeved. "I shall tell her later where her father lies. When you have opened the tomb and recovered my belongings and shut it again."

"Pharaoh is great." Horemheb bent himself down on his knees and kissed the floor.

Sennahet took Hapure on his shoulders up to Kalala, in the desert above the Royal Gorge. After three days Hapure was well enough to sit and eat a little bread.

"What happened to you?" Sennahet asked him. "Why did the soldiers try to kill you?"

Hapure fingered the long gash in his scalp. He felt weak all over, as if his bones were made of watery clay. They were sitting in his little garden. His beans had withered in the heat, and he fretted over that: Sennahet should have kept them watered. He put his head in his hands.

"I angered Pharaoh. It is his pleasure to punish me—if he wishes me to die, then I should have died." He wondered how he had failed the King; perhaps the command to find the old tomb had been a false one, not from Pharaoh at all, just a trap to see if he might reveal the hidden place of Akhenaten. He shook his head and the dull pain spread down the back of his neck and made his shoulders hurt.

"What did you do?" Sennahet asked.

Hapure said nothing, his eyes on the ground. His heart was sick. He had failed the King and should be dead.

"It was at Pharaoh's command that you were attacked," Sennahet pressed him. "Does that not anger you? Now, tell me where the gold is, and we will avenge ourselves together."

Hapure looked at him with horror. "Vengeance! No—no —Pharaoh is always right. If I failed him, then it is he who must take vengeance against me."

Sennahet began to argue. Hapure rose, carrying his throbbing head carefully on his shoulders, and went into his hut.

"I should have left you there to die," Sennahet shouted at him.

"I wish you had," Hapure muttered.

He sat down in a dark corner of his hut and brooded on his failures. Sennahet went away and did not come back for the rest of the day.

In the early morning, when Hapure was still asleep, Sennahet returned and shook him awake. Hapure cried out; the pain in his head wakened when he did.

"You fool," Sennahet shouted at him. "Pharaoh is right, is he? Then come with me! Come see!"

Hapure was trying to lie down again on his pallet. He pushed away Sennahet's hands. In the dark room Sennahet was but a shadow that pulled and tugged on him.

"Come with me. I will show you why Pharaoh struck you down."

Hapure rubbed his eyes with his fists. Sennahet was squatting before him in the dark.

"I will go," Hapure said. He knew it was his duty to find out what sin he had done.

Sennahet led him down the narrow path from his village to the Royal Gorge. They traveled single file, like jackals. The sun was hot. Hapure grew weak and tired. On the way down the steep side of the gorge, he stumbled, and Sennahet caught him in his arms. Hapure thrust him away. Panting, he sank down on the path and laid his head in his arms.

"I can go no farther."

"Only a little more," Sennahet said.

Hapure raised his head. He saw that they were nearly to the place of the secret tomb.

They went down the last few feet of the path to the floor of the gorge. Now Hapure could hear voices ahead of them. He put out his hand to Sennahet, and the other man took him by the hand and they went together to the side of the gorge and skulked through the shadows there. They bent their knees and traveled like thieves through the shadows. They went around the bend in the gorge.

Before them now lay the widening of the gorge where the secret tomb was dug. Hapure froze in his steps. His heart grew heavy. The tomb was secret no more. Three lines of soldiers encircled it, and three heavy sleds waited before it. Already two of them were piled high with goods. The entranceway to the tomb had been laid open. A steady stream of men came forth from it, bearing the grave goods of the King on their backs, and these they stacked up on the sleds.

"They are robbing it," Hapure whispered. He struck his breast with his fist. "They are robbing Pharaoh's house."

Sennahet whispered, "Be quiet—if they find us we shall die."

Hapure knew that was so. He knew now that was why he had been struck down. At first he told himself that these men had lied to him. It was not Pharaoh's work, what happened here. But the soldiers around the tomb were Pharaoh's soldiers. The oxen that stood in the traces before the sleds were the royal oxen.

"I have seen enough," he said. "Let us go."

He and Sennahet returned along the gorge, hiding as they had done before. The men of Pharaoh did not hide; they went about their work openly, carelessly. Hapure remembered that the soldier who had attacked him had called him a fool. For what: for obeying Pharaoh? His head throbbed and pounded unmercifully. The wound would ache him until he died. For obeying Pharaoh he would die.

For the first time he saw what death was. The priests taught that death was a passageway to life, but that was a lie. Death was the end. Death was horrible. He climbed the path after Sennahet, but his mind was not on the work of his feet, scrambling up the stony bank. His mind was on death. It was all a lie. Even when Kings died that was the end of them, and their successors were not reincarnations of the eternal spirit of the King, but mere men, who plundered the tombs of their predecessors. The King was only another man, richer, perhaps, but still one of a doomed race, that scratched and crawled across the earth until the time came when they should die. Then other creatures fed on them, their flesh was consumed, and their lives went for nothing.

The sun was heavy on him, greasing his skin with sweat. He stumbled along after Sennahet across the desert to his village.

Some few families had returned to their homes in the village. The women were spreading out their linen in the sun at the edge of the houses; they stared at Hapure and Sennahet as they passed. The two men went into Hapure's garden.

"You were right," Hapure said. "I should have helped you steal the gold. Then at least we would be comfortable. I was deluded. I was the slave of the priests."

"Yes," Sennahet said. His eyes gleamed.

"Now it is too late. I understand now, but it is too late."

"Our moment will come," Sennahet said.

In the midafternoon Ankhesenamun sent Meryat away across the Nile to the bazaar. Meryat did not go; she slipped into the garden behind the Queen's chambers and hid under the window, and presently she heard the Queen exchanging greetings with the Vizier and Horemheb.

The Queen said, "What news from the north?"

The wheezy voice that answered was the Vizier's. "The trouble has passed, although not without cost. There were men killed. We had to bribe the governor."

"I have sent another two hundred chariots north," Horemheb said.

"Without any authority?" The Queen sounded angry. "Do you think you are a kinglet, General?"

"A minor movement of troops," Horemheb said.

Meryat under the window listened keenly to all this. They spoke of Tutankhamun.

"He shows no interest in his role. No understanding." The Vizier was standing nearby the window. His tone was flat and lifeless. He was an old man and Meryat was afraid of him. He said, "I served Amenhotep and Akhenaten. To see the crowns they wore on such a head—"

"Peace," Ankhesenamun said.

"He is vain and silly, and dangerous," Horemheb said, crisp. "Let him take the notion, he will have us all knifed."

The Queen's voice grew indistinct. She was moving

away from the window, pacing down the room. Meryat could picture her, taut and lithe as a lioness. The servant closed her eyes. They were right about Tutankhamun. A vain, silly boy. Yet he was her lover, and she loved him.

"He is a child," Ankhesenamun said. "Easily managed. I mean to keep him on the throne—I can rule through him."

"You do not know him, my Queen," Horemheb said.

The Vizier spoke, his voice coming from directly above Meryat's head; she startled, turning cold as death, and pressed herself against the rough wall. He said, "She is right. There must be a King—there is none but Tutankhamun."

"The power to destroy us is at the tips of his fingers," Horemheb said. Meryat hated his round, convincing voice. "Let him merely guess at what we do—"

"Let him make a son, first," Vizier said. "The line must not be broken."

"He is harmless," said the Queen.

"I tell you, he is no stranger to murder," said Horemheb. "I myself heard him order a man slain for no more than obeying Pharaoh's will."

"What?" The Queen spoke sharply. She was nearer the window now than before. Confronting Horemheb. "When did he do this?"

"There is a tomb hidden, somewhere in the desert. He found a man who knew where it was, and when the poor peasant told him, Pharaoh had him killed."

Meryat bit her lips. He would not do such a deed. A vain, silly boy, only that. She rubbed her cheek against the wall.

There was an odd silence in the room above her. Finally Ankhesenamun said, "A tomb? Whose tomb?"

The Vizier said, "Why would he murder one who did him service?"

"To hide the disservice he himself did," Horemheb said. "He robbed the tomb of everything save the body."

The Vizier made a choking sound in his throat. "Blasphemy!" As he spoke he moved away from the window. Meryat sighed with relief. "I shall report this to the High Priest—"

"The High Priest is even now with the King," Horemheb said, "advising him how to avoid the vengeance of the gods for this sacrilege."

"He has robbed the tomb?" Ankhesenamun asked. "This cannot be the truth—he, not even he would dare—to rob my father's tomb!"

Meryat burst off across the garden at a run. The Queen's voice, shrill and strong, followed her across the garden to the hedge. "Let them who call my father scoundrel look on this—" Meryat dashed around a corner out of hearing.

Much later, in the evening, Meryat returned to the Queen's chambers. Ankhesenamun was sitting by a lamp, dressed in her nightdress. Meryat gave her the box that Ankhesenamun had sent her for. The Queen put it aside with only a look. She thanked Meryat, her eyes elsewhere. Her face was like stone. Meryat knew that Horemheb had prevailed, that they were set to murder the king.

Tutankhamun walked once around the Presentation Chair, admiring the way the gold was worked. Such a thing as this was fit for the King, an ornament to him. The little scene on the back depicted a King in the Crown of Sacrifice with his wife before him bowing and anointing him with the oils of life. The arms of the chair were shaped like winged serpents. The royal shield that bore the King's name carried the names of Akhenaten. It must have been made to celebrate the marriage of one of his daughters. Tutankhamun was unskilled at reading but he recognized the symbols at a glance. He would have the goldsmith of the palace pound out his brother's name and replace it with his own. He walked once more around the throne. It was beautiful work, and he grew light with pride at his own discernment. Let those who thought him stupid see how rare his senses were.

A servant crept in the door. Tutankhamun said, "You may speak."

"Life and death of Egypt, the High Priest of Amun awaits."

"I shall come."

Tutankhamun already wore a cloak heavy with gold. He needed no more to go out into the night. The High Priest awaited him in the next room, the Audience Hall, and at the approach of the King the bearers hurried out across the wide room with his open chair. With the High Priest running beside him, the King was borne in his chair through the dark courtyard to the palace gate, and then across the sleeping plain of the west bank of Thebes.

They traveled at a steady pace. The King's cheek grew chilly from the night wind. Irritated, he was about to call for a scarf, but then the litter carried him swiftly in through the gate in a high wall.

They set him down. The High Priest, out of breath, bowed before him. The priest was in haste; his eyes were white with excitement. They went into the house before them.

This was the workshop of the royal embalmers. No one else was there now. In the back of the central room, on a table, lay a corpse.

The King and the priest went at once to this table.

The priest said, short, "I shall speak the rites, your Majesty. Do nothing—say nothing. The slightest mistake, and the magic is fruitless."

With surprise Tutankhamun saw that the priest was frightened. He himself was unafraid. He looked down at the table, where the body of his brother Akhenaten lay, last of all the objects taken from his tomb.

The linen wrappings were stained dark from the oils that had sanctified them three years before. All the amulets and masks and shields that usually covered up the wrapped body had been taken away, and the corpse looked nude. Even the curved gold bands that held the body were gone.

The priest was speaking ancient words over the body. With a clap of his hands, he drew a knife and, leaning over the body, he slit the wrappings.

Tutankhamen jumped at the sound the knife blade made in the old linen. A tingle ran cold down his spine. He reminded himself that he was the King now.

The priest was saying, "Lose thy name, and be powerless." He pulled at the wrappings on the body. "Lose thy shape, and be powerless." The king swallowed the dryness in his throat. The priest freed the arms of the body, which had been crossed over its breast, and stretched out one arm down along the thigh. So were women posed; men were always buried with their arms crossed.

The priest said, "Lose thy seed, and be powerless." With the tip of his knife he cut off the phallus of the King.

Tutankhamun uttered a low cry. The priest wheeled on him. His eyes burned. Neither of them spoke again. The priest returned to his work. He laid the knife on the table and passed his hands over the body and made secret gestures. At last he backed away from the table.

Tutankhamun followed him through the darkened workshop. The place stank of natron. For the first time the King noticed how cluttered it was with tools and tables.

"That will protect us, I hope," the priest said.

"If it does not . . ." Tutankhamun said.

They were at the door; the High Priest glanced at him, his forehead puckered, and his small mouth pursed. In a dry voice he said, "I stand in more danger than you, Glory of Egypt. You are the master of all powers."

Tutankhamun heard these words with an inward shudder. He did not feel master of any magic now. He went forward through the door into the dark courtyard. There his litter waited. The priest bowed down before him and said ritual words to him. The King stood staring away into the dark. He put his hand down between his thighs and touched his organ. He longed to hold onto it, as a little boy might, falling.

The bearers brought over his litter. He climbed in among the cushions and they took him away to the palace.

In his innermost chamber a woman awaited him. He stopped on the threshold, startled at her appearance. It was one of his Queen's waiting women; he did not know her name. Her face was haggard. Alarmed, he stepped backwards away from her. She did not prostrate herself. She came at him, her hands outstretched, like a vulture.

"My lord, I have come to you—please, you must flee—"

"What?" he said.

It was hard to speak face to face to one so menial.

"They are plotting against you," the woman said. Her words tumbled out in a torrent from her lips. Her hands reached toward him, her palms up. He shrank from her profane touch. What she said made no sense; she said, "They mean to do away with you. You must save yourself. For the good of Egypt. Save yourself. Only let me go with you, Great One, my love."

"Save myself! From whom?"

Then, to his horror, she said the names of his closest friends. "The Queen. Horemheb, the general. And the Vizier."

"Ankhesenamun," he said. All his sense had fled.

The girl rushed at him. She flung her arms around him and pressed her face against his chest. "Take me with you—I will love you always. Have I not loved you so well, so much—"

He struck her down with his hand. "You touched me!" He raised his voice into a scream for his guard. She had touched him. She had polluted him with her common hands, now, when he required all his holiness untainted and intact. He scrubbed with his palms at his chest where her coarse face had pressed. She was coming at him again, speaking more foul words, things he did not understand, and her filthy hands out. Then his guards rushed into the room.

"Take her away! Drive her out—she is unclean, she—she—"

The men lifted her between them. She writhed, trying to free herself, and shouted to him again. He did not hear what she said. He turned away as they dragged her from the room, he turned and went into a corner, where there was quiet. Even when she was gone the clamor and disorder of her presence seemed to linger. The room was tainted now. He would never be able to come here again. He went out to the next room, his robing room, and there stood alone in the dark and silence until his mind settled.

When the Lord Sun appeared in the eastern sky, renewed in splendor after the terrors of the night, the King Tutankhamun went forth into the desert. He had determined that the strange girl's attack on him was retribution for his part in the destruction of Akhenaten and he meant to see that it did not happen anymore.

The bearers carried him along at a brisk trot through the desert. The dry heat and the dust annoyed him. He ordered a cloth brought to him, soaked in water, and laid it over his face, to preserve his face from the blistering sun. Halfway to his destination, the bearers stopped, exhausted, and the second group that had traveled behind them in chariots came forward to carry him the rest of the way.

They had no difficulty finding the place where Akhenaten had been buried once and would be buried again. The tomb had been left open. The doorway gaped hollow in the side of the hill. Just across the trail was another tomb; the two doorways faced each other like two shouting mouths.

Tutankhamun understood why his peace was disturbed. It was these two shouting tombs that robbed him of his serenity.

He stepped down from his litter and went to the tomb where Akhenaten had lain. To this tomb the dead man would be returned later in the day. Tutankhamun stood before the open door. The black shadows within were impenetrable to his eyes. A cold breath seemed to emanate from it.

He raised his hands. Summoning the powers of his godhood, he spoke into the mouth of the tomb.

"Cursed be this ground, and cursed him who dwells within."

Three times he spoke this curse. Then he spat on the threshold of the tomb; he pissed on the threshold of the tomb, and, turning his back and lifting his skirts, he defecated on the threshold of the tomb. "Let him be unknown, and all his works forgotten."

The bearers and the charioteers were gathered on the path. Their backs were turned to him. He understood that; the magic might burn them if they saw it, might rot them. He climbed back into his litter and lay down on the cushions.

He smiled. He knew that he had saved himself.

# 14

Meryat groaned with every step. The soldiers had beaten her over the back and on the legs before they threw her out of the palace. She could not go back there. If Ankhesenamun saw her, she would know immediately what had happened. Meryat limped down the road toward the ferry stage, sighing and moaning.

There, on the bench where people sat to await the ferry, she sank down and gave herself over to tears. The night was dark; she was alone on the ferry stage. She wept until her eyes were dry. Her throat was raw from crying, and her misery was like a stone in her belly.

She cursed those who had done this to her, Tutankhamun and Ankhesenamun, but she knew her words were only wind against such great ones.

All the night long she sat there on the bench, weeping when the reservoir of her tears was filled, and cursing when she had wept her eyes dry. Then the sun rose. People gathered on the ferry stage. They looked curiously at the wild-looking woman huddled on the bench, and no one would come near her, or even sit on the same bench with her.

She had no money for the ferry. Anyway, she had no place to go. She sat there the day long, no longer weeping, while hunger carved a hole under her ribs. She watched the common herd of people passing by her, coming and going. They looked on her with oblique glances, with shocked faces. She spat at them. They knew nothing of life—all they knew were the tasks of daily life. They knew nothing at all.

In the afternoon she saw Sennahet in the crowd.

She twisted her face away, ashamed. She prayed that he would go on by her without recognizing her. But he saw her and came and sat down beside her, murmuring in surprise.

"Meryat! I hardly knew you. What is this?"

She gritted her teeth together. If he knew what had befallen her he would despise her. "Go away," she said.

The hunger in her belly called to him in a rumbling voice. Humiliated, she closed her eyes.

He took hold of her hand. "Meryat, what has happened? Here—I have bread—I have some beer. . . ."

He drew her away to a shady place along the ferry stage, and from his wallet took a runt end of a loaf and a little jar half full of sour beer. She bit her lips, longing to eat, but afraid that he would mock her. He put the food in her lap.

"Eat."

Then she ate, and the food was delicious, far sweeter than the honey and milk of the palace. She began to weep again as she ate, and he put one arm around her and held her still. He fed her sips of beer.

"Why have you left the palace?"

"I can never go back—never!"

"I have a place to stay," he said. "You may stay with me and my friend."

She lifted her head. Her cheeks were rutted with the endless tears.

*

The sun had gone down. Beneath the world, Osiris was sailing back from west to east through the demon-ridden night. Above the world the great red star Sothis burned in the sky like a spark of flame.

Half-drunk, Hapure sat in the doorway of his house at the edge of the desert. Behind him Sennahet was sitting with the girl Meryat in the front room of the house. Hapure shut his ears to their talk. He groped beside him for the jug of wine.

Down the street two women were shouting insults at each other. The street was strewn with garbage; the rest of the villagers had come back to their homes and to their work in the necropolis of Thebes. Pharaoh had remembered them, too, and sent them bread and dried fish roe, beer and dates, linen and water and oil, and a new overseer who carried a whip.

Hapure took no comfort in this renewal of the village. He drank several deep swallows of the date wine without taking any comfort there, either.

"The Queen will not dare to doubt you," Sennahet said, his voice rising. "You misguess your power over her."

Hapure did not hear Meryat's answer. He turned his head slightly to see her. She sat huddled in the middle of the floor, under the lamp, her hands to her face. Sennahet crouched before her. He looked evil, his arms and legs crooked, his knees and elbows sharp as fishhooks. He never took his eyes from this girl. In spite of all that he and Hapure had seen at the looted tomb, Sennahet was ever more intent on stealing Pharaoh's gold. Now he claimed that the robbery of the tomb had brought the treasure within their reach. He was trying to talk Meryat into returning to the palace and finding out where the gold was stored.

Hapure leaned his head against the frame of the door and rubbed his hands together. A fly buzzed around him. He waved his fingers at it, irritated. Egypt would rise and fall and rise again, but the flies were eternal. He ground the heel of his palm into his eyes. The rage and pain had sickened his heart since the moment he saw that Pharaoh robbed Pharaoh; he felt clogged with the undigestible knowledge; his passions and his thoughts would not flow freely anymore, would not run themselves clear, or bring fresh thoughts and passions in their stream.

"She must take you in," Sennahet said. "Offer the flimsiest excuses of where you have been, and she will accept it, for fear of what you might say. She will not dare do otherwise."

"I can't go back," Meryat said. Her voice broke. She was near tears again. "If he sees me—if he summons the Queen again to his couch—"

"Let her alone," Hapure said, over his shoulder.

"You must go back," Sennahet said. "Just long enough to make us all rich."

"I don't want to be rich!"

"For revenge, then."

Meryat began to cry. Hapure almost twitched himself to his feet to defend her from Sennahet, but he stayed where he was. The evening was pleasantly cool; the stars were so bright they seemed almost within reach. He drank more of the sweet wine.

Sennahet said, "Only for a few days, Meryat."

The Queen Ankhesenamun dreamed of lions. Waking suddenly in the night, she heard an owl hoot in the garden. These portents of what she meant to do chilled her to the bone. Rising from her bed, she drew a shawl over her bare shoulders and went to the open window.

There were servants nearby, but she did not call to them. With her own hands she put the carved screen across the window.

But she could not sleep—would not, until the deed was done. She walked around the room in the darkness, the shawl caught fast in the meshing of her crossed arms. Her nerves fluttered like a bride's. She reminded herself of the lions she had killed, the horses she had mastered. Now she would avenge her father. She shut her mind to any thought of turning aside from that holy task.

It was her father whom she intended to avenge, yet her prayer was to her mother. Pressing her open hands to her breasts she spoke aloud: "Shining Woman, accept my thanks, that such a worthy deed should come to me."

She paced around her room, which she had furnished as simply as she imagined the barracks of soldiers to be. The bare floor chilled her toes. In the dark the low chest and bed were solid featureless shapes like stones. She strode from one wall to the opposite wall of the room. She knew that her father would hate what she was doing. He had wanted her to love everyone.

A rush of anger at him made her tighten her fists. He could believe that, preach that impossible ideal: he who had set himself off from the world in the isolation of his own city, where no one dared speak a word against him. But she lived in the world, in the midst of enemies.

Pacing around the darkened room, she paused before the marble chest, where a tray waited, with two cups. With one forefinger she traced the rim of the right-hand cup. When the time came, she would offer that cup to Tutankhamun. She quickened with excitement. She teased herself with the thought that she might not be able to do it, in the end, that some softness, some false pity, might betray her. She imagined what she would say, when the King lay dead at her feet. She imagined herself tall and cool, untouched. She longed for that moment, when it would be done, and the waiting over.

She sighed. Akhenaten had been a fool. If one loved everybody then how could one come to love a single person with the intensity and nobility that raised one above the common muck? To profess to love the world was an insult to those whom she did love. She loved her father, Akhenaten, and therefore she hated Tutankhamun. Tomorrow she would destroy him whom she hated. She began to smile. For the first time, she felt herself to be Akhenaten's equal, and she warmed with a fresh affection for him.

In his house in Thebes, the General Horemheb also walked sleepless through the deep of the night.

Horemheb's private chambers were as highly decorated as the altars of the gods. His chairs were of inlaid wood and his window screens of alabaster; his cups and mirrors were of gold. The floor was warmed and softened with many layers of carpet. The lamps that burned in the niches of the walls were made of the finest oils.

There the general walked alone. He had no taste for wine or food and no interest in sleep. Ever he returned to the window facing west, the window from which he could see the gilded palace of Pharaoh on the far bank of the Nile.

He wondered if the Queen would indeed kill her husband. She was not tough, not cold, like a true murderer. To herself perhaps it was not murder, just as to the lion the slaying of an antelope was only right and proper.

Thus far all Horemheb's plans had unwound without flaw, a golden thread of fate. He dared not consider what might happen to him if by some misjudgment he should break the thread. He was always careful, doing as little as necessary, nudging people a little, that was all. He stood at the window staring across the river toward the palace, longing for the sun to rise.

In the late afternoon the Royal Wife, Ankhesenamun, received her lord, Tutankhamun, in her bedchamber. She wore the sacred headdress of the Princess of the Sun, with the vulture goddess poised above her eyes.

Tutankhamun was brought in his chair. The bearers set down the chair and, without rising from his place, the King looked on his wife. She returned his looks with a calm face. She did not kneel to him.

The King arose from his chair. With a motion of his hand he sent away his attendants. All dressed in gold, his arms plated with bracelets and magic amulets, he stood stiffly before his wife.

"You are free before me," he said, "as no one else ever has been. Yet I do not find this unpleasant."

The Queen said, "I have summoned you here to give you news that will bring great joy to Egypt. It is my right to meet you now as your equal."

Immediately the King understood that she was with child. His delight was uncontainable. He clapped his hands.

"I shall build a temple. I shall dedicate five days of festival."

Two servants came into the room on their hands and knees, and the King bade them go for wine.

"We shall celebrate this news," he said.

The Queen nodded. "I anticipated that you would wish it. There is wine waiting. I will serve you with my own hands."

So saying, she went to a cabinet and opened it, and took out two cups of wine that she had prepared. She gave one cup to the King. Tutankhamun touched his scarab ring to his cup and to Ankhesenamun's.

"Blessed be the sacred life that has taken root in your womb."

"Blessed be it," she murmured.

"And for you, my Queen, another palace, the most beautiful in Egypt."

Tutankhamun drank from his cup. Immediately he felt a sickly fire racing through his veins. He cried out in amazement. He still held the cup; Ankhesenamun, with her cup, stood before him, her face immobile, and her expression distant. Tutankhamun sank to the floor. He coughed and moved a little and died there.

The Queen remained still a long while, the King dead on the floor at her feet. She put the cup down.

"As I told you," she said, "this is a great joy to Egypt, that you are dead. And you were right, in your promise to me.

Henceforth I shall rule from the greatest palace in Egypt."

She called to her servants; she sent to Horemheb and to the Vizier that the thing was done.

Although Sennahet argued and pleaded with her to go back to the palace, Meryat refused. Then the news came that Tutankhamun was dead, and she went back.

She went back at night. In spite of the late hour everyone in the palace was still awake. Idle servants roamed through the hall and gathered in knots in the courtyard. The great rooms and open terraces of the palace were meant for daylight and the night made them gloomy and the wind swept cold across the porches and the whole place seemed haunted.

Meryat went quietly toward the Queen's apartments. She passed by swarms of people, but no one seemed to recognize her. No one was crying or tearing up his garment or mourning in any other way; they stood close together and murmured.

The Queen's chambers were empty.

Meryat went through the robing room, painted with gold leaf, into the chamber where Ankhesenamun slept. No lamp burned there, but torches burned in the garden, and their hot fingers of light reached in through the tall windows. Without thinking, Meryat moved screens across the windows.

Heralded by voices, Ankhesenamun returned with her women. Meryat stood near the screened window. The Queen did not see her at first. Striding into the room, Ankhesenamun gave sharp orders about her to the servants. Two lamps were lit and the night retreated into the corners of the room. The Queen shed her light cloak. A servant caught it. Ankhesenamun turned and saw Meryat.

Their looks clashed. Meryat's muscles wound tight. With a little jerk of her head, Ankhesenamun sent away the other women. Hushed, the servants left by the door into the robing room. Their curious eyes sought out Meryat as they left. Meryat knew that they would listen from beyond the door.

She said, "Did you kill him?"

Ankhesenamun stood straight and lithe before her. "I did. Now what do you want?"

Meryat shivered. Her gaze fell to the Queen's hands.

"I know why you were driven away," Ankhesenamun said. "You tried to warn him. Then why did you come back?" The tall woman paced around the room. The heels of her sandals clicked on the painted floor. Her level stare returned to Meryat. It seemed to Meryat that the Queen's eyes glowed in the darkness like a cat's.

"Do you mean to make trouble for me, Meryat? Don't be a fool."

"I wanted—" Meryat began, and stopped.

"Before, you might have done some harm," Ankhesenamun said. Her voice was too loud. Surely she too realized that the servants listened to all that was said. She crossed the room with long, swinging strides. "But you have no power anymore, Meryat. You are nothing!"

"I shall go," Meryat said.

She started toward the door into the robing room, to chase away the servants. Ankhesenamun got in her path.

"No. Tell me why you have returned."

Confronted, Meryat said nothing.

"To accuse me," Ankhesenamun said. "It was to accuse me. Do you think, Meryat, that I can do the deed, but shrink from the word?"

She struck Meryat so hard that the sense left her; the next she knew she was sitting dazed on the floor, with Ankhesenamun shouting at her.

"You misjudge me—they all misjudge me! The Vizier thinks I will be mild and womanly, and make my husband King, and then sit at his knee. But I will place no man above me, and especially not one of my servants, who has bowed to me all my life!"

Meryat stood up on her quivering legs. Ankhesenamun

moved restlessly in a circle around her. Her forehead was puckered, and her shoulders hunched. She stopped before the veiled and canopied bed and placed her hand on the carved head of the bed, which was shaped like the head of a cobra.

She said, "I shall sleep with whom I choose henceforth."

"Remember," Meryat said, "that because of me you did not sleep with Tutankhamun."

Ankhesenamun gave her a fiery look. "Who would believe you? Who would ever listen?"

"You listen," Meryat said.

The Queen hesitated, and in the moment of hesitation Meryat knew that she had said truth, she knew that she was right. She stepped toward the door.

"I will prepare your nightclothes, my lady."

"You will leave me!"

Meryat said, "I will be in the robing room, my lady." She did not bow before the Queen; she only went out of the room.

That night Meryat slept in her old bed in the room behind the Queen's. She woke smiling, congratulating herself that she had the Queen in her grasp. Then when she went forth into the Queen's apartments her pleasure died.

The Queen was gone, and all her servants. The bed was gone. In the cupboards and the closets of the robing room only a few old clothes were hanging.

Meryat wandered around the deserted rooms, unable to decide what to do. Stupidly she went from room to room, as if the Queen might suddenly reappear. In the bedchamber there were marks on the floor, where the bed's feet had rested on the packed earth. At last Meryat went down into the quarter of the common servants, and there sat down among the porters and the sweepers.

On the western bank of the Nile, opposite the living city of Thebes and south of the palace of the King, was the City of the Dead. There worked the embalmers and the makers of tombs and coffins, and there many noblemen and princes were buried in great tombs, and there were the splendid temples of the dead Kings, who had become Osiris.

In the City of the Dead was a house called Per Nefer—the House· of Vitality. On the second day of Tutankhamun's death, the tent of Pharaoh was spread out above the Per Nefer, and Pharaoh was carried within.

The priests of Osiris who would justify Tutankhamun as Osiris were chosen by lot. In three rituals as old and sacred as the name of their god, the priests cleansed themselves and invoked the power by which they transformed the dead flesh of the man Pharaoh into the perfect and incorruptible body of Osiris. With their voices the priests said prayers. With their hands they prepared the body of the King.

They removed from Osiris' body all that might perish in the corrupting airs of the world of the living. They scooped out his heart and his spleen and gathered up his intestines in baskets, and they put hooks up through the nostrils of the King and drew forth his brains. Then they washed the hollowed body with wine and packed it with sacred oils, to dissolve away the fats that would putrefy. Thus they made perfect the body of Osiris.

The King's household was also busy. They had to prepare the goods wherewith the King's tomb would be furnished. For in the afterlife, in his eternal house, was he who had sat upon gold, dined upon rare meats, gone forth dressed in finest linen, was Pharaoh to sit upon the bare earth and eat of the wind?

For seventy days, thus, they would prepare to bury Tutankhamun.


On the fourteenth day after the death of Pharaoh, the overseer of Hapure's village ordered Hapure and some others of the village to follow him to the Royal Gorge.

Hapure walked just behind the overseer. The men behind him talked excitedly. All knew that they went to work at the tomb of Pharaoh.

The sun was still young in the east. Hapure's shadow ran on before him, sometimes to his right, and sometimes straight ahead of him. He carried his tools in a sack over his shoulder, as he had hundreds of times.

The overseer was a fat little man whose legs milled busily even at a walk. In his belt his coiled whip looked ridiculous and innocuous. He said, "Of course, the Sacred One cannot lie in the tomb we were making for him—it will not be ready for some years."

They went around a bend in the gorge. The overseer stopped. Before them the wall of the gorge rose in a massive natural parapet. The wind had worn and rounded the stone into great gross shapes like the knees and paws of huge beasts. On either side of the path, in the slopes above the path, was an empty doorway cut into the rock.

Hapure's sack slipped from his shoulder to the ground. He looked with horror on this place. The overseer went on a few steps.

"This eternal house shall be made ready for the Holy One," he said, and gestured to the tomb opening on the right. He nodded to Hapure. "Come with me, mason."

Hapure shook himself from the grip of his memories. Stooping, he reached for his tools and followed the overseer up the flinty path to the other tomb, the tomb on the left.

They went down a corridor that slanted into the rock of the desert. At the end was a single chamber. A lamp rested on the floor just beyond the threshold.

The chamber was unfurnished. The walls were covered with a white plaster that reflected the light in uneven patches and pools. The ceiling rose beyond the lamplight, so that the room seemed to go up and up into the darkness. Hapure's hackles rose. It was as if the room lay at the bottom of a well. He was afraid to look up; he longed to run.

At the far end of the room was an alcove, filled entirely by a huge stone sarcophagus. A man in a priest's white loincloth stood beside it.

The light of the lamp colored everything a deep saffron that wiped out all detail. Even the face of the overseer seemed composed only of flat surfaces. Hapure lowered his eyes. He felt the well of time above them, the raw future waiting.

The priest came out of the chamber. He stopped before Hapure.

"Who is this?"

"The mason," said Hapure's overseer.

"Mason. Tell me, who is God?"

Hapure opened his jaws; the words came forth from his throat. "Amun is God, and all the world is his work. Osiris is God."

"Good." The priest nodded. "Do your work."

The priest went away up the corridor. Hapure's eyes followed him. He wondered what his lot would have been had he answered that the Aten was God.

The overseer picked the lamp up from the floor. "You will stop this door," he said to Hapure.

The priest was gone. Hapure turned to stare into the darkened chamber toward the sarcophagus. He shivered all over in a sudden chill. This tomb had been empty before. For the first time, he put his mind to work at this. He said, "Whom are you burying here?"

"That does not concern you. Do your work, as the High Priest said."

Hapure sucked in his breath. Everything made sense to him now: the priest's charge, the preparation of the other tomb, where Akhenaten had lain, and whose position he had revealed to the thieves. He shook his head at the overseer.

"No. He does not belong here."

"Silence yourself," said the overseer. "You do not care, do you? You are no Atenist."

Then it was true: Akhenaten was being buried here. Hapure lifted his hands, pleading. "It is false and wrong to do this. The King must lie in his own tomb." He struggled for the words that would express what he felt, that if the King were not in his rightful house, then the whole world would fall out of its place.

"That tomb will serve to bury the King that's newly dead," said the overseer. "What does it matter? One dies, another dies."

Tutankhamun. Hapure let loose a burst of frightened laughter. Tutankhamun would lie in the tomb that he himself had desecrated.

"Collect your wits!" the overseer hissed at him. "Do your work. There will be gold—"

"Gold," Hapure cried. "Of what use is gold, when the world tumbles into ruin?"

The overseer took out his whip. At the sight of the long snake, Hapure giggled again; he shrank back, almost back into the alcove where Akhenaten lay.

"Will you block this door?" The overseer shook out his whip. "If not, I will dispose of you, and find another mason, who will not make trouble."

Hapure swallowed. The cold air of the tomb laid its hands over him. The smell of death filled the place. He felt the weight of the solid stone above him pressing on his mind.

"Where are my supplies?" he asked.

The overseer's face slackened with relief. He coiled his whip. "Near the entrance. Come and I will show you."

Tutankhamun lay in the Per Nefer, with his guts and his brain in jars. In the palace, the scribes of the procession went from room to room, making lists of the goods and furnishings that would be buried in the ground with the Eternal King.

# 15

Meryat was given linen to make into nightdresses and robes for Tutankhamun. She sat in the garden with some other women and embroidered the linen.

"Why take such care with this?" one of the other women cried, and cast down her work. "It will only go into the earth and rot."

Meryat's needle bit into the cloth. She spaced her stitches exactly and kept the linen taut, so that the lines of the embroidery were straight. She chose the colors with care. Everything she did was as fine as she could make it. The other women gossiped. They sent a boy for dates and milk.

"See Meryat, how devoted she is."

They giggled at her. She drew away from them and bent over her work.

"Soon you will make a wedding gown for the Queen, Meryat."

"And a nightdress," said another woman. "But you will

have to prick your thumb with your needle if that garment is to be properly blooded."

Their coarse laughter jarred Meryat. She thrust the needle down into the linen; the stitch was twisted. She picked it out with her nails. Then she clipped off the bit of thread; she would not use it twice; she would not defile the work by using the thread twice.

"Even were she a virgin, there would be no blood on the sheets the morning after her marriage—not with that old bridegroom."

The word around the palace was that Ankhesenamun would marry Ay, the Grand Vizier, who was past seventy years of age. Meryat straightened her back, one hand over her spine, and found the other women watching her expectantly.

"What?" she said. "Do you think I know any more than you? Or would tell you if I did?" She laughed. Quickly she bent over her work again, to hide the expression on her face. She had not even known where Ankhesenamun was, until a cook's boy had said within her hearing that Ankhesenamun had gone up the river to an old villa of her mother's. Yet she salved her pride with the rumor that the Queen had left her here to spy.

She finished a strip of the linen and folded it and laid the smooth cool folds in a box of cedar. Between the folds she laid sprigs of herbs. She took another piece of cloth across her knees. Bare and white as flesh the cloth lay on her lap. She dipped her needle into it and drew the red thread through it.

The gossiping voices around her stopped and all the women prostrated themselves. The Grand Vizier and the General Horemheb were strolling through the garden.

They walked side by side down the path of gravel, without remarking the women who were bowed down on either side. The Vizier was old and bent with his age, his head thrust forward, as if he searched the ground before him for the doorway that would let him out of this world and into the next. The general walked straight and young on springy feet.

"This shall be the most lavish funeral ever held here," the old Vizier said. "Yet what solace will it give to anyone? True is the old saw: *The more ceremony, the less understanding.*"

"What does that matter?" Horemheb said. They passed through the shadow of the palm tree, and his bronze armor grew dull. "Only the vulgar pay any heed to that."

"The less they understand," the Vizier said, "the more they cling to their beliefs."

They had passed Meryat. She lifted her head; she stared boldly at their backs, contemptuous, as the two men talked their way along. The general towered over the old man beside him. They walked as slowly as women. Did they think that Ankhesenamun who had murdered a King would give herself tamely to a fatuous old man? Meryat lowered her gaze to her work again. Her heart ached that Ankhesenamun had left her behind. With her whole heart she longed for the Queen's love again. Her hands were shaking, and her needle plunged into the linen; red stitches raced across the cloth.

The Queen was supposed to marry the aged Ay, Grand Vizier of Egypt, and by the divine union make him Pharaoh. Instead she sent messages to the King of the Hittites, in which she offered marriage and the kingly crown to a Hittite prince.

In her isolated villa south of Thebes, she waited for her unknown husband. Then soldiers came and took her villa as an army conquers a town. Horemheb commanded them. He said she was a traitor, and that the Hittite prince was dead.

In the bazaar along the east bank of the Nile three Persians in striped gowns were putting on a show with shadow puppets. Hapure stood in the little crowd before the stage, watching. The show was simple: a heroic thief, a land-owner with a big stick, chased each other here and there along the screen. Hapure had a handful of dates to eat, and nowhere to go; he loitered there, laughing when the land-owner beat the thief, and cheering when the thief stole the landowner's purse.

Sennahet came up to him, looking gloomy.

"What," Hapure said, "have you found her?"

The slightest movement of Sennahet's head indicated that he had not. Hapure grunted. He looked around them at the crowded bazaar. This day was dedicated to Ra; no one had to work, and all Thebes was searching through the booths and shops for something to spend their money on. Meryat had gone away on a day dedicated to Ra, and that returned Hapure's mind to Sennahet and his problem.

"You have not seen Meryat for eighteen days," Hapure said. "Why not admit that she has forgotten? She is happy there. She is not of our clay—leave her to her own people."

"Perhaps you are right," Sennahet said. He slid his hands flat under his belt, his face still very long. "If I could only see her, I know I could talk her into helping us."

"Not *us*," Hapure said. "Only you, Sennahet."

"You say one thing one day and the other the next day."

"I told you that if you find where it is and show me the way to steal it, I will help you—but it is your work to convince me."

"I will choose the day when you agree," Sennahet said.

At the end of the bazaar, where the great golden column stood, there was someone yelling, and around him people turning to hear. Hapure stood on his toes, trying to see better. He started down in that direction, curious: many others were going to hear.

Sennahet followed him, muttering under his breath. Hapure stole a look at him. Sennahet's singlemindedness alternately amused and upset him. The man did nothing else with such force as he plotted to steal Pharaoh's gold.

"Come," a voice was shouting, up ahead. "Come and see what has befallen the Queen!"

Sennahet's head snapped up. He exchanged a single fiery look with Hapure, and they ran forward, fighting their way through the crowd flowing past the Ray of the Rising Sun and into the broad street that led to the temple south of Thebes.

The sun was at its height. The gigantic sphinxes that crouched along either side of the street cast no shadows onto the yellow dust. Ten feet ahead of Hapure two boys were climbing up onto the paw of the first sphinx. Hapure cupped his hands around his mouth.

"You! What do you see?"

One boy squinted away to the south, his gaze like an arrow down the street. He cried out, "Chariots! Chariots coming."

Sennahet was already several yards ahead of Hapure, plowing through the massed bodies. Hapure struggled after him. They reached the edge of the road and spilled out onto it. The crowd followed them.

Ahead, above the columns of the Imperial Temple clustered thick with shadow even at midday, the three great columns of Amun blazed against the fathomless blue of the sky. Hapure blinked; it was a few moments before he saw the line of horse-drawn chariots trotting up the street toward him. The rest of the crowd had seen them also. They hushed.

It was many minutes before anyone could see what the chariots were or who was in them, but the crowd did not disperse; instead it thickened, clotting across the road. No one spoke. No one sat down or turned to gossip with his neighbor. Hapure passed his hand over his eyes. Beside him Sennahet heaved up a great hoarse sigh.

"It is she. Ankhesenamun—it is the Queen, bound in chains."

Hapure's skin prickled up along his arms and back. He strained his eyes to see.

There in the middle chariot, beside the driver, Ankesenamun stood. Hapure had seen her only seldom but he knew her at once by the slender straight figure and the proud pose of her head. She was bound with gold chains. Her hands were behind her.

Hapure clenched his fists. He wondered who would dare do this to Egypt's Queen. But Pharaoh was dead; anything could happen now.

The chariots on the wings were moving forward, swinging around to lead the chariot that carried Ankhesenamun. The driver of the leading chariot cracked his whip and the horses began to canter. They were going to try to break through the crowd.

Near Sennahet a man flung his arm forward to point. "They are Horemheb's men."

His clear cry brought the crowd to life. All around Hapure the voices rose.

"What are they doing? Where are they taking her? Come—come—"

The people broke and ran forward. Unused to being charged by such a rabble, the horses shied and stopped and reared. The crowd rushed forward and encircled the chariots and held the horses by the reins and the chariots by the wheels, and a thousand voices rose demanding to be told what was to become of the Queen.

Hapure was hanging over the wheel of the leading chariot. The driver whipped at him; someone behind Hapure caught the lash and yanked the whip away. The driver shrank back. His eyes were wild with alarm.

"Hear me," the Queen shouted. "People, hear me!"

Hapure turned toward her, in the third chariot from him. Like a lance, she was, unbending. Her voice rang out again.

"Hear me, Egypt. Will you let Horemheb and the priests

make themselves your masters? See what they have done to me!"

The people murmured. Someone brushed by Hapure; he glanced around and saw a thin man in a priest's loincloth clamber up into the chariot whose wheel he held.

"People," Ankhesenamun cried, "in the time of famine and plague, I saved you—I! I! Now you must save me! Help me, who has nothing but your good at heart!"

Above Hapure the priest thundered out, "People, she is Akhenaten's daughter! Remember what Akhenaten worked in Egypt!"

The crowd's muttering voice answered with a growl. Hapure clung to the wheel. The people behind him surged around him, pressing him to the rough wood, and the wheel rolled a little.

"I helped you—I put food into your mouths—I interceded for you with the gods—"

"Akhenaten attacked the gods," the priest roared. His voice was trained to carry. His words drew clamoring from the crowd. "Akhenaten hated you and Egypt!"

"Do not listen to him! They want me destroyed! Please —I rescued you—will you not rescue me?"

"She is Akhenaten's daughter!"

The people surged forward. Hapure was forced painfully into the wheel. A shower of stones flew through the air and pelted down around the Queen. The priest's thundering voice was lost in the mindless howling of the crowd. Hapure panted for breath. Ankhesenamun stood erect in the chariot, trying to call reason back to them, while the stones rained down around her. Blood shone on her face. Beside Hapure a man with twisted mouth and glaring eyes stooped for a stone and jumped up to throw it, wildly, without aim. It was Sennahet. Other misaimed stones were falling into the crowd. One struck the horse nearest Hapure, and the chariot lunged forward. He fell from the wheel and staggered to his feet. A mad panic took him. He bent and gathered stones and flung them, flung them anywhere. The Queen was gone. Her chariot looked empty. He turned and fought his way back through the crowd, his chest full of hurt, desperate for some open space.

In the Per Nefer in the City of the Dead, the priests of Osiris set a wooden coffin full of Nile mud. They sprinkled seed on this earth and watered it well. Seventy days after the death of Pharaoh, green shoots broke up through the surface of the soil. Then the word was sent about Egypt, that every man of the land of Egypt might rejoice: for the god that was dead had arisen, and Tutankhamun would now be placed in his eternal house.

The sun stood on the eastern horizon. The air retained the chill of deep night. Horemheb stood behind the sled that would carry the King's bier. The white linen coat he wore chafed his neck. He felt as if he had been waiting for hours, yet it was only a few minutes.

With him were eight other men of highest rank—the Nine Friends of the King—all dressed as he was in white mourning, with white bands of linen knotted around their foreheads. These nine stood a little apart from the great crowd of courtiers outside the palace. The dawn wind toyed with their white clothes, rippling and shaking like strange feathers.

The sun climbed into the sky. Its golden light turned the desert cliff first yellow, then orange; it danced on the breast of the broad, all-mothering river. No one spoke.

A brass horn blasted. Horemheb startled at the sudden sound. Now the procession would begin. He felt freed of the waiting like a bird freed of the tether.

The palace was hung with blue lotuses, the flower of rebirth. The priests led the vast procession around the outer wall, chanting hymns and scattering the ground with incense and the husks of seeds. After the priests came the sled, drawn by red oxen, the sacred cattle of the north. The Nine Friends of the King followed after the sled, and behind them, in five rows, were the hundreds of the courtiers and priests, each bearing some object for the Room of Eternal Royalty, in the tomb house where Tutankhamun would live forever.

As the procession coiled around the building, Horemheb could discern the wails and cries of the women inside, who were mourning over the dead King. The keening of the women was lovely and eerie. Horemheb could not hear it without a quickening of the heart. The priests burst into the palace through several doors and windows. Chanting ancient phrases, the women barred their way. They strove to hold back the King, to keep him in the world of the living, but the priests broke through their ranks and bore off the King's body.

As they came out of the palace with the body of Tutankhamun, the hundreds of people in the funeral parade bowed down to the earth. Horemheb bowed with them. Yet he lifted his head, at the last, to see the Grand Vizier, who paced solemnly along behind the body.

The old man wore the leopard skin of the Sem priest, who would hold the adz over Tutankhamun in the mysterious ceremony that freed the King's soul from the flesh. The sheen of the skin of the beast made the old man look older still, a walking corpse. Horemheb saw how the Vizier walked with dragging feet, his eyes downcast, weary already. The ceremonies were long. Horemheb could not help but smile. He bowed his head into its proper pose.

The Vizier would be Pharaoh, but no seed of his would quicken in the womb of Ankhesenamun. When the Vizier died, the throne would fall to him who had waited and planned and foreseen what was necessary. Horemheb's mouth was taut with his smile of triumph.

Two by two, crying out, the women were circling around the bier where the King now lay. Their voices lamented in the archaic words Isis had cried over the body of Osiris. Horemheb rose with the others at the jangling of the golden sistra. The front of his white coat was brown with dust.

Tutankhamun's transformed body lay now on the gold bier. Its canopy fringe was tied in the sacred knots; the sun cast the shadows of the knots across the King's arms. The Nine Friends went to take up the traces of the sled.

Horemheb passed by the dead King. Tutankhamun's flesh had been transmuted into the incorruptible gold, the metal of the sun. His hands and feet were masked in gold, and amulets and instruments of power weighted every limb. The huge gold mask was the perfect image of the King. The mouth curved in the same indulgent pout and the wide eyes were bright. The braided beard of Osiris hanging on the chin only emphasized the King's youth.

At the head of the sled, Horemheb found himself standing immobile, shaken by what he saw—by what he saw no more—the life counterfeited in gold, the death triumphant. Quickly the general turned away and went to take his place at the traces of the sled. He struggled to put his mind at rest. Yet he could not; all the years remaining of his life seemed to have shrunk down to a handful of days, and when he put his strength to the trace, it was himself that he drew on his inexorable path to the grave, and his triumph was lifeless, like the gold.

In the chambers of the Queen, Ankhesenamun was made ready for the night. She sat on a stool, and the strange women who served her now prepared her with sacred oils. She did not move; there was no reason to move.

Her head hurt, anyway, and it pained her to move. Her head had hurt ever since the stoning. And she was tired. It was easier to sit here and be tended, be cared for.

They lifted up the sacred crown and put it on her head. Her neck bent under its weight. She shut her eyes. They led her by the hand to her bed and she lay down on it, beneath the canopy of gold.

*

Hapure and Sennahet played at counters; Sennahet lost and began to argue over the stakes. While the two men were shouting at each other, Meryat came into the hut.

They goggled up at her, who stood above them. Her face was white and drawn, like fine linen.

"The gold is in the tomb of Osiris," she said.

Hapure sat back on his heels, the clay game chips in his hand. He watched Sennahet's face. Sennahet's eyes had narrowed, piercing as a hawk's.

"I need no one to tell me that," he said to Meryat. "All Egypt knows that."

"You need me," she said, "to tell you that there is a guard by night, and to help you distract him."

Hapure clinked the counters together in his cupped hand. His stomach turned over. He saw that the thing they had long discussed was becoming real; he saw it in Sennahet's face.

Sennahet rose up from his place. "Tonight," he said.

It was in Hapure's mouth to refuse. Crouched on his heels, he lifted his eyes to Sennahet's, and Sennahet seemed tall as the Sun. Alone of all men he had purpose, and it sanctified him.

"Come," he said to Hapure and Meryat, and they followed him.

They gathered up Hapure's tools. The sun was lowering toward the western shelf of the desert, there to begin the perilous journey through the underworld of night. In the village the women were cooking beans and millet together. With the tools on Hapure's shoulder, the three friends set off from the village on the path that led to the Royal Gorge.

Hapure walked first, because he knew the path best and the sun would set in the midst of their journey. He heard the others coming after him but he did not speak to them. None of them spoke. It was like a dream, what they were doing.

Hapure looked up from the path and saw the sun upon the horizon like a caldron of molten gold that tipped and spread the burning color all along the edge of the world. The path turned downward under his feet and he led his friends down into a little dip in the desert where the shadows were already dark and the night had come early.

The darkness fell over them. They went down the steep slope in the wall of the Royal Gorge. In the chill Hapure shivered and could not stop shivering.

Sennahet murmured, "Where is the guard?"

Meryat pointed ahead of them. "I shall go," she said, "and see what might tempt him away from his duty."

"What?" Sennahet asked her.

"I have gold," she said, "and if that fails, I have honey in a secret jar."

Hapure averted his face from her. She was too delicately bred to speak like that.

She went away down the gorge. She walked down the middle of the narrow valley with the two steep walls on either side of her like the pillars of a temple. She grew smaller with each step until she was only a white grain that walked between the raw pillars of the desert.

"This is unlucky," Hapure said. "I feel that we shall not succeed in this."

"You are a fool," Sennahet said. "There is no luck. There is no god. There is only what a man might seize with the force of his arms and the wit of his brain."

Hapure did not reply to that.

They waited there for more than three hours, until the moon was coursing high in the black sky. Then Meryat returned.

"He is asleep," she said. "Now, come."

She seemed no different, her clothes unrumpled, and her arms as smooth as wax; her face was smooth, as if what she had done could not touch her. She led them down through the gorge, and they came into the widened part of the gorge where the King was buried.

A stairway led down into the hard rock of the earth. At its foot the door was blocked with stones covered with plaster. Hapure took his mallet and a chisel. With the mallet he tapped at the plaster. It crumbled and fell in sheets of dry plaster and crumbs of still-damp plaster, and he scraped it away from the top of the doorway.

His heart began to pound hard. He hastened, and Sennahet came to help him. They pounded wedges into the cracks between the stones that filled the wall and worked loose the topmost stone.

"That is too small a space," Hapure said. "We shall have to remove another."

"No," Meryat said. "There isn't enough time. I can fit through a smaller space than you."

"You are mad," Hapure said roughly. "A woman—"

"You do not know what a woman can do," she said.

They set to work again, all three of them. The passageway beyond the door was full of small stones and pebbles and earth. They dug through it, making a tunnel back toward the tomb. Hapure dug as much as he could reach, but then Meryat had to climb within and dig her own way through. Hapure and Sennahet cleared away the dirt she cast out behind her. They carried it up to the top of the stairs.

They tied a rope to the sack where Hapure carried his tools, and gave it to her, and she took it into the tunnel. She heaped up the dirt she was removing onto the sack and the two men pulled it out. The dirt showered down over them; Hapure's arms and shoulders were caked with dirt and bruised from the stones. At last Meryat put her head out of the tunnel.

"I have come to another doorway," she said.

Hapure and Sennahet looked at each other. That was the way into the tomb.

"Here." Sennahet stooped for the mallet and the chisel. "Can you open it? You saw how the mason did it."

She took the tools. Her face was stained now; what she was doing could not leave her clean. Her eyes were wide in the moonlight. She looked blind, like a mole whose life-time is spent underground. She disappeared down the tunnel.

Hapure leaned against the doorway and brushed the dirt from his arms. Foul thoughts swarmed in his idle mind. He could not meet the gaze of Sennahet, who stood so unconcerned before him.

Deep inside the slope, something fell with a crash.

"She is through," Sennahet said.

Hapure licked his lips. He pressed his hand over his heart, which seemed ready to break through his ribs.

Then suddenly Meryat's hands thrust out of the opening in the doorway, and a shower of gold cascaded down over the two men. Laughing, she put her head out after it.

"There! Take it—take it—there is more—so much—" Her head popped back inside the tunnel and she was gone.

Sennahet whooped; he crouched and gathered up the gold and scampered around the corner steps over the loose dirt and stones picking up the stray bits. Hapure stooped down to reach a shining thing on the bottom step. It was a ring. The image of the scarab was cut into the stone. His fingers clenched around it. Now the madness took him. With Sennahet he scurried about hunting for the bits of gold.

Another wild laugh issued from the mouth of the tunnel and more gold streamed down around them, tinkling on the rocks.

Hapure tore off his garment; he formed it into a sack and began to pile the jewels inside. In his haste he gathered up stones as well, and chunks of earth. He collided with Sennahet and they both fell.

"Don't steal my gold!" Sennahet cried. He lashed out at Hapure with his clawed hand.

Hapure was already lunging across the ground for a thing that winked in the moonlight. Meryat's voice

228

sounded above his head and a cup bounced down on the rocks before him, and he seized it.

His sack was so heavy that he could lift it only with both hands. He slung it over his shoulder.

"Let's go," he said. "I have enough."

Sennahet nodded. He put his head into the tunnel. "Meryat. Meryat."

The girl's voice answered, the words indistinct.

"Come out. We are going now—we must hurry."

"No," she called. "No, I will stay here a while longer, with my love."

Hapure startled at her words. She was mad—he should have guessed it, from the strange calm on her face.

"Come out, Meryat. The guard will return."

"I will stay here," she said, from deep inside the earth.

Hapure started away, his sack on his shoulder. Already they had spent too long on this work, which should be done as fast as possible. Behind him Sennahet was arguing with Meryat.

Sennahet came after him, grumbling, his loot wrapped in his skirt. They went off down the gorge.

"Hurry," said Hapure. "Before the guard comes."

"Oh, the guard will sleep until dawn," Sennahet said. "It is only that I can carry no more."

He was struggling with the great weight of his goods. They reached the foot of the path back to the village and he set down his bundle with a sigh.

"I must rest."

Hapure lowered his sack to the earth. He cast a long searching look about them. The gorge was still and barren in the moonlight. The top of the cliff stood out sharp against the sky. The moon was still riding well above the horizon.

"Here." Sennahet opened his bundle and spilled out the heap of loot that he had taken. Hastily he covered it over with loose dirt. A cup rolled away; he kicked it under a

229

rock. "I am going back for more." Shaking out his skirt, he hurried away down the gorge.

"Sennahet!" Hapure cried.

His friend disappeared around a bend in the gorge.

Hapure stood there awhile, staring after Sennahet. He thought of going back to the village; he would have to hide his loot before daybreak, when the other villagers would waken. He was tired and longed for sleep. He was hungry. But he did not move; he waited for Sennahet to appear. Finally he started down the gorge after his friend.

While he was walking along the gorge the soldiers came.

He saw them from a distance. They had come out along the desert so that their chariots would not give warning of their presence, and then they had climbed on foot down the cliff, and Hapure saw them climbing on the cliff. He turned and took flight. They swarmed after him. He wondered if they were real men, or demons loosed on him, a swarm from hell. In his terror he heard the flapping of their leathery wings. He raced up the path, but they caught him there, and a blow struck between his shoulders, and he fell. He knew no more.

The sun rose. Sennahet stretched his legs, cramped from sitting so long. He could not stretch his arms, which were bound behind him.

Meryat sat beside him. They were sitting near the wall of the gorge and the rising sun drove his rays like poisoned arrows into their eyes.

Around them there were many soldiers. None of the soldiers spoke or looked at them. The only voices were the voices of the priests, down at the foot of the stairway inspecting the damage that had been done within the tomb and to the doorway of the tomb. Now the voices sounded clearer and the priests began to climb back up the steps from the doorway of the tomb. They came up to the surface of the gorge, dusting their hands and shaking their heads.

Sennahet did not try to beg them for mercy. He sat still in his place. Beside him Meryat was singing to herself.

On the other side of the gorge were men digging a pit. The dirt and stone they dug up they flung into the stairway of the tomb. They would bury it, to hide it from other robbers. The rhythmic grinding of the shovels in the earth rang on the walls of the gorge. The priests walked up and down past the tomb, talking and casting looks of indignation at the tomb robbers.

Meryat sang, rocking herself back and forth. Sennahet did not speak; he did not move.

At last the pit was finished. The priests stood back, and the workmen stood back, and the soldiers cut away the bonds that held Sennahet and Meryat and threw the man and the woman down together into the pit. A few moments later Hapure's dead body was flung in with them.

The soldiers and the priests and workmen went away. Meryat sat in the corner of the pit; but now she did not sing From the sleeve of her robe she took a knife, so thin and fine she had concealed it even from the priests who bound her, and she put the knife to her breast. The blood welled up from her breast. She put her head back against the wall of the pit and shut her eyes.

Sennahet sat still a long while, until he was sure that no one had waited on the surface of the gorge. He chuckled. He had fooled them to the last. Carefully he unwound his loincloth. He had hidden gold and jewels from them. They had not found what he had stolen; he had stolen it all away. He held the baubles in his hands, smiling. Now at last what he had sought was in his hands.

He sat there in the pit, laughing now and then. The bodies of his friends lay nearby. Truly the priests had given him choice meats for his eternal house. He laughed again, fingering his priceless gold.